a novel

Sharon Kreider

Sylvie
a novel
© 2021 by Sharon Kreider. All rights reserved.

This book, is a work of fiction.
Names, characters, places, and incidents either are products of the author's imagination
or are used fictitiously. Any resemblance to actual events or locales or persons,
living or dead, is entirely coincidental.

Book Consultant: Judith Briles, The Book Shepherd
Editor: Barb Wilson
Cover illustrator: Natalie Aline Kreider
Author photo: Julie Ulstrup Photography
Cover, Interior Design, and eBook conversion:
Rebecca Finkel, F+P Graphic Design

GRAY WOLF BOOKS

Books may be purchased in quantity by contacting
Gray Wolf Books | www.graywolfbooks.com

Library of Congress Control Number: 2021910728
ISBN trade paper: 978-1-7372393-0-7
ISBN eBook: 978-1-7372393-1-4
ISBN audiobook: 978-1-7372393-2-1

Women's Fiction | Mental Health | Grief

First Edition
Printed in the USA

For Natalie

PROLOGUE

Moonlight grazed the tips of the trees. Stars sprinkled like sugar across the sky as she looked deep into the shadowy alcove of her heart. It seemed she was in the most fragile moment of her life.

She thought of the people she loved the most. Her mom. Her dad. Tim. Naomi. Jaycee. How could she bother them with the mess she was in?

"Oh, God…," she muttered to herself. Her heart felt like a small dead creature.

In a haze of muddled thoughts, she walked back to her dorm room. Once there, she pulled open her bedside table drawer, took out a small plastic bottle filled with twenty-six yellow pills and lined them up on her bed, evenly spaced in neat rows. Soldiers prepared for battle.

Propped up on her elbows, she ate the soldier closest to her and gazed at them as if they could show her a way home through her seemingly never-ending maze. Then she downed the three others, closed her eyes, and remembered eating M&Ms with Tim. How he opened the package with his teeth and positioned the candy on the rug between them.

She'd shouted with glee, "Can I have the red ones?"

Tim laughed. "Sure." He carefully picked them out, one by one, and placed them in her tiny hand.

She bit into the hard coating and allowed the chocolate to rest on her tongue. "Mmm." Sylvie thought about how much she missed her brother and made a promise to herself to call him.

She heard her dad's strong voice. "Hey, Sylvie-girl." He lifted her onto his shoulders and they watched the sun head for the horizon, lit up with beautiful brushstrokes of scarlet, sunflower, and ochre. It was the loveliest moment of her life.

How she loved her dad. He'd never been anything but the best dad in the whole world. She couldn't wait to hug him when she saw him again. Not one of those wimpy embraces she'd given him these last few years, but a big bear of a hug. Like what Hagrid would've given Harry Potter.

And her mom. Sylvie remembered how she scooped her up to be cuddled and held and loved. Smiling wide, her mom whispered, "My special girl." Her mom would waltz her around the kitchen, singing a nursery rhyme. She adored her mom. She missed her so much.

Yes, that's it, she thought. *I'll talk to my mom. I'll be honest about everything. She'll show me the way. I'll absorb all her good judgment into my skin and things will sort themselves out. I'll go home.* Sylvie felt her mother's heart pulsate in tandem with hers.

Her head lolled to one side and she gathered the rest of her army and cradled them close to her chest.

one

MIA

A few months after—Memories

Born a little after midnight on a clear spring night, Sylvie weighed four pounds five ounces, and spent thirty-six days in intensive care; nurses monitored her breathing, and doctors charted progress and relapses. When allowed to bring her daughter home, Mia became a cautious parent, heedful to any sign of distress. She even took to whispering when she checked on her, afraid her voice might disturb Sylvie's sleep.

Mia kept her vigil for about a year or more, until she was sure Sylvie had met her milestones and relaxed a little, but still hovered more than necessary throughout Sylvie's childhood.

Strange thing about habits: once rooted, they become difficult to eradicate.

When Sylvie started school, Mia watched her little Sylvie play teacher in her make-believe Animal Elementary school from the sidelines, amazed at her daughter's creativity and the kind words Sylvie offered to her imaginary friends. While hugging her stuffed border collie tightly to her chest, she said things like *don't be afraid to start over*, or *be patient like our tree out back—it has big, deep roots.*

In a small, unfinished back room in the basement filled with some discarded exercise equipment, Animal Elementary had an old easel with a chalkboard and a teacher's desk made from two cinderblocks and an unfinished door. Animal toys were designated as her students. And her "students" sat on the floor on random pieces of pressboard taken from her father's workbench. Completed homework, scrawled on quarter-sheets of paper, and returned to the appropriate bin on the teacher's desk, earned extra recess time. Each student had a journal, an improvised backpack, a sack lunch, and a bus schedule. She held parent-teacher conferences, sharing a full-year curriculum and lesson plans. She retaught everything she learned at school each day; the solar system, multiplication tables, Shakespeare's *Twelfth Night*, field hockey, "Mary Had a Little Lamb" on the alto recorder, and all the countries in South America.

Scooter, a girl dog with her soft floppy ears, was a special-needs student. She positioned her in a wheelchair, which was just a pink stroller that never saw a true doll in its time of service. Mia marveled at the way she took such good care of the stuffed animal, even making a ventilator out of plastic straws and paper towel rolls, mimicking one of her classmates.

Squirmy, a blue-and-black striped snake, and Al, a plump tabby cat, were best friends. Sylvie would often comment, "Mom, I need to find some rules for these two. They always sneak out of their boxes." Her all-star students were Kinta, a border collie, and India, the tiger foreign-exchange student. When she was finished playing teacher for the day, the stuffed animals were gently placed in a big box to keep them clean and safe.

Sylvie, whose heart was as big as tomorrow, cared for her imaginary students as if they were real.

She spent so much time on her make-believe school, Mia eventually started donating things: rubber stamps and a stamp pad, paper clips, sticky notes, art supplies, folders, note pads, even a discarded overhead projector found at a rummage sale. With the unnecessary wood from a partial basement remodel, Sylvie's dad, Jack, made several desks for Animal Elementary. Three were painted a creamy white. Some had stickers, while a few sported colorful designs.

Sylvie played Animal Elementary every day for several years, from about second grade through fifth. Sometimes, she'd invite a few classmates over to play teacher with her. But the other girls didn't seem as enthusiastic and lost interest early. They were too young to understand Sylvie's world. And Sylvie didn't have the vocabulary quite yet to explain what she saw.

Because of this, Sylvie experienced difficult times with social settings. She disliked day care, crying when a babysitter arrived to take care of the kids when Mia and Jack went out on a rare date, and she screamed and clung to Mia when someone else tried to hold her.

Mia thought Sylvie's peculiarities were not unusual. Instead, they were what made her daughter distinctive—her extraordinary little girl. Mia showered Sylvie with the attention she deserved, thoroughly trusting her love could conquer any uncertainty Sylvie might encounter with the outside world.

Mia's pride gushed and rushed through her veins like quicksilver when Sylvie tried out a new set of watercolors and painted her first picture—a remarkable rendition of Squirmy and Al drinking tea. Mia put the drawing on the refrigerator where it stayed for months.

A little while later, Sylvie drew a portrayal of her school with Scooter situated in her wheelchair by the flagpole and won her school's award for best artwork. The principal hung it on the front entrance bulletin board. "Man, that kid has talent," she said to Mia as they both admired Sylvie's uncanny ability to blend colors, the blue concrete a stark contrast to the red brick. "That stuffed animal almost looks like our little Amanda."

Sylvie wrote her first poem in third grade. Her teacher noticed. "Sylvie, would you mind if I showed your poem to a few other teachers? We might like to print it in our school newsletter. Would that be all right with you?

Sylvie, always a touch shy, didn't know how to respond. "Okay," was all she thought to say at the time.

Mia was simply astounded when she opened the monthly school newsletter and saw Sylvie's poem on the front page. "Sylvie! Why didn't you tell us?"

Sylvie shrugged. "I dunno. Doesn't everyone get in the newspaper?"

As unfair as kids can get from time to time, they said mean things to her. One kid sneered at her picture in the front entry-way. "Doesn't even look like a dog. Why would a dog be in a wheelchair? Doesn't make sense."

Sylvie pretended she hadn't heard, but she thought about what that classmate had said many times, and wondered how she could help people understand what went on inside of her.

Sylvie's insecurity was a slippery thing, like trying to hold a tiny fish—there one moment and gone the next. But looking back, Mia thought Sylvie might have started to feel a lack of confidence in herself starting in sixth grade when a group of popular girls, interested in boys and rap music, gossiped behind her back. They shunned her at recess. Not having anyone to associate with on the playground, she continued to draw in her little leather-bound notebook her dad gave her and wrote whimsical poems. Unfortunately, that only encouraged the popular girls to laugh at her even more.

She found one other girl, Nancy, who did not fit into the popular crowd either.

One evening while Sylvie drew a bath, just a few months after beginning her friendship with Nancy, she asked, "Hey, Mom, could you help me wash my hair?" Sylvie had trouble washing her thick, blonde hair. She couldn't get all the soap out.

Mia noticed Sylvie's eyes were slightly puffy and pink. "Everything okay?"

Sylvie didn't respond right away, waiting until her hair had been rinsed, and tied up in a towel. "No," she replied.

Mia took a breath. "What's up, honey?"

Sylvie's eyes filled with tears. "I don't know how to tell you."

Mia's heart started to beat a little faster than she would've liked. She tried to keep her composure. "Tell me what?"

She searched for Mia's eyes and when she found them, time seemed to hang between them, like a suspension bridge over a mountain canyon. "Nancy tried to strangle me."

The voice inside Mia went still, the blood pounding in her ears strong like ocean waves. She didn't know what to say at first. Fear, like a cold hand, gripped the back of her neck. She swallowed a few times. "I don't understand…she strangled you? Where? How? When?" Mia tried not to let her sense of panic show.

Sylvie crossed her arms, held her shoulders tight, and began to shake. "I'm cold."

Suddenly, she realized Sylvie was likely feeling as vulnerable as a newly-sheared lamb. She wrapped a warm towel around her and hugged her tight to her chest. Tears pooled in the corners of Mia's eyes. She let them fall onto the towel on Sylvie's head.

"I love you. Tell me what happened." Mia couldn't imagine anyone wanting to hurt someone as innocent as Sylvie. And those eyes. Who on earth would ever consider wanting to harm such a beautiful child?

Sylvie told Mia that Nancy had hurt her a few times before —hit her with a stick when she refused to play one of Nancy's games; punched her in the arm at lunch; threatened her with small acts of violence. Two weeks prior, on a snowy day, lunch recess happened to be in the classroom. For unknown reasons, Nancy didn't like the game Sylvie chose to play.

Sylvie said, "She blew up and ran over to me, grabbed my neck like this." She demonstrated by wrapping her soft hands around the sides of Mia's neck and squeezing. Sylvie couldn't continue with the story because she started to cry—big sobs, her chest moving up and down.

Mia held her for a long time, waiting until Sylvie's weeping became noiseless. "It's all right," she said. But she knew it wasn't.

Mia vacillated between waves of shock and anger to hurt and bewilderment. She couldn't wrap her head around the implications. Even today, she wondered if she should've done more, seen the incident as a red flag. At the time, though, she tossed back those feelings, trying to maintain self-control. She didn't want to upset Sylvie any more than she already was.

Mia consoled herself with a plan to take care of things, certain it would be a one-time thing. After all, her daughter just might be the next Picasso or Jane Austen.

After several school meetings with the principal, teacher, counselor, and Nancy's parents, she found out that Nancy suffered from an anxiety disorder, among other things. Her parents were apologetic and stated, "Our daughter sees a psychiatrist and is on medication. I'm sure she didn't mean any harm."

Mia wasn't convinced and put an end to the only friend Sylvie made that year, firm in her belief that Sylvie could channel the tentative times of preadolescence into her art and writing, or maybe even discover something else. "Just think of the possibilities," she said to Sylvie.

Mia believed that Sylvie's peers were jealous of her daughter's exceptional talent and physical beauty—symmetrically flawless face, delicate frame, fair-haired. Not everyone came out winners in the genetic pool.

Sylvie retreated into her artistic world, sorrow spiraling into her bones like a thousand metal screws, but she also half-believed her mom. Not yet equipped with the emotional maturity to process these overwhelming feelings, she did what she knew best. She wrote. She painted.

Mia bought her acrylic paints and canvases in various sizes. Jack built her an artist easel.

Not long after her encounter with Nancy, Sylvie looked at her room and decided she'd outgrown the pink and white theme. The comforter with embroidered roses, the eyelet lace skirt around the twin bed with matching curtains and her cherished stuffed animals—albeit a little too loved as they were beginning to appear shabby—were okay when she was seven, but not for a budding teenager.

She brought the subject up at the dinner table. "Mom, I think it's time for a remodel."

Mia perked up. "Really?"

"Yeah, I'm feeling the need for something more grown-up. A place to put up my easel and paints." She paused, expecting an argument.

But Mia didn't object. "That's a great idea."

Upon hearing her mother's approval, Sylvie lit up. "I mean, a real big remodel! A new queen-size bed and a desk and a laptop, not some hand-me-down from Tim." She added, "I'll need a hardwood floor, too, you know." Her eyes were as big as splashes from a spring thunderstorm.

Mia laughed. She hadn't seen Sylvie that excited in a while. "What are we waiting for?"

When Sylvie entered junior high, Mia trusted Sylvie's camaraderie with her peers would improve. She'd outgrow her shyness and learn to have faith in her remarkable talent that Mia had never lost sight of.

She delighted when Sylvie joined the Science Olympiad team and attended after-school gatherings. "I'm so proud of you."

Sylvie excelled in the extracurricular club and qualified for the national Science Olympiad competition in Iowa. She talked about sharing a room with a friend she met on the team.

"I'm sharing a room with Caitlin." She clapped her hands in anticipation of being on her own with her new friend. She'd be gone five whole days.

Mia breathed deep and long, delighting in the milestone, hopeful Sylvie would learn to feel comfortable in her own skin and see what she and so many others saw: a uniquely beautiful and talented young woman with forever potential.

Just around that time, Mia's friend, Kerry, invited Mia to hook up with two women from their book group on a camping trip to the Great Sand Dunes National Park in southern Colorado. It was going to be a fun getaway with friends. The weather channel forecasted clear, warm days and cool, possibly cold evenings—not bad for the end of April.

Mia's husband Jack, and her son, Tim, were going to catch up on a few movies, play some tennis, and enjoy having the house to themselves.

The group of women left early on a Saturday morning, relishing the drive over still-snowy passes. They soaked in a hot spring near Buena Vista and ate lunch at a picnic spot, with the mountains and blue sky surrounding them. The sun, ready to dip below the horizon, still felt warm when they arrived at their campsite.

Mia helped put up the tent. Kerry started the camp stove to heat up rice and beans. The other two women gathered firewood and assembled four camp chairs. It didn't take long for the tasks to be completed, or for the temperature to drop quickly. They sat close to the campfire and chatted about their families, the glow from the coals highlighting their rosy cheeks.

Kerry opened a bottle of wine. "This is great. Should we talk about the next book we're going to read, our kids, or work?"

Mia laughed. "Definitely not work. Let's talk kids."

When it was her turn, Mia shared, "Sylvie is at the national Science Olympiad competition this weekend in Iowa. She loves this science stuff. For her exhibit, she collected glass bottles of various shapes and sizes, and can mimic the sounds of the *Star Wars* theme song when she blows into them. It's so impressive." Mia also told her friends about the metal flute Sylvie made using a blow torch. "She painted the flute a silver color and inscribed several Native American symbols using contrasts of navy blue, lime green, and deep red." Mia smiled broadly. "Oh, she even added some leather pieces and feathers she found."

Images of her beautiful daughter receiving her medals floated through her head: her blonde hair bouncing in rhythm to the spring in her step while everyone clapped, her peers in awe.

On the way home, Sylvie called using the then-latest technology: the cell phone. "Hey, Mom, the reception isn't so good but wanted to let you know I came in first for the music invention competition." Static kept her from saying much more.

Everyone in the car heard, clapped, and whistled. "Way to go, girl!"

A small lump formed in Mia's throat. "Wow. First place. That's fantastic! Woohoo!"

Relief like a cold breeze washed over Mia. She needn't worry anymore, certain the reticence of childhood was behind Sylvie and that her confidence would continue to grow and blossom, the beginning of long and fortuitous successes. "Safe travels home. See you soon. Love you."

For the next several hours, the women talked about all the good things their kids had done or were doing. At one point, one of the women said, "Amazing our kids have come through this crapshoot society we live in unscathed."

Mia nodded in agreement, awash in mirages of Sylvie growing into a strong, successful, independent woman, imagining her as the valedictorian at her high school graduation, getting her doctorate, creating a masterpiece or discovering a cure for something. Maybe she could even win a Nobel Prize.

In May of that year, the Board of Education wanted to honor Sylvie's Science Olympiad team. Mia took Sylvie shopping for a new outfit, and she insisted Sylvie buy whatever she wanted. "Don't look at the price tag. Pick out exactly what you want."

As they browsed the clothing racks, Mia eyed a dress she thought would flatter Sylvie's petite figure. "Hey, look at this." Sheer gauze floated over the bodice and came together at the side, stitched at the waist, and then fell over the supple skirt. "Oh, and how about some chic pumps to go with it?"

Sylvie shook her head. "Nah. Think I like this." She pulled a plain white shirt from the rack. "Maybe after I get my braces off. It's not a big deal."

Mia's pride drifted a little. She couldn't help it. She wanted Sylvie to look her best, get an updo at her favorite hair salon, wear that mauve sweater she thought highlighted Sylvie's eyes. Mia always dressed well, even at home and she never missed appointments with her hair stylist or manicurist.

Just before they left for the acknowledgment meeting, she noticed Sylvie's medals hanging from a thumbtack on her bulletin board. "Aren't you going to wear those?" Mia couldn't imagine why Sylvie wouldn't choose to show off.

Sylvie looked at the medals and touched the gold one. "Nah, I don't want to wear them. They make too much noise."

At the dedication, Sylvie downplayed her award and compressed her lips into a simple line. Mia thought she was being too humble but didn't push, chalking her reluctance up to adolescent sensitivity.

But pesky little thoughts—like mosquitoes after a summer rain—popped into her head: Was she missing anything? Why couldn't Sylvie bask in her gifts and her achievements? What was in her way?

At the end of Sylvie's seventh-grade year, Mia and Jack gave up their vacation savings to send Sylvie on a school trip to Italy with her classmates. Sylvie spent hours anguishing over what to wear, packing and unpacking her suitcase, indecisive about her choices.

Mia watched, amused at her daughter's entry into teenage-land. "Do you need some new capris and tank tops?"

Sylvie placed her fingers under her chin. "Hmm. You know, that might not be a bad idea."

Mia agreed. "Okay, then. Let's go shopping!"

〜

Sylvie was gone for two whole weeks.

When she got back, Mia asked, "Do you want to get together with Katie or Emily and reminisce about your fabulous time in Italia?" Mia thought she was such a clever mom using the word *Italia* instead of Italy. "Let's buy a photo album and develop all your pictures. You love to write. How about describing your experiences as well?"

Sylvie shook her head. "No. I don't want to see Katie or Emily right now. But the scrapbook thing sounds like fun."

"Great. You decide on the book, including stickers and paper. I'll see if I can get your pictures processed." Mia exhaled slowly. She thought Sylvie just needed time to herself—time to write and paint again.

Sylvie spent the summer designing, writing, drawing, painting, and decorating her newly-remodeled room. Her walls were now a pale blue in sharp distinction to the bold colors on her bed and the dark walnut wood flooring. Her stuffed animals were packed and sealed in a box under the stairway closet. A modern floor lamp fit right behind the easel, and a state-of-the-art laptop sat on the barnwood desk her dad had made.

Mia ordered an exclusive Persian rug online to match the wall color and the throw pillows on the bed.

Sylvie spent four weeks painting an otherworldly landscape of some of her favorite moments in Italy and hung it over her bed. On one wall, she posted her poetry, loose pages haphazardly secured with bright push pins. In someone else's room it might have looked tacky, but Sylvie's artistic flair made it appear inventive.

Mia admired the room and felt lucky all over again to have such an amazing daughter. Maybe Sylvie didn't need friends. She seemed to have everything she needed right there inside of herself.

When Sylvie went back to school in the fall, her brother Tim started college. Mia focused her energies on helping her son get settled into his dorm and begin his new life in Washington.

Almost every time the three of them sat down to eat, Mia would talk about Tim: Tim this, Tim that. She never noticed Sylvie roll her eyes or how many times she left the table early.

When Tim came back to visit for a long weekend, Jack rented a yurt in the mountains. He thought it would be a wonderful way for the "fam," as Tim called them now, to spend time together.

Mia loved backcountry skiing. "Excellent!" She could hardly wait to see her son.

Sylvie took an exceptionally long time arranging her little backpack for the weekend. She put three sweaters on the bed, folded them carefully, unwrapped them, and then put them back in her dresser drawer.

It drove Mia a little crazy. To get things moving, she just wanted to pack for her. Mia pinched the bridge of her nose. "Hey, girl. Ready yet?"

Sylvie stared at her rucksack. "Do I have to?"

"Of course, we can't leave you by yourself. It'll be fun. The yurt will be warm once we get the wood stove going. I'm making pasta for dinner, your favorite." She looked in Sylvie's bag. "It'll be fantastic to spend time with Tim, don't you think?" Mia didn't wait for Sylvie to answer—of course, she would want Tim to be part of their adventure. "Don't forget an extra pair of socks. The nights will be cold."

The family set out for the ski to the yurt under a clear, blue sky, the sun warming their backs. A recent snowfall silhouetted the trees. Mia inhaled deep and full, the mountain air unclogging her thoughts. "This is fabulous."

Mia looked back at Sylvie, who didn't seem to be enjoying herself very much. "It's not much further. Tim's already at the yurt and probably melting snow for tea." Mia's heart warmed at the thought of Tim. He'd matured into such a confident young man.

When they got to the yurt, the thermometer next to the door indicated the temperature was twelve degrees. Inside, there were two rustic bunk beds with two-inch-thick foam pads on each sleeping space, a two-burner propane cooktop, and a folding table and chair set. Pops and hisses emanated from the cast-iron wood stove.

As he saw them arrive, Tim shouted from a pristine snow pile, "Hey there. This place is amazing! I'll be there in a minute. Just filling up the pot with snow. Teatime soon."

Mia's joyous laughter echoed in the still air. "Can't wait."

Everyone got to work getting things set up before dark. Jack chopped wood. Tim made numerous snow trips, filled several pots with snow, and placed them on top of the wood stove, eager to make tea and hot chocolate for everyone. Mia unpacked sleeping rolls, food, and opened the outside canvas flaps over the plastic windows.

Sylvie decided to forget about her painting and pitched in to help, too. "I'll get the food out and start cutting up veggies for the salad." She created letters with the carrots and spelled out "love u" and placed them over Tim's plate. Mia's heart swelled.

After dinner, everyone played card games. Tim teased Sylvie. Sylvie goaded him back. Jack threw his ballcap up in the air.

Later, Mia and Jack went outside to look at the stars. The Milky Way looked like thousands of diamonds on a bed of velvet. Mia squeezed Jack's hand. Happy and secure, she whispered in Jack's ear, "I love it when it's just the four of us."

After Tim left, Sylvie spent more time in her room, writing on her new laptop, painting, drawing, and studying. She also made friends and socialized more. Sylvie even began to dress better, which pleased her mother immensely. Mia knew it would happen; she just knew it.

Sylvie won an award for her art in tenth grade, and then another for a poem she submitted to the school's student paper.

At parent-teacher night, Sylvie's art teacher commented, "Mrs. Weaver, your daughter has exceptional talent. Have you thought of where she might go to college?"

Mia hadn't thought about it yet. Her baby going to college already? "Actually, no."

The teacher went on to describe elite schools in the eastern part of the states. It seemed like a long way away to Mia.

Unwilling to consider the teacher's suggestions, Mia cut her short. "I think we have time." She wasn't ready to send her special girl to some faraway university just yet.

Mia positioned Sylvie's awards in the front hallway right by the door so everyone could see them first thing upon entering the house. She'd asked Sylvie if she wanted them in her room.

"Nah. Go ahead. Place them where you want. I have other plans for my room right now," she said.

Confident Sylvie would find her path, Mia didn't fuss. Sylvie spent time in her world; Mia spent time in hers. To Mia, everything felt balanced.

For Sylvie's sixteenth birthday, she organized a surprise birthday party. Gina, an artist friend of hers, created the invitations using depictions of Sylvie's favorite things in an array of colors: images of animals; musical notes; drawings of science icons; and famous writers.

Mia asked Beth, Sylvie's best friend from eighth grade, "Could you deliver these to her friends?" Beth hesitated.

Mia couldn't understand why. She added, "If it's not too much trouble."

Beth stared at nothing for an extra long moment before she said weakly, "Okay."

When the big day arrived, Jack took Sylvie shopping for the afternoon, stopping for milkshakes on the way home. It gave Mia time to coordinate the arrival of the ten girls she'd invited, decorate the great room with sixteen balloons, and pick up the two-layer vanilla cake with chocolate frosting from Fiona's Cake Shop. Fiona's specialized in making the finest cakes in the area. Nothing but the best for her little girl; Mia wanted to do something special for Sylvie. Turning sixteen only happened once.

Sally, Jill, Heather, and Ava arrived first. Sally wore a tight-fitting tube top with bright red lipstick, her long hair recently styled with a few highlights. Mia thought it was a strange outfit for a sixteenth-birthday party.

She said, "Girls, nice to see you. It's been years. How have you been?"

She sat around with the girls drinking iced tea and greeted the other girls when they rang the doorbell. Everyone helped put out appetizers. Beth got there just in time.

Just before Sylvie got home and made her way through the kitchen from the garage, Mia stopped for a moment and looked at the decorations, the girls, the presents, the cake. *Beautiful.* She couldn't wait to see Sylvie's face.

Mia winked at the girls. "Hey, Sylvie, I'm in the living room."

Sylvie rounded the corner to the shouts of "Surprise!" from everyone. Shocked, she simply stood there and eyed the girls, one by one. "Uh, thanks." She clasped her hands tightly.

Mia hugged her. "Happy sweet-sixteen birthday!" She must have really amazed her daughter because Sylvie just stood there, seemingly unsure what to do next. "Do you want to open your presents now or after cake?"

Sylvie stepped back from the group as if she needed space. "I think I'll sit down for a moment." She sat on the coach and listened to the girls talk about sixteen-year-old things. At one point, she got up and changed into a nicer outfit, brushed her hair out of her braid, and put on some lip gloss.

Mia left the girls to party on their own and found Jack in the study. She placed her arms around his shoulders. "Thank you for taking such good care of our daughter today. Isn't it lovely?"

Jack nodded. "Mia, you did an outstanding job. I think this will really help connect her with her friends again. Thanks."

Tears rose in Mia eyes. "I do believe this is a turning point."

It was. Just not in the way she had presumed.

two

SYLVIE

Before—Sylvie's Childhood

appy memories: sitting on her dad's shoulders, pointing to a store window display filled with soft, floppy stuffed animals. Twirling around and around, her blonde hair following her as she tried to catch a few raindrops with her tongue; Tim holding her hand; making snow angels with her mom.

She didn't care much for school. The outside world felt as bristly as a thistle. By contrast, home was soft and smooth, like a perfect summer day.

Sylvie attended half-days in kindergarten and attempted to do what was expected of her. She learned the alphabet, numbers, games, social time, and participated in group activities. But her heart ached the whole time as she waited for her dad to pick her up at lunchtime, or for the smell of her mom's home-made cookies, or to hear the sound of the classical music her parents played at dinnertime.

She acquired the ability to lie by the time she was five. "Yep, I had a good day," Sylvie told her parents. She also learned that when she smiled, people left her alone and didn't ask her any more questions.

In first grade, she transitioned to full-day schooling, which wore her out: kids laughing and shouting on the playground, the rhythmic whoosh of swings going back and forth, stepping on sticky floors from juice spills, trying to memorize assignments stretched across the whiteboard in the classroom, students moving around her, the sound of chairs scraping against the tile floor, the frenzied rush of everyone unzipping and zipping their backpacks, the chewing sound of the pencil sharpener.

Not chosen for a friendship circle or team, she retreated to her inner world: a place filled with faeries and wizards who could talk, fly, cherish her secrets, and best of all, love her. Every day, she drew and painted and wrote about her magical world: a world where everyone belonged, and where days were full of sunshine, good wishes, and happiness.

In second grade, Sylvie graduated from her dad picking her up after school every day to riding the bus; an older, big yellow bus with leather spinach-green seats. By the time it arrived at her stop, the popular children who lived up the hill behind her neighborhood had the back seats, behind the rear wheels. When the bus windows fogged up, they drew silly pictures and notes with their fingers on them.

Sylvie liked her seat—number sixteen—because it had the heater right at her feet. For most of the school year, she wore a puffy coat, her misty breath forming dense vapor clouds as she waited on the sidewalk for the bus to turn the corner. She imagined her favorite stuffed animals, Scooter and Squirmy, right there next to her.

In third and fourth grade, she watched the other kids and didn't raise her hand much in the classroom. She stayed in her seat and didn't rush to the front of the line. The more vocal peers got first pick and that was fine with her.

But a perplexing disquiet stewed within her, like a strange concoction from a witch's brew. Sylvie wanted to fit in, but felt more secure in her imaginary world. Sometimes when her teacher singled her out to answer a question, her mouth felt as dried up as an autumn leaf. She could barely get the words out, rehearsing the answer in her head over and over and over. Her palms were covered in sweat. Even if she knew the answer, she said, "I dunno," more times than she should have. She kept this charade up through fifth grade.

But by sixth grade, a few things changed that would have lasting consequences.

One cold February morning, Sylvie got on the bus and shuffled down the aisle. She sat closest to the window and placed her alto recorder and her heavy book bag on the seat next to her, like she had done for the past several years.

In seat seventeen sat her former friend from third grade, Samantha. She didn't talk to Sylvie anymore. Samantha wore makeup and close-fitting shirts, painted her nails, and much to Sylvie's fascination, even self-tanned. Boys liked Samantha. She had a lot of friends who giggled about kissing or pointed to suggestive pictures in teenage magazines like *Seventeen*.

That February morning, Samantha held a stack of red and blue envelopes and began to pass them out to the other kids on the bus. Some kids yelled when they opened them. "Birthday party, yeah!" Almost everyone on the bus received an invitation.

Not Sylvie. She just stared out the window, pretending that the lack of an invitation didn't bother her. But it did. She kept her lips securely closed and feigned indifference. She thought about painting Samantha a picture for her birthday; the colors she'd use, maybe even write her a short poem. Do something nice, letting her know she still cared about her.

Maybe Samantha didn't think Sylvie liked her anymore. Sylvie's lips curved upward.

At the next stop, Sylvie's friend Nancy waved and took the empty seat next to Sylvie. Sylvie and Nancy talked about inconsequential stuff—their shared love of animals and a cartoon they liked. Sylvie didn't feel as isolated anymore.

Once they got to school, Sylvie went to her classroom door and Nancy to hers. Sixth-grade kids had to wait at the outside doors.

Nancy said, "See you at lunch."

Sylvie was glad she had someone to sit with in the boisterous cafeteria.

Some of the sixth graders started a snowball fight in the tetherball courts. The playgrounds and recess fields looked like a vast expanse of white—still, serene, cold. The snow-capped peaks of the Rocky Mountains, visible through the fog, blended well next to the gray, cloudy sky. Icicles like frozen spears fell off the roof of Sylvie's elementary school. The air smelled icy— crisp, sharp, tingling her nose like peppermint.

Mr. Stevens, one of Sylvie's favorite teachers, was late opening the classroom door. Often the last teacher to his classroom, Mr. Stevens appreciated a chat with a fellow teacher, filling his coffee cup, or answering an email or two before a long day with his sixth graders.

Mrs. Jones' class, next to Mr. Stevens, had already let her students inside. Nancy was in her class.

Sylvie waited in the cold, but in her opinion, spending a school day with Mr. Stevens was worth it. He taught her real, useful skills, and encouraged her to explore her creativity, often imploring her to "reach for the stars."

Sylvie liked her class, except for the fact that she didn't have friends. She tried to conform, but she enjoyed things her classmates were not interested in. Sylvie still relished living in a make-believe world: playing Animal Elementary, writing fantasy tales, and drawing whimsical designs. She didn't like rap music, shopping at the mall, discussing the latest fashions, or any of the activities the other girls seemed to revel in.

Those red and blue shiny envelopes Samantha had on the bus were still in Sylvie's mind as she looked around at her class. Most had one in hand. Some didn't. Heather didn't, and neither did Kristy or Ava. Those three girls sat together near the benches, talking about anime, covered in dog hair, with backpacks smelling like cigarette smoke. Sylvie wondered if they were more like her.

Then just before the bell rang and Mr. Stevens came, Nancy burst through her classroom door. The heavy door slammed against the brick wall. Nancy ran out, screaming, "I can't take it anymore!"

She sprinted across the tetherball courts, pushed a few of Sylvie's classmates aside, and ran as fast as she could toward the edge of the school property, kicking up snow like a hare loosed from a trap, her long limbs seemingly with a life of their own. Mrs. Jones called after her, while the rest of Sylvie's class watched Nancy make a dash for the chain link fence.

A few days before, Nancy had told Sylvie, "I hate school. I'm gonna run away the next time someone tries to touch my rucksack or take my pencils without asking again."

"How would you run away?" Sylvie asked.

Nancy pointed across the playground to a gap in the fencing. Sylvie had never been in that neighborhood, and she didn't think Nancy would actually do it. But there she was, racing through the snow like a mad person.

"Nancy!" Mrs. Jones yelled. Her voice echoed off the playground equipment.

Sylvie's entire class alternated between gawking at Nancy, and then at Sylvie. Sylvie stared at the snow and her boots. She wished she could just coil into herself, like a piece of yellowed paper. Sylvie thought Nancy might just keep running, but she stopped before she reached the edge of the field. Nancy balled her fists, turned around, and walked back to class, muttering under her breath, kicking at chunks of ice, tugging on her ponytail.

Sylvie didn't like it when Nancy got wild like that. It scared her.

Finally, Mr. Stevens unlocked the door, oblivious to Nancy's outburst, and the class shuffled inside, stomping snow off their boots on the doormat. Sylvie's classmates talked animatedly about what just happened with Nancy. Sylvie tried to ignore the comments.

"Good morning, Sylvie," Mr. Stevens said cheerily. "How are you?" He lightly rapped his fingers against his leg as if to some internal music.

"I'm okay," she said. She gazed up at him, questioning whether he'd understand her dilemma with her classmates. Probably not, she thought. "I wrote a story about a rainbow-colored cat that swims across the ocean."

Mr. Stevens beamed. "Keep writing, Sylvie. You've got talent." He added. "Oh, and I'd like to see any new artwork."

The encouragement lifted Sylvie's spirit and her worries about Nancy drifted away. Sylvie immersed herself in her morning assignments. By midmorning, snowflakes as big as pennies started to fall and cover the playground in sheets of white. The principal called for indoor recess. Kids groaned.

Because they couldn't go outside, the sixth-grade classes mingled for lunch hour. Boys played board games or cards. The girls sat huddled in tight groups, tittering, flipping through periodicals with pictures of celebrities Sylvie didn't know.

Nancy coaxed Sylvie to practice dance routines on the tile near the sink in the back of the room. At her mom's insistence, "to build character and discipline," Sylvie studied tap dance at one of the town's studios and decided to rehearse her newest routine.

A ballet student, Nancy kept correcting her. "You have to keep your back straight," she said.

Sylvie knew for a fact that wasn't true for a tap dancer. "No, in tap we don't have a straight back."

Nancy, who had taken ballet classes since she was three, fumed. "My teacher said you have to keep your back straight."

"But I'm in tap. You're in ballet. There's a difference. And in tap we're supposed to bend forward." Sylvie demonstrated by posing. She couldn't understand why Nancy had to be so antagonistic.

Nancy snapped, "I know better! You're doing it all wrong."

Sylvie inhaled, struggling for calm. She tasted coppery anger on her tongue, and then, before she could stop herself, she blurted, "Well, then why don't *you* come up here and show me how to tap dance, since you seem to know everything."

Sylvie put her hand over her mouth, afraid she might've gone too far.

Nancy gritted her teeth and stomped to within an inch of Sylvie's face. She wrapped her hands around Sylvie's neck and gripped tight. Nancy, who was at least four inches taller, fixed her razor-sharp gaze on Sylvie, and squeezed.

Sylvie couldn't breathe. Nancy pressed harder and shook Sylvie's head back and forth, back and forth. Nancy's hands were cold. To Sylvie, Nancy's long fingers and nails felt as unyielding as steel.

"It's not fair!" Nancy shrieked. She let go of Sylvie's neck and dropped her hands to her side, quickly surveying the room. "I hate you! I hate all of you!" She dashed into the hallway and shouted, "I'm going to the restroom. Leave me alone!"

Girls stopped their snickering and looked up from the magazines. The boys suspended their board games in a momentary silent pause. They watched Nancy leave. Then they looked at Sylvie.

Sylvie touched her neck where Nancy had choked her. Her skin felt hot and flushed. An ache expanded in her chest. She searched for Mr. Stevens, but he happened to be just outside the door, conversing with another teacher. He hadn't seen what had happened.

Embarrassed, she dropped her eyes to the floor and went to her desk, folded her arms and rested her head on her hands, careful to snuff out the desperate sob waiting to surface.

For two whole weeks, before she told her mom, Sylvie worried about what would've happened if Nancy had squeezed her neck just a little longer or just a little firmer. Of course, her mom took charge and she lost the only friend she made that year. It was a lonely time for Sylvie, but it also inspired her to retreat into an enchanted dreamland.

"Mom, would it be okay with you if I painted a mural?" she asked.

Her mom pondered Sylvie's request for a moment. "I don't know about splattering a wall with paint, but I'd buy a large canvas, extra brushes, and paint."

"That'll work," Sylvie agreed.

For six months, Sylvie coated the canvas with intricate designs of her spiritual world. A place with jagged mountain peaks sprinkled with snow, lush green valleys, waterfalls, lakes, elk, buffalo, elephants, giraffes, monkeys, eagles, owls, hawk, songbirds, and a slew of wildly colorful butterflies roaming freely throughout the landscape. She even captured faeries and elves sitting on rock ledges, and a magician flying in the almost-purple sky.

Her father sometimes watched her paint, mesmerized by her focus and attention. "Wow. I don't think I've ever seen anything so beautiful in my life." He observed the way she delicately dipped her brush into a bead of silvery-gray paint. "Do you have a name for this place?"

Sylvie lifted her brush off the canvas and placed it on the palette. "No, not really."

"Maybe we could find a name together," Jack said. He continued to watch her for a while. His daughter was truly talented.

Despite focusing on his daughter's work, he missed the troll she drew hiding in a bush, the butterfly with devil horns, and the more obvious ogre chasing a little pink piglet.

three

JACK

A few months after... Owls

Jack let the car idle for a moment, before turning off the ignition, and admired the golden aspen leaves quivering in the morning light. As he watched some of the leaves fall to the ground, he wondered when the first snow would come this year, covering everything in white. There was a certain beauty to the starkness of winter, but he'd miss the autumn colors.

He grabbed his briefcase and the coffee he had just bought at a local drive-through and headed for his office, arriving a little before eight a.m. He always liked to get to work before Ben, his three junior staff members, and Monica, his dedicated administrative assistant.

Glad to have a moment, he closed the door to his office and sipped on rich espresso. The sound of the Roaring Fork River drifted through a marginally opened window. He could see the sky edged with clouds.

On his desk stood a picture of Mia taken years ago, showing her copious brown hair, her tender smile and open eyes. He felt lucky the day he met her. Hiking on a trail near Maroon Bells, he'd seen her sitting on a boulder near a stream.

He dipped his hands in the creek. "Nice day for a walk."

She looked up. "Yes, it is."

Jack, struck by the color of her eyes, a mixture of topaz and aquamarine, asked, "Where are you headed?" He hoped they might be going in the same direction.

"Back to my car."

His heart sank a little. "Oh. I'm on my way up to the ridge."

She didn't say anything. He mumbled something about maybe next time, which sounded a little corny, considering he'd just met her. He had his camera out and snapped a photo of her just as she turned to glance his way, her mouth slightly open.

"Hey, I could send you the photo, if you'd like?"

She laughed and gave Jack her phone number.

That was thirty-five years ago. To him, her energy had always seemed measureless. He likened it to the ocean, bottomless and endless. Yesterday, when she quietly returned home from work, she looked tired, worn out, as if her heart was all zipped up.

Tilting his head back slightly on his soft leather desk chair, his heart skipped a beat or two when he eyed another photo on the top shelf of his bookcase: Sylvie when she was about three, holding a stuffed dinosaur they had just bought at the local mercantile shop down the street. Her smile was just like Mia's, that delicate crooked grin, pinching up her cheek as if she had a dimple there.

Sylvie was a daddy's girl. Born premature, she became Jack's universe. Unable to stop spoiling her, he bought her baby toys every week—rag dolls, stuffed animals, books, trikes. Rearranging his schedule, he worked from home a lot before she went to school. When he took time for lunch, he packed her in a snuggly feather-down onesie, and went for a long walk.

The waiter, at one of their regular bistros, would light up when he saw them. "Ah, Mr. Weaver, nice to see you. And Sylvie —what a gorgeous girl."

Sylvie giggled when he tickled her chin, her blonde curls bobbling up and down.

Those were the best years. Jack never wanted anything bad to touch her. Overprotective, yes. But he felt that was okay. After all, his daughter was special—no, *super*-special. Maybe all fathers felt that way.

Jack convinced Mia to let Sylvie attend only half-day kindergarten and insisted that he could take care of her in the afternoon. "I can easily work from home," he assured her. In his opinion, Sylvie wasn't ready for the onslaught of peer and academic pressure. Jack thought nine a.m. to noon seemed like plenty of time to begin the schooling process. When noon came, he'd be there waiting for her at the front door of her elementary school.

She'd burst through the doorway. "Daddy, Daddy, guess what I learned today?"

He feigned innocence, so she could tell him all about it, his heart like a bowl of jelly—gooey and soft. They spent the afternoons of that year playing imaginary games, tea parties with her beloved stuffed animals, and watching cartoons.

At three p.m., they drove to pick up Tim at his school. Sylvie adored her big brother and watched his every move. She tried to imitate him reading a book or playing a video game, and even asked for licorice (Tim's favorite) instead of ice cream (her ideal treat).

Mia, often running late after a speaking engagement, would breeze through the front door, holding her arms out wide as if to hug the world. "Hey, my beautiful family, how was your day?"

Jack would sit around their hand-carved walnut dining room table listening to his family talk about the weather, the new kid at school, the upcoming science fair, who moved to town, a movie coming out, Mia's impending conference, or where they wanted to vacation that year. If he'd known that was happiness, he would've savored the moments more and not have taken them for granted.

Monica tapped at the glass window separating his office from the lobby. Jack motioned for her to come in.

"Hey, Monica, what's up?"

"Morning, Mr. Weaver. Jess from Mountain Spring Builders is on the line. Said something about needing a revision on the Morrie residence."

For the rest of the day, immersed in the details of his job, he didn't think about Sylvie until just after he'd locked up the office. The wind swirled around him, and a few scattered drops of cold sleet froze on his coat. He shivered. As he walked toward his truck, he saw a set of wings fluttering in the dark.

An owl.

Sylvie loved owls.

One January night, he and Sylvie went owl-spying when she was just about seven. The sliver of moonlight allowed them to see the outlines of the trees. They ambled down the path behind the house to an open meadow, a flashlight tucked away in Jack's flannel coat. Sylvie's eyes were big and round; excited. She'd been waiting for this.

For the past several nights, Jack had heard a great horned owl hooting and he had scouted the trees before dawn that morning. Finally, he found the owl perched high in a blue spruce. The owl watched Jack carefully. Then, without warning, the owl rose and was gone, its silent wings a thing of beauty.

Sylvie grasped Jack's hand and squeezed his fingers. He whispered, "Almost there. Remember when we get to the field, not a sound, okay?" She nodded, revealing her new front tooth, a tad uneven.

Their boots made crunchy noises on the packed snow, otherwise nothing. When they got to the clearing, he placed a finger on Sylvie's mouth. "Shh. We might not see the owl right away. We'll just have to stand still and wait. Can you do that?"

She nodded again, maintaining her silence.

They stayed there in the snow waiting for about twenty minutes. The temperature had fallen, and their breaths made ribbons of fog. Sylvie scuffed her feet from side to side. He draped his arms around her, pulling her in close.

"Just a few more minutes." He was beginning to lose hope they'd see the bird.

Then, *whoo-hoo, whoo-hoo* echoed through the trees.

Jack lifted his face and searched for where it might be coming from. He thought he saw a large shape in the top of a ponderosa pine. He lifted Sylvie on to his shoulders and before he could show her where to look, the great horned owl swooped in front of them, her wings barely three feet from Sylvie's astounded face.

They didn't linger after that, the night air ice-cold. At home, they drank hot chocolate and looked up owl facts in the bird book he'd given her. That week Sylvie drew a picture of them and the owl, her talent evident to him even then.

Jack hung the picture on his work bulletin board and smiled every time he saw it, even years later when it was covered by other job stuff.

⟍⟋

The car took a moment to warm up.

Jack sat there, not turning on the lights quite yet and thought about how hard it was to not let his mind drift into the past. The effort to try and stay present sucked the energy out of him, his Sylvie memories more precious than ever. His hands trembled as he reached for his keys in his pocket and started the ignition.

Two large tear drops, one from each eye, rolled down his cheeks and into the collar of his shirt.

four

SYLVIE

Before—Junior High

When she walked through the doors of her new, much larger junior high school, Sylvie hoped making friends there would be like trying to learn her locker combination—just keep trying until she felt the click.

But it wasn't like that.

Rapidly, tight-knit peer groups formed and blatantly excluded her. Cohorts who had the new flip phone texted their friends during school. Peers sported the new hairstyle with side bangs. Girls kissed boys and buddies rode in a limo to the formal dance. Many of Sylvie's female classmates started wearing high heels and delicate underwear, spritzing themselves in the latest "So Sexy" Victoria's Secret perfume.

Kids left her alone. Isolated, Sylvie found comfort in reading fantasy books.

Her seventh-grade science teacher, Mrs. Magma, noticed how often Sylvie sat in the hall before class, her face covered by an opened novel or her hair falling in front of her. One day, she asked if Sylvie could stay after class.

"Sylvie, I think you'd be a great asset to our Science Olympiad team. Would you consider joining? We meet after school on Tuesdays and Thursdays." The teacher reached out her hand as if to stroke Sylvie's hair and then pulled it back. "There are some great kids on the team."

"Really?" Sylvie had spent the entire class period worried that she might have done something wrong.

"Yes, I personally think you'd be excellent. I think the other kids would like you, too," Mrs. Magma said.

Sylvie felt a bolt of joy. Other kids might like her? She jumped at the opportunity to be a part of something, to have a place to go after school, meet new people, and maybe just be herself. After school that day she noticed her mother's car in the driveway. She ran toward the house, sprinted up the front stairs, and opened the door.

"Mom, Mom! Guess what?" she yelled, slightly out of breath.

"What?"

Sylvie dropped her books and hurried to the kitchen. "My science teacher asked me to join the Science Olympiad team! They meet after school on Tuesdays and Thursdays. Can I join, please? Can you pick me up on those days?"

"Of course, you can." Smoothing a crease in her skirt, she motioned to Sylvie. "Come here, give me a hug."

Sylvie excelled in the extracurricular activity, making new friends with kids who enjoyed invention, discussing scientific theory, and speculating about diverse ideas. She medaled first in regional and state competitions, and competed nationally twice. She loved the *clink-clang-clink-clang* of her medals worn around her neck in the hallways the day after a competition, especially the first-place ones. They shone with a golden hue.

But Sylvie didn't wear them again after Sally, who sat behind her in her social studies class, turned to her friend and whispered, "Those medals sound so annoying, oh, my *God*!"

Sally's friend, Maggie, snickered in agreement. Sally bared her teeth like a beaver and mocked the *clang*. "CLINK-CLONK-I'm-a-dork-CLINK-CLONK!"

Maggie laughed harder.

"You know what I think?" Sally hissed after a minute, her voice audible only to Maggie and Sylvie. "She should just take those medals and use them to hang herself...."

Sylvie knew she should just ignore her, but she peered over her shoulder anyway.

Why would Sally say such a thing?

Sally caught her glance. "Oh, did you hear what we said? You know we're just kidding, right?" She flashed a fake-sweet smile, crossed her arms tightly across her chest, and fixed her gaze on Sylvie.

Sylvie had never met anyone as glamorous as Sally—tall, beautiful, fashionable, long lashes with impeccable makeup, no acne, ears pierced twice, a series of silver rings on her fingers and bangles on her wrists. She carried expensive face cream in a designer bag and had a phone, just like in the commercials. Everybody knew her name; she'd dated boys, and sat at the "cool" table in the cafeteria for lunch.

Sylvie didn't believe her for a second, but she nodded anyway, and faced forward, pretending to be interested in the teacher's lecture. She felt a sadness uncoil, taking up space inside her. Looking out the classroom window, she saw white clouds drifting across a pale blue sky. She wished she could float away, get lost there.

When the bell rang, she forced herself to pick up her books and walk out of the classroom without looking at Sally, concentrating on other things. An image of princess with a black heart surfaced in Sylvie's mind.

She wanted to tell her mom what happened at school and what the other girls said, either to her face or behind her back, but Sylvie shied away from sharing the way she felt because whenever she shared bits and pieces of the harassment, her mom's face changed. Anxious ripples grew into deep canyon contours.

Like the time she finally told her about Nancy.

After she related what had happened, Sylvie knew her mom was so upset she couldn't sleep. Instead, she hovered. Her wide, sharp eyes watched Sylvie's every move, waiting for her to show the slightest sign of distress.

The thought of burdening her mom with the drama about Sally, or rumors and gossip seemed to hurt more than the tyranny. She decided to hide her feelings. But it left her feeling like a stranger in her own body.

Awkward. Alone. Adrift.

five

MIA

A few months after... Memories

t had only been a few months since that dreadful day, but to Mia it felt like years.

In her office at work, she tried to focus on the sixteen year old talking about her recent breakup with her boyfriend. To the girl, it mattered a lot—but Mia only half-listened to the teenager talk about her troubles. Memories of Sylvie flooded her mind.

Bobbing her head at the proper times, Mia offered, "Try to concentrate on just today and not worry so much about tomorrow." She ended her session with a few mindfulness techniques. "Breathe in. Breathe out. See if you can feel your abdomen rise." She did the exercises, too; heaven knew she needed it.

At lunch she met Holly—a colleague and psychologist like Mia—at one of her favorite restaurants in town, or at least it used to be. She hadn't been out much for fear of running into somebody she knew. They'd ask questions about Sylvie that she wasn't ready to talk about.

Holly hugged Mia and stepped back to look in her eyes. "How are you?"

"I'm fine," she fibbed. Her smile felt stiff, like clothes left to dry in the cold.

Holly paused, but didn't press. "How is your caseload this year? My schedule is already full of seniors falling behind and afraid of not graduating. I can't believe the district has asked our team to take on two additional schools." She laughed.

The sound of her mirth jolted Mia slightly. She hoped it didn't show. When was the last time she had felt the tickle of pleasure?

The waiter brought two Caesar salads topped with plump grilled shrimp. Holly stirred the dressing in her salad and began to tackle the crisp bite-sized lettuce pieces. "Delicious."

Mia watched Holly eat and played with her own food, making little roads, cutting up the shrimp. She listened to Holly chat about her kids, the delight obvious in her voice.

"Holly, that's wonderful," Mia said. "I'm glad Travis made the football team." But she wasn't glad, not really.

Holly asked. "Aren't you going to eat?"

Mia looked down at the mushy salad. It didn't look right. "Oh. Guess I'm not that hungry."

"Well, maybe next time. Maybe we can try the new sushi place downtown."

Without thinking, Mia said, "Looking forward to it."

She had no intention of following through.

That afternoon she wrote up a few treatment plans, attended a family meeting, answered emails, and made a phone call before leaving the office. A light drizzle had begun to fall, smearing the dust on her car. She made a happy face on the window, then changed the smile to a squiggly line.

She took the long way home and passed Sylvie's old elementary school. Back in those days, they were so happy—Sylvie, Jack, Tim, and Mia. People used to call them "the quintessential family."

Willing herself not to get out, Mia kept driving past the school and arrived at her contemporary mountain home a little after five. Jack's black truck, clean and dry, was parked in the garage. She stayed in the car for a few minutes before entering a quieter-than-usual house.

"Hello."

Jack appeared, wearing a Broncos apron, trying to cover the extra weight he'd recently acquired. "Hey there. Tim said he might call tonight. Thought you might like some quiet before dinner." He peered over his glasses. "How was work?"

Work—at one time, she loved going to work. She packed a healthy lunch, sometimes going to a yoga class during her lunch hour or meeting up with friends for happy hour. But mostly she dedicated her working hours to helping teenagers "find themselves."

She worked for the Maple School District as a psychologist. When she started the job, there were very few mental health professionals offering services within schools. But times changed; then came Columbine, and her life got busier. Soon the school district had a team of therapists offering mental health assistance: counseling for youth experiencing emotional distress; psychological testing; assessments; even support for emergencies, like a teacher or student death. Her reputation as a skilled specialist grew and she had more speaking engagements than she could fit in a week.

Now her days were filled with administrative duties, with the occasional volunteering to coach kids. Like today.

But her heart wasn't in it.

She thought about retirement. But then thoughts of *what would I do?* crept into her head, and she lost the guts to begin the process.

"Oh, you know. Same old, same old," she said. "What's for dinner?" Mia had become a master at switching the topic away from anything that had to do with her feelings.

Jack brightened. "Picked up some wild salmon today at the Flying Fish. Thought we could grill out. Would you like a glass of wine with dinner tonight?"

Jack and Mia used to share a glass of wine or two in the middle of the week. They'd lounge and talk about their kids and their milestones, all sources of pride.

Tim's successes: valedictorian at his high school graduation; getting into University of Washington and then Stanford; his medical degree. They relished delighting in Sylvie's art awards, the medals she won in Science Olympiad, her poetry, her style and grace.

Mia tried to sound cheerful, but the thought of wine made her throat close. "No, I'll pass tonight. I'm going to run a hot bath instead. Maybe use some of those new bath salts you bought me. Give me about an hour and I'll join you for dinner."

Years of working as a mental health professional had taught her how to mask shock, concern, alarm, and how to be the consummate listener. She attended to Jack's account of his day and nodded her head accordingly.

She was happy for him—or maybe not.

Jack continued, "We closed on the Johnson project today. That house is going to be spectacular and I can't wait to start the drawings. Think I'll go in early tomorrow."

Jack worked as an architect at Weaver and Olsen Design, a firm not far from where they lived. Jack and his partner, Ben Olsen, built the company from Jack and Mia's kitchen table and over the years the firm triumphed with consistent demand from clients. She knew he didn't want to retire just yet.

"Okay. Sounds good. I'll do the dishes if you'd like." She felt like a fraud trying to be civil. How long could she do this?

In the middle of the night, she woke and couldn't fall back to sleep. Jack's light snores were no help. She found her soft wrap —a recent gift from Tim—and shuffled out to the screened-in porch in her sheepskin moccasins.

The full moon cast a blue-white light on everything; the coolness was pleasant on her skin. She let out a long sigh, and then another and then another. Had she been on edge?

She pulled her legs up into a cross-legged position on the wicker rocking chair and willed herself to meditate. After all, she knew what to do—she gave advice all day long.

Her mind, though, like a thousand monkeys, jumped all over the place and landed on nothing. It was no use. She stretched out and let her thoughts drift, hoping they'd be like flower petals carried away by the breeze. But they stuck quickly on things she'd rather forget.

Especially Sylvie's last year of high school, when Mia believed Sylvie had weathered the worst of the adolescent angst that almost every teenager she worked with went through.

～⌒

Sylvie came up the stairs from the finished basement, holding hands with her then-best friend, Naomi, sobbing uncontrollably.

"Don't. No, I can't tell her."

Mia put on her psychologist face. "What can't you tell me?"

Sylvie's face, flooded with tears, looked like a little girl. She eyeballed Naomi and pleaded with her. "Can we just stop? I can't bear it." She wrapped her arms tightly around her middle as if her insides might spill out.

Naomi crossed her arms. "Well, if you don't tell them, I will."

Sylvie continued to cry as if one of the water faucets had been left running. She seemed a little unhinged and that scared Mia. She had never seen her daughter cry like that.

Mia delayed saying anything, counting her breaths. *Breathing in, breathing out.*

Time slowed and a couple of minutes passed. She waited for Sylvie to speak.

Finally, Sylvie shook her head. "I can't do it."

Naomi looked at Mia and then at Sylvie, and blurted, "Sylvie has been having lots of suicidal thoughts. She doesn't want to live anymore. She also tried a few times."

Tried what *a few times?*

Surely Naomi must be mistaken. Mia knew her own daughter.

Mia would've known if Sylvie was suicidal. She was a psychologist, for heaven's sake! Naomi did not know who she was talking to.

Mia assumed Naomi to be a negative influence on her daughter; planting pessimistic seeds in her head or egging her on to do something dangerous. She was sure this was Naomi's doing, not Sylvie's.

Facing Naomi, she put her game face on. "Thank you for sharing this with us. Perhaps it would be wise for you to allow our family some time to absorb this shocking news and to talk to Sylvie in private."

Mia's skin felt prickly and taut. She should've been grateful to Naomi, but she was deeply shaken. *Just leave already, I can't stand you being here.*

Naomi got up off the couch. The way she grabbed her coat and slammed the door—Mia still couldn't understand the friendship. Naomi seemed a bit too tactless. She probably bought her clothes at Walmart.

Sylvie didn't say a word, just placed her hands over her face, and rocked back and forth, like one of those roly-poly bugs.

"I'm going to call your dad. He's in his workshop." Dialing Jack's phone, Mia felt shaky. Right then, she needed Jack. Luckily, he picked up on the first ring. "Hey, Sylvie's not doing so hot. Can you come in and talk?"

Jack and Mia each took a seat next to Sylvie on the couch. They looked at each other. Sylvie crisscrossed her arms and held her shoulders. Her knuckles were white.

Mia couldn't help but stare at them.

Why were they so bony? Who was this frightened, slightly emaciated seventeen year old?

Mia's thoughts seemed thick and gluelike, sticking in the corners like they were not making the right neural connections. Anger and sadness pulled her in all directions.

After what seemed like an unbearable amount of time, Sylvie unfurled her limbs, grabbed a tissue, blew her nose, and stood up. "I can't talk about it right now."

Mia watched her move toward the coat rack. "Wait. Please don't go out. Are you safe? Can we talk later? Tomorrow? Please?" She scrutinized Sylvie's face, searching for clues, part mother, part investigator.

Was she really suicidal or was Naomi overreacting? She suspected Naomi envied Sylvie. Either way, Mia would find a good counselor for Sylvie. Maybe the therapist could help Sylvie end her crazy friendship with Naomi.

Sylvie sighed. "I just want to be left alone. I need to call Naomi and tell her I'm all right. I won't go anywhere, I promise. Just outside." She walked to the front closet, put on her down coat, took out her phone, and turned to face her parents before closing the door.

Sylvie's tired smile did little to mollify Mia's rising angst. An uneasiness trickled into her bones. In the middle of the night, having surrendered to insomnia, Mia found her bathrobe and went to check on Sylvie.

Asleep, she looked soft and tender—the way Mia remembered her as a child. Her angelic face full of wonder whenever she touched a butterfly. Running as fast as her little legs could go to keep up with her older brother.

Mia's heart contracted a little, recalling her beautiful daughter, and wondered what in the world might have happened. The pain of not being able to protect her stung.

But the bite of what was to follow hurt a lot more.

six

SYLVIE

Before - Junior High

When her eighth-grade PE teacher paired her with Beth for all the upcoming sport activities and challenges, she thought she'd won the lottery. She'd made a few friends from Science Olympiad, but they never shared any classes together and didn't have the same lunch period. Beth shared her exact schedule.

Beth was on the gymnastics team and she performed her backflips and cartwheels flawlessly. Everyone in class clapped when she landed a dive roll. After school, Sylvie would stay and watch Beth practice.

"Can you do *this*?" Beth's voice echoed off the high rafters. Nimble and slender, she sprinted, seemingly effortlessly, across the gymnasium floor and flew into a forward flip.

"Uh, no," Sylvie responded shyly.

"Try," Beth encouraged, beckoning Sylvie to join her on the gym floor. "I'll spot you. Come on, you can do it, Sylvie. Just try!"

Sylvie tried. After weeks of practice, she managed to do a handstand—even if she only held it for a second. Working out with Beth helped Sylvie's confidence. She became physically stronger than she'd ever been before, and passed all of the physical stamina tests in her physical education classes.

Beth openly admired Sylvie's artistic aptitude and also urged her to enter the schools' most prestigious award—the Almost Famous contest. Every year the school honored an individual who showed the most promise.

"Your artwork has won first place in our region for three years in a row!" Beth nudged Sylvie's side. "And the principal asked you to write a poem about our school. C'mon, you can't win if you don't try."

Beth and Sylvie's friendship flourished. They did everything together: shared inside jokes; laughed at the lunch table; walked through the hallways with arms interlocked; went shopping and even explored fashion ideas.

Sylvie finally felt like a teenage girl like everybody else, doing girly things with her best friend, discovering what all that lingo meant in magazines, and all the hip fashions on television. Sylvie bought thongs and perfume, and started wearing makeup and jewelry.

Her dad noticed. "Sylvie, I saw you downtown today with Beth. She seems like a nice friend."

When Sylvie told Tim about her BFF, he scoffed. "About time." Making friends was easy for Tim.

For spring semester, Sylvie could hardly wait for her new creative writing class. With her friendship with Beth solidly in place and now finally in a course where she could explore her ingenuity, Sylvie felt buoyantly self-assured.

She entered the Almost Famous contest, submitting a portfolio of selected photos of her art with captions of the ribbons and medals she'd won, along with her state and national accomplishments in Science Olympiad, and her poetry, which was really what she was most proud of. She spent extra time on the cover—a 3D rendition of the mountains surrounding the town.

When one of the contest committee members reviewed Sylvie's work, she lifted the portfolio and said, "Isn't this something?"

Sylvie walked through the classroom door, head held high, took her seat, and peered at her fellow classmates. She sighed and thought about Beth, who had decided to take a math tutorial instead. Most of the students were boys—goofing off on the other side of the room. The only girls were Sally and Maggie in the seats behind her.

Sally flicked her hair and flashed Sylvie a sugary-rich smile. Sylvie didn't acknowledge her.

At lunch, Beth said, "You have creative writing with Sally and Maggie?"

"Yeah." Sylvie wondered why Beth seemed so happy.

"Oh, cool. They're awesome. I'm jealous—I wish I had that class with them."

"You know Sally?" Sylvie let out a nervous titter. Surely Beth wouldn't like someone like Sally.

She nodded. "We went to the same elementary school. Sally and I were good friends in fourth grade."

Her chest tightened. "Oh. That's nice." The tension spread down to her stomach.

Sylvie arrived late to her class on the second day. Under the bright fluorescent light strip, she saw Sally and Maggie chatting with a few boys. Other students laughed and shouted greetings to their friends. Sylvie thought she should just forget about what happened in seventh grade.

Maybe Sally and she could even be friends. Beth liked her. Sylvie thought she should at least say hello and try to be nice. Glancing in Sally's direction, she placed her things on her desk and thought about what to say to her.

"Wow, I like your planner," Sally said, pointing to the front of Sylvie's spiral notebook covered with several chemistry formulas. Sally wore a sequined skirt, enormous hoop earrings that chimed when she bent to take a closer look at Sylvie's planner.

She stared, mesmerized by Sally's glamour. She had no idea how Sally managed to look like that every day—mascara, eyeshadow, manicured nails, designer clothing. Sylvie's hello got stuck somewhere between her head and her tongue.

Sally was yet again looking at Sylvie's notebook cover. The formulas were so artistically drawn. "That's interesting."

Sylvie wasn't quite sure how to respond. "Thanks. I'm not quite finished." She shrugged and wondered what Sally might be drawn to.

Sally folded her arms, jangling her wristlets, and lifted her eyebrows. Maggie and the two boys chuckled. "Oh, I know what you should write."

"What?" Sylvie innocently asked. Maybe Sally liked chemistry.

"You should write 'dyke' on the side there, instead. You know…it's just a little bit more honest." She pointed again to the corner near Sylvie's name.

She felt her cheeks warm. She was confused. What did *dyke* mean? She looked at Sally and wanted to ask, but she and her friends started to laugh so hard that they had to put their hands over their mouths.

Sally said, "Think about it." She straightened, adjusted her skirt, and sashayed back to her desk. Maggie's laughter rebounded off the adjacent wall.

The teacher came in and said, "Okay, enough fun and games. Time to learn."

Sylvie tucked her planner into her backpack and kept her head down for the entire class, too humiliated to raise her hand, or look at anyone. She felt like a mouse in a herd of gazelles.

After school she went to the front office and asked for a schedule change. As much as she wanted to stay in creative writing, she just didn't know how to be in there with Sally and Maggie. She didn't tell anyone why she wanted to switch, not even her mom. Her mom wouldn't understand anyway, considering how she couldn't stop talking about how happy she was to get into the class. Her mom knew how much writing meant to her. Whenever her mom brought up the subject, she just kept repeating, "Maybe later. I've got too much to do."

The office gave Sylvie a student-aid job in the tech wing. There she was left alone to fiddle with equipment, organize circuit boards and wires, clean workbenches and sinks. She didn't see Sally much at school, but she always worried she'd find her in the restroom or in some other unsuspecting place.

When Sylvie googled *dyke* and read what it meant, she was bewildered. Why would Sally call her that? What gave her the impression that she was interested in girls? Was she saying that only to be cruel?

She tried to talk to Beth about it. "Sally called me a dyke."

Beth straightened her back. "What?"

"I don't know why she'd say that. Do you?" Sylvie implored.

Beth took a step away from Sylvie. "I can talk to her and ask."

She exhaled. "Thanks, Beth."

She didn't know if Beth had talked to Sally or not, because over the course of next few weeks Sylvie's friendship with Beth teetered. Beth came to school crying, telling Sylvie all about her parents' divorce and how she caught her dad cheating on her mom. Sylvie also noticed that sometimes, when she was busy with Science Olympiad or spent time in the tech room, Beth hung out with Maggie.

Beth started to make excuses about lunch. "Sorry. Can't sit with you today."

One day she found a note in her locker, a torn-up lined piece of scrap paper shoved through the cracks: *dyke*. It looked to be in Beth's handwriting, though she couldn't be sure.

Jostling past a line full of teens, Sylvie rushed to get to the lunchroom first and save Beth a spot. At the first chime of the bell, she sprinted out the classroom door, waiting for her friend in the hallways. But the more she did this, the more Beth seemed annoyed. And, eventually, when she walked into the cafeteria, Beth would already be there, sitting next to Maggie and Sally.

At the end of her eighth-grade year, Beth walked through the halls with Sally and Maggie, wearing new clothes, and changed lockers so she wouldn't be next to Sylvie.

At lunch, Sylvie sat with her Science Olympiad friends. They talked about odd things—aliens, calculus, and the world ending. She listened and watched Beth grow into someone she hardly recognized.

The school assembly for the winner of the Almost Famous contest was on the last day of school. The principal walked up to the podium and addressed the four hundred students assembled on the bleachers.

"Before you rush out these doors for a much-deserved summer break…" Kids cheered. "I'd like to take this opportunity to announce the winner of this year's Almost Famous contest." Students settled down, quiet, eager to hear who had won. "By unanimous decision from our dedicated board, the winner is…" He paused just enough to create a bit of drama.

A few teens groaned. "C'mon, tell us."

The principal spotted Sylvie sitting in the front row. "Sylvie Weaver."

Everyone clapped and applauded. A few shouted, "Way to go, Sylvie."

One of Sylvie's classmates clapped her on the back. "Go on! Get up there!"

Sylvie's cheeks warmed as she made her way to the stage. The principal shook her hand and placed the trophy in her hand.

"Congratulations, Sylvie. It's an honor to give this to you." He beamed. "Is there anything you'd like to say?"

Sylvie struggled for control. "Uh, thank you, Mr. Albright." She turned to face the audience and saw a few of her peers. One of them had told her how much he wanted—no, *needed*— to win. "And thank you to all my talented classmates." She held up the trophy. "This is for you." Some kids gave her a standing ovation.

Sylvie couldn't wait to share the good news with her family and almost jogged out of the auditorium. Classmates she'd known over the years shouted praise. A few whistled. Sylvie wrestled with how to accept such sudden admiration.

On her way to her locker, Sylvie stopped to use the restroom. Sally followed her. Before Sylvie could open the cubicle, Sally slammed into her and folded her arm across Sylvie's neck, "Be honest with me. Are you a lesbian?"

Sylvie had a hard time breathing, but managed to spit out, "No. Of course not."

Sally loosened her chokehold. "Leave Beth alone. She's creeped out by your weird crush on her."

Sylvie felt a trickle of pee. "I don't have a crush on her. I just wanted to be her friend."

Sally whispered, "Yeah and I'm one of the Pussycat Dolls." She stared at the trophy in Sylvie's hands. Sally's eyes held more than a trace of malice.

Sylvie didn't know what she meant, but didn't stick around to find out and sprinted out of there as fast as she could, hearing a few kids call her name.

Thoughts of reporting Sally drifted into her head, but in the end she didn't. How could she go to the office with a grievance after just winning the school's most esteemed prize? Wasn't that hypocritical?

Sylvie spent the summer alone, writing poetry and short stories about illusory things. She repainted the canvas over her bed using a larger brush. Instead of creating complex lifelike sketches, she branched out, applying big wide strokes of various tints and hues, unlike anything she'd done before.

At first it didn't look like much. Her mom didn't like it. "You could've at least asked for a new canvas. I loved that picture."

Sylvie dissented. "It's my room." When she finished coating the picture with an array of lopsided color, it resembled a thousand snakes intermeshed in a mound of hay. It had an eerie appeal.

Sylvie stood back and admired her work. Then she observed her room. Everything was too matchy-matchy.

She went to a thrift store and bought red sheets. A blue pillowcase and an orange one. A faded quilt. She repainted an old end table and lamp gold, then filled an entire wall with her canvases. They fit together like puzzle pieces. She rolled up the Persian rug and put it in the basement, exposing the walnut floor. After that, she framed her recent poems around the door and pushed the barnwood desk her dad made against the naked adjacent wall. The vacant wall was in sharp contrast to almost everything else in the room.

There, Sylvie thought, now I'm ready for high school.

Her mom gave her pep talks about branching out in high school and making new friends.

She's right, Sylvie thought, just stay positive, not let Beth or Sally get to her. Ninth grade would be different.

seven

TIM

Seven months after... Home to Colorado

He stretched his legs into the aisle. He hated flying. But the Dreamliner he'd chosen to fly on for his journey back to Colorado to be with his family provided much more comfort than he'd had in several months.

A few friends thought it was foolish for him to sign up for the Doctors without Borders program instead of accepting a position at Stanford Health Care. True, he could've made more money. But he needed to get away from it all—the States, the politics, *everything*. Not to be cliché, but the rat race. And he wanted some time to sort things out; to let things settle.

Lilly had officially ended their relationship. "It's over, Tim. Let's just be friends."

The lease on his apartment expired. When the landlord asked if he needed a few weeks to think it over, Tim replied, "No need. I won't be coming back."

Worried about him, his mom called often. "Tim, it's Mom … call me, uh … when you get a chance … I know you're busy, but … are you okay?" The texts from his dad were only slightly better. "Hey, buddy, got time to talk?"

He didn't want to talk. He'd rather just work; keep himself occupied. Talking made him remember. The memories were like gnats buzzing around his head.

His parents would want to talk about Sylvie; they'd ask him for guidance. Tim didn't have the answers then, and he didn't have them now.

It was not that he didn't want to help; he did. It was just... well, complicated. They would likely never be able to figure out all the pieces, and he knew that frustrated the hell out of them, especially his mom.

An image of the new house his father recently finished floated through Tim's head—a mountain contemporary home built on a few acres of land his parents bought several years ago. The picture they sent featured a downsized version of the home he grew up in, smaller but more elegant somehow. A glimmer of hope flickered near his heart, anticipating spending time there.

The airline attendant motioned to him. "Sir, could you kindly put your feet back under the seat in front of you? We need to keep the aisle clear." Her synthetic smile matched her uniform.

Adjusting his posture, he nodded. "These long flights are killer."

"Can I bring you anything?"

Reluctant to engage in chitchat, he shook his head. "No, I'm okay." Closing his eyes, he dozed for a bit, with thoughts of Sylvie drifting in and out like a sailboat lost at sea.

As far back as he could remember, Sylvie, his baby sister with her emerald eyes and blonde hair, followed him around everywhere, at times annoying the hell out of him. He'd see her out of the corner of his eye: sitting on the stairs, staring through the bar rails, peeking from behind a book, fidgeting with her hair, apprehensive about joining the crowd, afraid she might not fit in. He wished she could've been more forthright, cheeky even.

Just before he started second grade, his mom went back to work in the afternoons. Sylvie was maybe a year, or a year and a half old. His mom sent them to a local day care and Sylvie was there for a few hours before he arrived for his after-school care.

He met a few other boys his age interested in the newest game technology then. They'd spend the time talking about how to progress through the levels, draw cartoon versions of their accomplishments, laugh, drink chocolate milk and munch on cookies.

He would hear Sylvie crying in the next room and the caretakers trying to calm her down. It would be a matter of minutes before one of the caregivers found him and asked if he could sit with her, to help quiet her wails.

Of course, as soon as he entered Sylvie's area, she'd toddle over and grab his hand. Even though he was angry, he just couldn't walk away. He'd end up reading her a story or asking the teacher if she could come to his room and watch the guys play.

When Tim's mom came to pick them up, she'd ask, "So, how did it go? Did you have fun playing with the other kids?"

He protested. "Sylvie cries a lot. Are you sure you want to go back to work?"

His mom twisted her mouth to the side and the crease in the middle of her forehead formed such a deep trench, Tim swore he could drive one of his Matchbox cars through it. She never did answer his question and Sylvie sobbed every time she was at day care for the rest of the year.

Tim loved school. He excelled at anything the teachers threw at him, finishing tasks earlier than his classmates. Then he'd have extra time to do things like looking up interesting statistics in the *Fact or Fiction* books, or think about what he might do when he grew up. He wanted to go to Mars, invent something that nobody had even heard of, explore the deepest part of the ocean, or maybe even find a hidden treasure.

His elementary school teachers often congratulated him on his efforts with comments like, "Tim boy, you just aced another test. Way to go! Maybe we should send you to high school." He didn't mind when they suggested he help his classmates struggling with math or reading. It was the least he could do.

When Sylvie started first grade, Tim was in junior high. They never shared the same school. But he noticed she got off the bus alone, didn't have friends over on the weekends, preferring her own company. She created mini-masterpieces and wrote for hours, or followed him around the house, then planted herself in his room while she sketched.

Sometimes he lashed out. "Sylvie, would you get out of here? Go to your room. You're such a loser." He knew it hurt, but she exasperated him. When she slammed her bedroom door, he'd add, "Grow a backbone." At times it was difficult for him to believe they came from the same parents.

He had a blast in high school, mostly because of his awesome peer group. Josh, his best friend, lived down the street from where Tim grew up. They went to elementary school together followed by middle school, high school, and college. In eighth grade, Josh was easily a foot taller than Tim.

Josh teased, "Hey, Tim, my little buddy. What, are you still in fifth grade?" His guffaw sounded like a jackal.

The jeers hurt a little—okay, maybe a lot—until he caught up in high school, more than caught up actually. He surpassed Josh's height by at least two inches.

Before the end of Tim's sophomore year, Josh grew a moustache and the cutest girls noticed. Tim liked that. Their friendship circle flourished at the start of their junior year and Tim ended up bringing home at least a dozen friends on the weekends. Some weekdays Josh and Tim formed study groups in the Weaver residence's rec room.

Not that they did much studying.

Tim liked this girl named Maggie. She had long, red hair that flowed like a river down her back. When he touched her hair, his heart quivered like the trembling aspen outside his bedroom window. One time, he brushed his hand under her shirt and squeezed her side.

He whispered in Maggie's ear. "Your skin is so soft."

Her hand found Tim's and she guided him to explore more. She cooed. "Your touch feels wonderful."

For a blissful moment, Tim was transported into paradise until he opened his eyes and saw Sylvie staring at him. How she showed up at precisely that moment was a mystery he never figured out, but it pissed him off. Not because she saw him flirting with Maggie, but because she stole his moment.

Seemed like he had felt that way since the day his parents brought her home.

After Maggie left, he saw Sylvie's bedroom lamp on, walked in without knocking, and sat on her bed.

"You little cunt." He was so angry. "Can't you just leave me the fuck alone?"

Sylvie put down the book she was reading and pulled her quilt up to her chin. "Sorry, Tim. I was just looking for my Game Boy. I thought maybe I left it on the couch in the rec room. I didn't mean to disturb you."

"Too late now. Jeez, Sylvie." He punched her in the arm. He'd meant it to be just a friendly knock, but he could tell it hurt by the way she jerked and then frowned. Still, she didn't cry—he gave her that much.

Better than the days when she always cried.

Sylvie preferred being home to almost anything, and that bothered him because he liked going out, especially for dinner. Tim's dad relished in taking Tim to new restaurants, even driving over the pass to try "the new bistro." Even though she went with them, Sylvie picked at her food and didn't seem to enjoy it at all. Tim thought Sylvie destroyed the whole evening.

To alleviate the tension between Tim and Sylvie, Tim's dad often joked. "Hey, Mia, maybe we should try that new Mexican place down the street. I hear they've added mole and homegrown tamales." He kicked Tim's foot under the table and winked. Tim would offer a weak smile, shuffling his feet under the table.

Tim usually pretended it didn't bother him, trying to be oblivious to the obvious. When he got home from these outings, he made a beeline for his second-story bedroom. His dad converted the bottom bunk of his bunk bed into a desk, with books and games filling up the spaces. Tim felt relief when he closed the door and put his headphones on, tuning out what might be going on in the rest of the house. Sometimes he wished he had a brother...and closer to his age.

One day it occurred to him that maybe if Sylvie got interested in his video games, they'd develop a shared interest. He began to tutor her in the art of video-gaming by allowing her to just watch him while he played at first. Sometimes he talked through the games. "See, you hold the controller like this and push the buttons using both thumbs. You gotta be fast."

Sylvie picked up the controller and started to play. At first, she was horribly slow. But she kept at it, over and over. Impressed, he said, "You're learning quickly."

Sylvie liked the attention and before he knew it, she was playing right along with him. When she advanced to new levels, he'd exclaim, "Whoa! Sylvie, that was awesome!" And a smile appeared on her face. He liked that.

When Sylvie smiled, her eyes changed from a soft jade-green to a bright lime color as if the sun got caught there. A dimple formed in her right cheek. It could take his breath away.

Tim wished she knew how beautiful she was.

For his eighteenth birthday, she painted a picture of him on top of a mountain, feet spread apart, arms open wide, his face lifted toward the sky, sunbeams shining on his silhouette.

He was blown away and hung it in his college dorm room until some jerk knocked it down and stepped on it.

Whenever he came home from college—granted, not that often—he'd find her behind a computer screen, playing his video games or writing. He could tell it made her happy, but he felt guilty because she grew increasingly more introverted because of it, especially when she mastered a game or evolved into more sophisticated virtual worlds.

One time he saw her dance from her room, down the stairs, and into the living room, shouting, "I did it! I beat the Boss!"

He laughed. "Sylvie, you are becoming just a nerd." But secretly he was proud. There weren't many girls who could do what she just did.

When she hugged him later that same day, he wanted to tell her how much he loved her and to take care of herself in high school. But he didn't.

Now, he wished he had.

The lights flickered and the airline attendant announced, "Please stow your belongings under the seat in front of you and bring your chair into its upright position. We'll be landing soon. The temperature in Denver is twenty-one degrees." She chuckled. "Make sure you have your coat handy."

Jet-lagged, he raked his fingers through his shaggy, too-long hair, and zipped up his carry-on, filled with gifts from Africa. Out the window, the jagged line of the Rockies formed an impressive sight, silhouetting the morning sky. He remembered the white mountains, the cloudless sky, and the crystalline blue river of his childhood home; tall trees rising out of the earth to brush the sky, the wind rustling through the leaves—the colors so vibrant they sometimes didn't look real.

Soon he'd be on the ground, his parents waiting for him.

Tim suddenly had an overwhelming feeling of dread. His fingers tingled.

They had to visit Rosewood before driving over the mountains.

SYLVIE

Before – High School

igh school terrified her. Bigger corridors filled with boys growing into men and girls who didn't look like her. They all seemed like adults. Sylvie's small stature seemed remarkably different; lean, with petite buds on her chest, and slight curves.

A teacher mistook her for a visiting younger sibling of a student and directed her to the office. "Honey, someone in the office will help you find your older sister or brother."

Sylvie tried to reach out to Beth, Sally's friendship circle, even her Science Olympiad classmates. But everyone had leaped into areas Sylvie had no knowledge of—sex, drugs, alcohol, vandalism, defiance, and rebellion.

She did what her teachers told her to do; she didn't have any reason not to. She liked her teachers. Her experience with sex was zilch, zero, nothing. No one had so much as asked her out on a date.

In her Spanish class, she struck up a pseudo-rapport with Maria, a daughter of a Mexican immigrant. Confused by the large building, Maria asked, "Sylvie, could you help me find these classes?" She pointed to her planner. "I want to do good here."

Pleased to see Maria would be in her next class, Sylvie suggested, "Hey. I'm in that class, too. Want to walk together?"

Maria grinned. "Thank you."

Maria looked twenty. She had thick, black hair that fell to her waist, along with full breasts and hips, and straight white teeth. Some of Sylvie's classmates thought they looked weird together. Sylvie didn't notice. She was just glad to have at least one person to sit with at lunch and wave to between classes.

However, rumors circulated. Sally said to Beth, "I heard Maria and Sylvie kissed in the bathroom." Maria heard the rumor, too, and got scared.

One time just after lunch, two Latino boys slammed Sylvie against the lockers and pinned her arms behind her back. One of them hissed in her ear, "I catch you hanging out with Maria again and I'll smash your face, you filthy bitch. You tell anyone about this and I'll find where you live." His spit wet her ear.

Sylvie feigned being sick and went to the nurse's office. "Could you call my mom and see if she can pick me up?" Her mom came and she lied all the way home. "I'm having these migraines. Maybe it's my period. I think I need to rest for a bit."

In the aftermath of her most recent bullying incident, Sylvie found herself between worlds. A virtual world where she played *World of Warcraft*, *Diablo*, *Final Fantasy 7*, spending hours on the computer, even a few nights, falling asleep just before dawn, and avoiding the real world of high school—the clang of metal doors opening and slamming shut; items from lockers hitting the floor; cool concrete walls; mushy food left on cafeteria trays; voices over the intercom calling someone to the office; classmates gossiping; school cliques that excluded her.

In her virtual world, she felt smarter than other people; advancing her skills, even developing as sense of elitism—loving the rush, like a megadose of adrenalin, especially when she beat the Boss.

One of her fellow students remarked, "What does Sylvie do all day on that laptop of hers? Write to her boyfriend? Or should I say girlfriend?" Two other kids listening couldn't stop laughing.

Sylvie tuned them out and made her online name *Born Winner*, in hopes she would be just that someday.

Although not included in ninth-grade circles, she gained respect, and even admiration, amongst her fellow gamers. They'd leave chat messages: "When can you get online?" or "You are so dope!" One fan even hailed her as the best gamer ever. Eventually she gained a sense of dominance and control that had eluded her for years.

In her real world, she repainted a few of her wall canvases. Depictions of the cybernetic characters she identified with— a powerful swordswoman who conquered her enemies with skilled tricks, a limber female ninja, a domineering sorceress. She wrote short stories and poems about them, too.

Her ninth-grade art teacher urged her to submit one of her art pieces to the Colorado Arts Institute's annual young talent achievement competition. "Sylvie, you really should enter that dragon you did using all those black ink dots. It's truly impressive."

Awards didn't mean that much to her. "Sure, okay." She shrugged. "I really don't care if I win anything." However, she did win—first prize in the freshman category. With the award still attached, she gave the picture to her teacher. "It was your idea."

Her teacher's eyes widened. "Thank you, Sylvie." She reached out and grabbed Sylvie's hand. "I'm going to hang it right over my desk."

In tenth grade, she met a girl in the school cafeteria who would end up being her best friend. The girl purposely dropped her books next to Sylvie, which made her jump. A flush of adrenaline tingled through her body.

The girl slowly smiled and then chuckled. "Hey, no worries. It's 'Merica, girlfriend. We can do what we want." She gazed at Sylvie. "What's your name, anyway? Mine's Naomi."

Sylvie blinked. "Sylvie. I didn't know if this was your spot or something." She pushed her hair out of her face. "I think you sit next to me in English Lit." Sylvie took in Naomi's short haircut. "Like your hair."

Naomi flipped one of her longer hair strands. "Oh, this? I cut it myself."

Sylvie's eyes widened. "Really? That's so cool." She had not even dared to cut her own bangs.

Naomi and Sylvie talked for the next two hours, mostly about superficial stuff: a television show they both enjoyed, teachers they liked and didn't like, favorite foods.

Sylvie didn't realize she had missed her computer science class. "Oh, crap." Sylvie grabbed her new friend's arm. "I missed my class."

Naomi scoffed, "What? You mean you've never skipped class?"

Sylvie shook her head. "Nope." Her chin trembled slightly.

Naomi burst out laughing. "Sylvie, you've made my day."

After that, they met every day for lunch and talked about all sorts of things. They got close, traded secrets.

Sylvie confided, "I always feel like I'll never be what my parents want me to be." Her eyes filled. "I don't think my mom ever asked me what it is that I want."

Naomi turned her head to the side. "My mom's an alcoholic." Her lip quivered. "At least your mom doesn't hit you."

They also talked about boys.

"You've got to be kidding." Sylvie pressed both hands to the sides of her face. "Two?"

Naomi stroked her throat. "Well, yeah. I liked them both and couldn't decide which one to sleep with, so I thought, *what the hell.*"

"In the same night?" Sylvie tried to imagine Naomi with two boys, but couldn't.

Naomi egged her on. "Need to expand your world there, little Sylvie. Why don't you play around in this computer stuff you've been into?"

Naomi's words stuck in her head. *Why not,* thought Sylvie.

So, one night she played well into the early morning and met a fellow gamer named Bandit. They played for hours. Amid one game, he sent a message: "Hey, you are pretty awesome." She answered with what she thought Naomi would say: "Of course." They exchanged several posts and signed off.

In the subsequent days, whenever she logged on, there'd be a memo from him. One time he typed, "Are you a girl?" She hesitated for a moment, not sure if she should respond. All sorts of *what-ifs* rolled around in her head: would he respect her if she was a girl? Could this lead to something? Did she want it to lead to something? She decided to reply with a simple *yes* and waited.

Bandit sent a long communication that started with something like: "I knew it! This is so totally cool. I can't believe I've found someone like you." Their chat notes got longer and longer every time they found each other on the internet. Sylvie couldn't wait to get home just to check if he sent anything.

She told Naomi, "I have a boyfriend."

"No way." Naomi jerked her head back. "Who?"

"A guy I met online." Sylvie giggled. "His name is Bandit."

"For reals?" Naomi mumbled. "Sounds like someone I might like."

They laughed like the teenagers they were and went shopping after school.

Sylvie bought a rose-colored lip gloss and panties with lace. She stood tall, chest puffed out. "This is so much fun."

Naomi didn't buy anything. "I just like watching you." She laughed for a little longer than normal.

"Okay," Sylvie responded. "I should get home anyway." She wondered if Naomi didn't have any money. "Besides, I'm hanging out with Bandit tonight."

When Bandit asked for Sylvie's phone number, she didn't respond for a few days, mostly because her conscience got to her. It felt fine to have shared intimate conversations in the safety of cybernetics. But she hadn't even kissed a boy, let alone had sex or participated in all those things she told Bandit about— went to a strip club, wore see-through panties, attended a rave, smoked weed, drank alcohol. She had not done even one of those fabrications. She imagined the stories she invented were no different than one of her online games.

But her phone number…that felt as real as an intruder in her home. Her throat tightened and she couldn't eat, lost sleep, and didn't get online for days. Unease took up space in her mind.

Time crawled forward. Sylvie constantly looked at the clock. She missed Bandit like a sickness. She knew it was daring, but she couldn't stop herself. She waited for her parents to go to bed and counted her breaths, her heartbeats.

Sylvie thought it seemed to take forever until she could turn on her computer. And then, there they were, popping up one after another, love notes that felt like warm towels right out of the dryer.

Sylvie caved and gave him her number.

She lay in bed with the comforter over her ear, her phone right by her chest so she could feel the vibration if he called. Around midnight, her phone lit up. Bandit texted if he could call.

Sylvie texted back. "Give me five minutes."

She slipped out the side door of the house and huddled inside the cab of her dad's truck to take Bandit's call. They talked for two hours. A steroid-big excitement bubbled up and her chest expanded. She felt light-headed…elated, almost high.

Walking back into the house, she noticed every whisper of the wind. The smell from a recent rain made her feel giddy with joy.

At breakfast, her mom remarked, "My, aren't you happy today." She poured orange juice and fixed French toast, her movements fluid and light.

Bandit and Sylvie continued their late-night phone calls for about a month before he insisted, "I have to see you. Tell me where you live."

She wanted to meet him, but she just couldn't give him her home address. She didn't know who he was.

This occurred right around the same time Sylvie's school introduced internet safety classes, with shocking stories of girls and boys lured into sex trafficking or worse. Sylvie didn't want to admit that the class scared her, but it did. So much so, she didn't answer any phone calls or go online for what seemed like ages to her, but was really maybe a week...a terrible week.

She felt a blackness descend as if someone had stolen the sun. A weight sat right in the middle of her breastbone, making it hard to breathe, not knowing what was worse: that things could go terribly wrong if Bandit found out where she lived, or if he would ditch her for someone else if she didn't give him her address.

Sylvie shared her dilemma with Naomi, who promoted the idea of setting up a rendezvous. Her friend thought it was thrilling. "Think of it. He could be older. Maybe rich. Sounds exciting. Dangerous, even." She winked.

Sylvie settled on the word *dangerous*. "I don't know, Naomi. This could just be plain stupid."

Bandit's messages held a hint of urgency. When she reread them, her mouth tasted like a copper penny. She replied with half-truths. "Busy right now." "Got a test." "Out tonight."

Sylvie wondered if they could backtrack; return to playing games and flirting. She needed time to think through the consequences.

His responses were filled with a passion that both excited and terrified Sylvie. No one had called her "my darling" before.

She felt as if she were poised on a great precipice. After much deliberation, she suggested a compromise: they would exchange pictures.

Bandit called later. "Baby, send me your sexiest photo."

She spent the rest of the night trying on clothes—slipping the sleeve out of her black tank top and letting it rest on her shoulder, allowing her hair to graze over her eye, her mouth in a pout. *Snap, snap, snap.* By morning, she had three photos she liked and sent them.

When her mom came to wake her up, she feigned illness and slept until late in the afternoon.

Sylvie felt a need to run, jump, scream, or simply whoop it up, every time she sent suggestive texts or called Bandit, delighting in her clandestine world. But as she engaged more, a worry nipped at the edges of her psyche. *What were the next steps?*

She asked Naomi, "How do you know when to go further?" Her eyebrows lifted, waiting for the answer.

Naomi chuckled. "You mean sex?"

She wanted to appear self-assured, but she didn't know how to begin to explain. "Umm. Yeah."

In response, Naomi gave her a website address for buying sex toys. "My favorite is *Lacey's Choice.* Oh, and *Banana-oh-rama* is good, too."

Sylvie thought they were odd names, but wrote them down anyway. She waited until after her parents had gone to bed and all the lights were out. Picking up her laptop from under her pillow, she turned it on.

When she browsed the website, she felt slightly ill. It wasn't what she expected: images of naked men having sex with each other, and girls wearing pasties on their nipples and see-through underwear. Pulling the covers high over her head, she rubbed her eyes before closing down her computer.

nine

NAOMI

Before - Memories

Naomi lived in "trash town." Not in the new modern trailer park across the street, but the older one stuck behind Newman's Waste Management. Mobile homes sprawled haphazardly across a dirt road. She resided there, in a two-bedroom worn-out trailer with her mother, an embittered woman who had recently divorced Naomi's father. Two plastic chairs, a cooler, and a garbage can sat on their miniscule porch with a low power line connecting the trailer to the main power source; a pile of debris on a tiny lawn with a few spotty grass spots.

An army veteran who served three tours in Iraq, Naomi's father suffered from PTSD—post-traumatic stress disorder. Each time he returned home on leave from his posting in Baghdad, his mental health worsened. He hollered at empty television screens and jumped when Naomi accidently slammed the front door. Unable to stop, he raked his hand through his hair over and over and over. Worst of all, he hit Naomi's mother for no reason.

Her mother screamed at her dad a lot. "I've had it! Get out! You're nothing but a loser."

To get away from her mother's increasingly difficult mood swings, her father moved to a tiny settlement in Utah when Naomi was about fourteen. There, he managed a meager gas station at the edge of town, with nothing but red dust for company.

Life was somewhat peaceful for Naomi until her mom got fired from several waitressing jobs. After that happened, she settled on living off the government, drinking during the day, and watching her favorite soap operas on TV. She took her internal frustrations out on Naomi: slapped her in the face when she asked for money; ruined her favorite T-shirt by throwing it in the wash with the filthy kitchen rugs; and yelled at Naomi when she asked why there wasn't any food in the refrigerator.

Naomi learned to stay out of her mother's way.

When she met Sylvie in her sophomore year of high school, she'd just about given up on trusting anybody. Sylvie's type of folks—not to be sterotypical, but people who lived on the other side of the tracks, so to speak—weren't her type. Yet something drew her to Sylvie, an openness like the shiny glass globe she got one Christmas, shattered long ago from one of her mom's throwing fits.

The first time she went to Sylvie's house, Naomi could hardly believe what she saw. "You live here?"

Sylvie nodded. "Of course. Why?"

Naomi shuffled on her feet, back and forth. "Well, I mean, I don't get it." She opened her arms. "You have all this: your own room and bathroom, nice cars in the driveway, classical music playing in the living room." She paused briefly to collect her thoughts. "Picture perfect."

"That's just it." Sylvie covered her face with her hands, then pulled them away. "I want to mess up sometimes, like you."

"What do you mean?" Naomi asked.

"I wish I could wear black fishnet stockings. Get in trouble." Sylvie murmured. "Not feel like I have to get A+ in everything I do. My parents think they know what's best for me."

Naomi listened as Sylvie continued to talk about the way she felt. She used words like *hollow*, and expressions like *wanting to be alone* and *afraid of making a mistake*.

Naomi's heart fluttered slightly every time Sylvie confided in her. They got close, and for Naomi, that was intimate. Sometimes she even mirrored Sylvie's body language and thought they complemented each other like a jigsaw puzzle, fitting into all those just-right places.

Because Sylvie was her friend, she supposed helping Sylvie discover how to "mess up" was the least she could do.

Besides, Naomi figured she'd be the best person for her to turn to if anything went terribly wrong.

ten

SYLVIE

Before – High School

"Naomi, what kind of, uh, you know, things should I buy? Can I send them to your place? Just buy one for now?" She was thrilled at the prospect of trying these grown-up playthings.

Naomi moved her thumb up and down. "Try a vibrator."

Sylvie whispered. "A vibrator?" She looked around to see if any of her classmates had overheard.

"Yes, silly. It'll give you a sense of what the real thing is like." Naomi lifted her chin. "It's easy."

When the vibrator arrived at Naomi's home address, she called Sylvie. "It's here."

"Oh, my gosh!" Sylvie exclaimed. "I'll be right over."

"Um, let's make it tomorrow. Ah, my mom's gonna be out late." Naomi cleared her throat. "Gotta go, bye."

All the next day, Sylvie couldn't concentrate on her studies, excited at the prospect of finally understanding something about sex. After school, they went to Naomi's place.

Sylvie unwrapped the box and picked up the sex toy as if it were made of glass. "What do I do with it?"

Naomi laughed. "Here." She grabbed Sylvie's hand. "Let's watch a video." Naomi turned on her outdated computer. "It'll take a few minutes."

Sylvie watched. A few times, she closed her eyes—it all seemed too much. "Think I'll wait 'til I get home."

Naomi shrugged, clearly disappointed. "Whatever."

Sylvie quickly switched topics. "Let's make popcorn and watch a movie. I'll call my mom and let her know I won't be home for dinner."

Later that night, Sylvie took out the vibrator she hid between her mattress and springboard and replayed the video she watched in her head. When she got into bed, she removed her panties, and turned the vibrator on. She took a deep, pained breath and closed her eyes.

What am I doing…?

Cautiously, she placed the vibrator between her legs and slowly inched the toy close to her private parts. Rubbing the vibrator in a gentle, gradual rhythm caused tingling sensations she'd never experienced before. As she relaxed, a warmth spread through her chest. She didn't know if she was doing it right, but it felt good. *This must be what sex was about.*

She texted Naomi. "Feels nice."

Still up, Naomi replied with a thumbs-up emoji.

Now she had something to talk to Bandit about. Not only Bandit—she could converse with kids at school and feel part of the high school crowd. Her imagination took off and she started telling stories at school, as if the line between fantasy and reality had suddenly gone astray.

"Saw John this weekend. We went up to Copper Mountain. He has a condo there. We were supposed to ski, but you know we never got to the slopes."

Sylvie thought the lies weren't hurting anybody. It was just her way of fitting in, of finally catching up to her peers—more like Naomi.

"Can you take me to that thrift store you go to?" Sylvie implored. "I want to get some different clothes, like those mesh leggings you wear and a miniskirt, if I can find one."

Smiling, Naomi shook her head slightly. "You know, your mom's gonna freak out if she sees you wearing stuff like that."

Delighted, Sylvie clapped her hands. "I know. I'll hide them in my locker."

Electrified by her fabrications, Sylvie grew daring in her late-night phone calls with Bandit and told him she was eighteen. He seemed to take her age as a sign, and asked, "Wanna hook up?"

Her heart raced as if she had just drunk an espresso. "What do you mean?"

He exhaled noisily. "You know, meet in person."

She thought about what confident Naomi would say. "Sure. Where?" She bit the inside of her cheek.

"How about Sin City?"

Oh, my God, Sylvie thought. "You mean Las Vegas?"

He laughed quietly. "You got it, baby," he assured her. "People do things like this all the time."

She wasn't sure, but listened to Bandit as he made plans. "There's this hotel I go to for gaming conferences. We could meet there." He continued, "It's a great place with a pool and a casino. There's a restaurant near the lobby. Lots of people go there on vacation. We'll blend in so easily."

"I have some saved birthday money from my grandparents." She didn't know that what she just said was a dead giveaway she wasn't an adult.

Not deterred by her naïve confession, he told her to buy a plane ticket and he'd reserve a hotel room for one night. "I'll meet you at the Aria. How about this Saturday around 4:00?" His description of the hotel made it sound like an inn from Disney World.

She relaxed. It was only Sunday. "Okay. I'll meet you there. Give me a few days to work on it." She needed Naomi's help.

When she told Naomi about her secret rendezvous with Bandit, Naomi shook Sylvie's shoulders. "You are growing into such a badass."

Sylvie felt a jolt of surprise, never thinking anyone would think of her as a badass. "For reals?"

"Well, yeah. Flying to a different state to meet someone you've never met. Do you even know his name?"

Sylvie didn't know his name. "Uh, not exactly." *What was she doing?*

Naomi's mouth opened into an airy grin. "No worries, Sylv. You got this." She nodded. "Okay, let's make a plan."

Next day while sitting around the dinner table with her mom and dad, Sylvie announced, "Naomi is going to visit her dad in Utah this weekend. Would you mind if I went with her? You know, to keep her company?"

Her mom raised her eyebrows. "Really? I didn't know her father lived in Utah or that she had a car."

With a sweet singsong voice, she added, "We're using her mom's car. You know, the white Subaru." Naomi's mom's car was at least twenty years old.

"Why don't you use my car? It'll be safer," her mom countered.

For once, she wished her mom didn't have to be so concerned about her safety. "No, we're fine. Thanks anyway." Quickly diverting the conversation to Tim's medical school attainments, she continued, "How about Tim receiving that award at Stanford? Wow, impressive." She'd watched her mom enough over the years to know how to deflect unwanted attention.

The frown on her mom's face changed to a bright smile. "Oh, gosh, yes. I can't wait to visit him." She carried on about Tim and his recent achievements.

Sylvie didn't listen much. She'd accomplished her mission and had better things to think about. Should she wear her stretch jeans, white top, and black pumps? Take a backpack or a small overnight bag or buy new underwear? Would they really have sex?

On Friday, she went to the bank and withdrew two hundred dollars. On Saturday, she asked Naomi if she could drive her to the airport. "I got the last seat on the plane."

In the car, Naomi nonchalantly asked. "Are you scared?"

Sylvie didn't want to admit it. "Not at all." Despite her brave words, she felt a prickling along the back of her neck.

"Text me anytime you need to, okay? It's only one night. You'll be back tomorrow." Naomi tightly gripped the steering wheel. "Everything will be okay."

Sylvie, wanting to be as bold as Naomi, lifted her chin. "Yeah. I've got this."

At the airport, she waved goodbye and watched Naomi speed back onto the highway. She slipped her overnight bag over her shoulder and searched for her driver's license in her jeans pocket. In the airport restroom, she applied a layer of her favorite pink lip gloss, trying to appear older than her seventeen years, and walked up to the ticket counter. "Las Vegas."

The attendant peered over her chic-looking glasses. "Any checked luggage?"

"Nope. Just this carry-on." She bit her upper lip.

"Departure will be in forty-five minutes." She handed back Sylvie's ID. "Have a good flight."

Wow, that was easy. Excitement bubbled within Sylvie like an opened bottle of champagne. She found a discarded magazine and flicked through it without reading a word. When the boarding call was announced, she breathed deep and long, consciously forcing her limbs to move toward the kiosk, handed her boarding pass to the attendant, and walked onto the plane. Giant butterflies bounced around her stomach as she held her bag to her chest and found her aisle seat.

An older gentleman in a business suit sat next to her with his laptop opened and earplugs in. Halfway through the flight, she struck up a conversation with him, trying to appear casual, as if she had been flying on her own for years.

The gentleman was from Las Vegas, and suggested, "Take a taxi to the Aria. Easy, fast." Once they landed, he even helped her pick out a taxi. "There, take that one. They're a better company. Good luck, have a good time visiting your aunt."

Sylvie had told him she was visiting family. She figured she shouldn't tell him that she was hooking up with an online boyfriend she'd never met.

She looked out the backseat cab window at the maze of tall buildings. Garbage strewn in the street gutters made Las Vegas seem less attractive than her daydream about the city. The late afternoon sun filtered through a haze of dust.

A group of men smoked at a corner stoplight. Billboards advertised a new housing development, lingerie, and perfume. One ad displayed a picture of two women, with the words "Need help?" The phone number was painted in big, bright orange numbers.

The driver pulled up to the hotel sidewalk. "Here we are, miss." The Aria had a tall tower on top of its many floors. A group of foreign tourists posed for a picture by the hotel's front fountain.

She paid the driver, got out, and stopped for a moment to watch a man and a woman kiss. A gust of wind raced behind her and lifted her hair from her damp neck. Heartrate quickening, suddenly her throat felt uncomfortably dry. Looking around at the tall hotels, she felt she'd just shrunk by several inches and everyone else had grown taller.

Entering the lobby of the Aria, she decided to find a chair while she waited. It was 3:45 p.m. Watching the front desk with an intensity bordering on mania, she chided herself every time she bit her fingernails.

Thirty minutes.

Forty-five minutes.

Increasingly uncomfortable, Sylvie twisted her wrists. *What am I doing here?*

Any moment someone might come up to her and expose her recklessness—*you're not supposed to be here, isn't that right; we're taking you to the police station.* Sylvie vacillated between tapping her leg and tucking her hands behind her elbows. If he didn't show, she could abort the whole thing.

After a little over an hour, a man walked up to the inn's booth. He wore a faded tie dyed T-shirt and his unkempt, greasy brown hair fell to his shoulders. His belly stuck out from over his baggy jeans. He looked like one of the homeless people Sylvie passed on her taxi ride from the airport.

"I've reserved a room under the name Bandit," he muttered to the receptionist. He scratched his crotch.

Sylvie's mouth dropped open. She had envisioned Bandit being more her age, lean and tall, with a modern haircut, wearing stonewashed jeans, and a denim jacket over a clean shirt.

Sickened, she sunk down into the comfortable recliner and pulled her hoodie over her head, afraid he might recognize her. Eying the exit door, she bolted from her seat, and dashed through the revolving glass doors.

Her fantasy about meeting Prince Charming dissolved with each breath. An aching sense of disappointment expanded in her chest, trading places where cheerfulness once lived only moments ago.

"Taxi!" she shouted and quickly jumped in the car. "Airport. Right away, please." Once there, she ran up to the reservations desk.

"Are there any flights to Aspen, Colorado? I have a ticket for tomorrow, but I need to change it." Sylvie took a sharp intake of breath. "Uh…I can pay the extra fee. And I only have this carry-on."

The attendant peered over his glasses. "Last flight of the day leaves in fifty minutes. Ticket?"

Sylvie reached into the pocket of her daypack and pulled out the folded voucher. "Thank you."

Once on board, she kept the hood of her sweatshirt over her head and stared at the night sky through the plastic window. Her heart pounded as half-forgotten warnings rushed into her head. Regret elbowed her at every turbulent bump. She scolded herself for being so damn stupid.

When she landed at the Aspen airport, she called Naomi. "Naomi," she whispered, "Can you pick me up?"

"What the hell, Sylvie? It's almost midnight."

She told her what had happened, exaggerating a bit to give her story more substance. "He was so gross. He looked at least forty. His teeth were crooked and he looked dirty and smelly. I swear he might've been running from the law." She gulped. "Please, I need your help."

Naomi pulled into the arrival zone about thirty minutes later. Sylvie got in. "Thanks."

Naomi had both hands on the steering wheel instead of her usual one-handed, relaxed style. "I told my mom you had a fight with your parents and needed a place to stay."

Sylvie searched her face for clues. "It's all true, you know."

Naomi didn't respond. Maybe her friend thought she'd chickened out about Bandit.

Once back at the trailer, Sylvie got under the blanket on the couch, but was unable to be still or relax. Remorse needled her and she couldn't fall asleep. After an awkward breakfast with Naomi and her mom, Sylvie went home.

She told her parents, "Naomi didn't want to stay with her dad. She said it was too weird. I'm pooped. We drove all night. Think I'll spend the day catching up on sleep." Guilt snapped at her heels like a rabid coyote.

The sudden precariousness of Sylvie's world made her want to run and hide. Her hopes pulled out of her like plucking petals from a daisy, replaying the Las Vegas trip over and over in her mind. Even though she wanted to apologize, she realized there was no one but herself to ask for forgiveness.

The river near her home flowed all year long, swiftly absorbing anything thrown into it, making it the perfect place for Sylvie to erase Bandit from her life. Watching her cell bop along the current for a mini-second before sinking, she threw pieces of her smashed-up laptop into the churning waters.

Gone.

"Someone stole my phone and laptop. Honest." Her arms hung by her sides as she pleaded with her parents. "I'll help out more around the house and at your office, Dad." Sylvie tried to think of other ways she could repay her debt. "Sorry...."

Things felt a little surreal as if she were in a movie, warped into another dimension. Sometimes she couldn't eat or drink, her breathing as shallow as a tropical lagoon. Her thoughts flew around in her brain, quick as a Japanese bullet train. Good makeup did little to mask the dark-blue circles under her eyes. At times, she felt paralyzed by guilt and dread, and she lost weight.

Her mom remarked, "Anything wrong? You haven't been out much lately. What's up with Naomi?"

Sylvie offered a tired smile. "Gotta get into CU Boulder. Make Tim proud." She had always looked up to her big brother and didn't like the thought of him finding out about what she did with the gaming stuff he taught her.

Sometimes she contemplated what could've happened if she actually had met up with Bandit. Suddenly the computer games felt just like that—games. They weren't real.

She realized that she had narrowly missed making a serious mistake. She wasn't Naomi. At school, she made excuses, and thought up ways to avoid her friend.

"Can't get together with you this week. My mom wants me to help around the house." Sylvie stared at the floor. "Oh, and I have a big project coming up."

Naomi drew her eyebrows together. "Thought you didn't want to be hanging out with your mom."

Sylvie swallowed, talking fast. "Um, I just don't want her to suspect anything. You know…about Las Vegas." Quickly glancing toward the school doors, she moved away. "Gotta go, bye."

When she got home, she rummaged around her closet until she found her paint jars and her soft flannel brush holder. She took out her favorite medium-sized brush and stroked her cheek. The delicate filaments felt like home.

She closed her eyes. A slideshow of wraithlike images fluttered around her brain: water crashing against glass, white sand dunes shifting in the wind, a woman emerging from a cocoon, people with no faces, a flock of migrating bluebirds.

Sylvie took down the canvas above her bed and began to repaint it for the third time.

When she didn't come down for dinner, her mom brought up a tray of food and set it down on the floor next to her. "Redoing that thing again?" she inquired.

Sylvie, too engrossed in her vision, hardly responded. "Yep."

For the next few weeks, Sylvie went to school, came home, and painted or wrote poems. The tightness in her chest began to loosen. Her fear that others might know about Bandit or Las Vegas—or worse, judge her for it—subsided.

Chores around the house provided a welcome distraction. "Hey, Mom, I'll fold the laundry today," she offered in a cheery voice.

Later, in her room she wrote short, succinct verses about change and tacked them all around her canvas painting as if the poems were part of her art. She placed one beside a depiction of a dolphin leaping through a circle of flames:

My soul led me into a dark land
without light, without night
and stripped away my very flesh
and then my bones
said to me—awaken your heart
illuminate the darkness
walk the earth
and not cease until you are transformed.

Naomi dialed Sylvie's number again. No answer. "Damn," she mumbled. She slipped her phone into her pocket, got in her mom's old car, and drove to Sylvie's house.

When she got there, she sat in the car for a minute or two before ringing the doorbell.

"Oh, it's you." Sylvie's mom twisted her mouth to one side. "Sylvie's in her room if you'd like to go on up. She's been painting like a madwoman."

Once upstairs, Naomi watched Sylvie for a moment before announcing her arrival. "Hey there, Sylv."

Sylvie tipped her head. Her smile slowly widened. "Naomi!" Stretching her legs, she got up and quickly moved toward Naomi, surprised by how much she had missed her friend. She wrapped her arms around her. "Glad you're here."

Naomi sighed and hugged Sylvie back. "Glad I'm here, too." She noticed pieces of torn paper on the wall. "What are those?"

Sylvie pulled away. "Oh, just some poems."

Naomi inched closer to the wall and leaned down to read the script, halting to read some of the verses twice. "These are incredible, Sylvie. You're really something special. You know that, right?"

Sylvie tried to laugh it off. "Yeah, right." Shrugging, she quickly changed the subject. "So, what's up? I'm assuming you didn't come here just to read my poems."

Naomi glanced at Sylvie's painting before responding. "Tyler's parents are out of town this weekend and he's hosting a party for just about everyone in town." She sucked in her breath. "Would you like to go?"

Tyler Greenwood was lean, muscular, smart, and well-liked. Sylvie doubted he had ever even said hello to her. *I don't want to go* popped into her head, but the apprehension in Naomi's request changed her mind.

"Yeah, okay. Can you pick me up around seven? Is it alright to use your mom's car?" She didn't want to borrow her parents' car. "I'll need to shower and change." Her stomach clenched. "I don't know what to wear."

Naomi laughed, grabbed Sylvie's hand, and bounced in place. "You'll be a knockout just the way you are."

Sylvie felt the throb of her heartbeat. "I don't know about that."

Before Naomi left, she pointed at Sylvie's wall. "Oh, and by the way, that painting is just about the most awesome thing I've ever seen."

Sylvie pursed her lips in thought. "Um…thanks."

Later, on their way to Tyler's party, Naomi chattered nonstop. "Psyched you're going with me, Sylv; we're going to have so much fun."

Sylvie listened, attempting to show some excitement. "Yeah, it'll be nice." Still, her gut kept flipping.

There must've been at least sixty people already at Tyler's when they got there. Outside, the night was clear and bright. A sliver of moon peaked above the mountain ridgeline. Inside, people were sitting on the stairs and crowding onto couches, pushing through packed hallways and rooms. Rap music blasted from the great room speaker. Beer bottles lined the outside of a large coffee table. A tray of red and green gelatin shots jiggled when anyone ran or jumped.

Sally came up from behind Sylvie and whispered in her ear. "The red ones are tequila and the green are vodka." She glided over to the table like some game show host and picked up one of the shots. "Try one. They're delicious."

Sally wore a tight-fitting lace bodice with no sleeves that accentuated her rounded breasts. She chugged down the liquor in one gulp. A few kids shouted their approval and she hollered back, "Nothing like being part of this awesome crowd!"

Naomi yelled, too. "Love a good party!" She grabbed a beer and slugged down a green gelatin shot. "Fuckin' A!" Several partygoers cheered.

Sylvie had not drunk much alcohol, even though she led others to believe she had. Naomi assumed Sylvie had got drunk at least once and offered several times to get "plastered" with her. But Sylvie had politely declined.

She looked around at her peers, watching Sally dance with someone she didn't recognize. Her hips swayed in rhythm to the music. Everyone seemed to be having so much fun.

Uneasiness pecked at her temples. *Wish I could erase all my memories of Bandit...and Sally and Maggie and Beth and Maria and...* Nancy? She hadn't thought about Nancy for ages. But there she was, in a corner kissing some guy.

Sylvie's gaze flicked over to Naomi, laughing and kicking off her shoes. *If only I could let go like that…just for one night….*

Watching several partyers gulp down the red and green gelatin shots, Sylvie figured just one of each would be okay. To her surprise, the shooters were tasty. Even after swallowing one of each color, she couldn't taste the bitter tang of alcohol. A tiny smile crept across her face as she started to feel giggly and light-headed.

Ben, one of Tyler's friends, slapped her on the back. "Whoa, Sylvie. Never thought you had it in you." He handed her two more.

Sylvie chugged down eight shots. The room whirled like the spinning wheel on *Wheel of Fortune*. "I'd like to buy a vowel." Everyone laughed.

She felt like part of the pack. *Included.*

Another shot.

Sylvie danced on a table and raised her T-shirt over her head, swinging it like a rotating fan. The crowd clapped. Adrenaline gushed through her body and a rush of excitement at being validated emboldened her to down several more gelatin shots before she hopped from the table to a chair to the couch as if she was on the track and field team.

The air was tight and hot, flavored with the odor of cigarette smoke. Music blared from two ceiling speakers, the bass rattling some of the pictures on the walls. A cluster of partygoers started to dance and pulled Sylvie into their circle, jumping up and down and around and throwing off their clothes; the girls leaping onto some of the guys' shoulders and yelling and tossing away more clothes.

At one point, Sylvie stumbled into a group of kids passing around a bottle of tequila. She took a swig—and another—and then everything faded away.

When she opened her eyes, it was eerily quiet.

A cold draft swept over her body. Her arms ached when she tried to lift them and her throat felt dusty dry. She elevated herself onto her elbows and blinked a few times.

A sudden feeling of cold expanded in her core. From the waist down, she was naked, with spots of blood on her right thigh. A flaky trickle of vomit laid in a zigzag pattern across her belly. Empty plastic cups littered the floor.

A few partygoers lazed on the couch. One slouched in a recliner.

Appalled by her physical state, she searched for her clothes and running shoes. Finally, she found them in a heap in one of the bathroom tubs. Her chest burned and a dizziness overwhelmed her every time she bent down. A gluelike substance stuck between her legs was chafing her bottom.

She scanned the room before she left, but didn't see Naomi or anyone she knew.

Outside, the predawn light seemed abnormal as if a ghost might suddenly appear.

As she walked the three miles home, she tried to recall details of what happened. No matter how hard she tried, she could not remember anything after she danced on the table. Her body felt hot when she thought of what she might have done.

A dog barked as she crept down her neighborhood street, keeping her head down, afraid someone might notice her.

Careful not to make a sound, Sylvie gently unlocked the front door, and waited a moment, listening.

Whew.... They're still asleep.

She showered and watched the pinkish gummy mess float down the drain, like washing a filthy car. Just the thought of those red tequila shots made her gag, heaving and puking three times.

Before turning off the water, she spotted two bruises—one on the underside of her arm and another near her hip. She wasn't sure, but to her eyes, one of the contusions looked like teeth marks.

Nestled in her childhood bed with a pair of PJs she hadn't worn in years, she sobbed. An unrelenting pounding thumped at the base of her skull. Despair clung to her bones and a blackness exploded inside her head, as if she had just stepped on an unexpected landmine.

Curled into herself like an infant, she tried to recall the evening, but just couldn't remember when she took off her clothes....

Or worse...what could have happened after that.

Her heart felt like it ached all over.

eleven

JACK

Jack placed his and Mia's daypacks in the right-hand corner of the backseat, leaving room for Tim's gear and anything they might pick up in Denver.

When he stepped out of the truck, a cold wind whooshed past him. He shivered and zipped up his coat, noticing the saucer-shaped clouds. The snow swirling around the mountaintops suggested a change in weather.

He closed the door and looked up. Mia's brown hair, flecked with streaks of gray, fell over one eye as she laced her boots. Jack's heart contracted, amazed she could still take his breath away.

"Hey, could you bring my phone? I left it in the den." He smiled sheepishly, always forgetting something.

Mia cocked her head, rolled her eyes before she went in to get his phone. When she came back, she carried two steaming cups of tea. "Phone is in my pocket. Looks like we might get some weather," she added, glancing at the sky.

After checking they had everything, he hopped in the truck and closed the garage door. "If the roads are good, we should be in Denver in a few hours." He looked at the clock on the dashboard; it was seven o'clock in the morning. Tim's plane was scheduled to land in a few hours.

With his left palm on the wheel, he reached over and squeezed Mia's shoulder. "Excited about seeing Tim?" He felt her tense at his touch.

She nodded. Just a few short months ago, she might've returned the affection—held his hand or patted his cheek. She did neither.

Quiet music played as he drove through town and on to the freeway. Jagged mountain peaks came into view from time to time. Frozen water formed into bluish ice sculptures, a startling contrast to the black rocks on either side of the road. A few semi-trucks passed splashing the windshield with highway grime. He switched radio stations to more upbeat tunes.

Mia closed her eyes. A few minutes later her mouth opened slightly. A soft snore followed.

Mia often struggled with insomnia, especially when she worried about the kids over the years, the many restlessness nights she spent agonizing about Tim or Sylvie coming home late from a party. She fussed about the *what-ifs* until the wee hours. Then her overtired mind would succumb to slumber around four or five in the morning, waking up several hours later.

"Oh, my gosh, I can't believe it's ten o'clock," would be her frequent remark.

Jack would grin. "Hmmm," and hide behind the morning paper, feigning indifference.

He concentrated on the curving road, watchful for any icy spots. Then he stole a glance at Mia, all curled into herself like a puppy.

An aching sense of loss expanded in his chest. He wished he could go back and change what had happened. It was his job to protect his family.

Sighing, he let his mind gravitate to the past.

When Sylvie was seventeen, he saw her sitting at a booth in Henry's diner, a local joint with great lunch food. He'd just run an errand and was walking back to the office when he happened to look up and noticed Sylvie's distinctive hair through the restaurant window. Her head was bent over her phone, her fingers moving quickly over the keypad.

He watched for a moment, thinking he'd join her, but then Naomi rushed in. Sylvie lit up when she saw her and the two of them instantly engaged in back-and-forth banter.

Jack couldn't understand their friendship. They seemed like odd ducks together, even physically. Naomi—tall, dyed black hair, piercings in her lip and nose, tattoos on her leg, and one on her upper arm, papers falling out of her backpack. Sylvie— petite, long blonde hair, straight white teeth, nice jeans, her things in a neat pile on the table.

Sylvie didn't ask for his advice much anymore. And she didn't reach out to him like she once did. In fact, they rarely conversed. After leaving early for school, she came home late, uttered a quick hello, and usually made a beeline for her room. Family dinners became less and less frequent. He thought her behavior normal—a teenage girl thing. Not many adolescent daughters seemed to spend time with their dads.

On weekends, she preferred to go over to Naomi's place, even spending the night. He offered, "Our house has more room." But the two girls rarely had sleepovers at Sylvie's home.

One time, Sylvie and Naomi went to a party at the Greenwoods. He knew the Greenwoods, a well-respected family in the area, and had designed their home several years ago—a beautiful hand-crafted timber home with vaulted ceilings and distinctive windows.

Jack thought they needn't worry if the Greenwoods were hosting a party for the senior class at their house. He told Mia, "The Greenwoods are good people. Sylvie will be fine."

Sylvie didn't come home at the expected time. Mia couldn't sleep; instead, she paced and looked out the window. Jack thought she fell asleep around four in the morning. When he got up to go to the bathroom, Mia was all snuggled in the down comforter, her breathing slow, heavy, and long.

Before climbing back into bed, he checked Sylvie's room and saw she had not yet come home; the bedding smooth and even. His throat tightened, tried to squelch any anxious feelings; not wanting to assume worst-case scenarios, trusting his daughter could handle things. *Mia doesn't need me to overreact.*

Maybe a half hour later, he heard the front door open, followed by the familiar footsteps of his baby girl. A few minutes later, the murmur of the drainpipes suggested she showered.

He must've dozed off because when he finally did get up, he peeked in her room and saw her nestled in a pair of PJs he hadn't seen her wear in years—soft flannel jammies with animal-paw pictures. Her face looked innocent and childlike against the blue sheet.

Later, when Mia joined him for coffee and scones he'd picked up at a nearby bakery, he said, "Sylvie got home after you fell asleep." Leaving out the *when* part, he quickly added, "She's wearing a pair of those cute PJs she used to wear all the time." He chuckled. "Some party, I guess. Think there was alcohol?"

Mia let out a nervous laugh. "As if we never did things like that, right?"

She stirred creamer into her coffee. "I guess everything's okay. I mean, she's sleeping in her own bed, right?" Clearing her throat, she picked up her mug, blowing little ripples on the hot liquid as if pondering something.

Jack thought he'd know if something was wrong. "Right."

That same day, Sylvie surprised her father by draping her arms around him in a hug. "Sorry for being out late. Hope you didn't fuss." She sat down at the dinner table. "I'm not that hungry. I just want to be with you guys."

Mia lied, "No. We didn't worry." She searched for Jack's face. "We know these things happen."

Sylvie got up from her seat, went over to her mother, and placed her chin on her mom's shoulder. "I love you, Mom."

Mia startled. "Uh, love you, too."

Sylvie straightened. Her chest rose as if she was holding in a breath.

Jack noticed. *Did anything happen?* He searched her face and saw how she was just like Mia. They both found it so hard to admit they needed anyone.

Maybe he should say something…but he didn't, and let the moment fade like a photo left out in the sun.

A few days later, he came home for lunch—a rare occurrence —and heard what sounded like a cat crying, a high-pitched wailing. He thought the noise was coming from the backyard, but when he checked, nothing was there. Then he noticed the open window in Sylvie's bedroom. When he went upstairs, Sylvie slammed her door.

"Sylvie, everything all right?" He tried to sound cheerful, hoping she'd reach out to him if she needed. "Thought I'd make a sandwich. Want one?"

A near-flawless silence before she answered. "I'm not feeling well. Came home from school. You go ahead."

The urge to hold her nearly sent him to his knees. *How I miss the days when she wrapped her arms around me, giggling in my ear....*

No longer hungry, Jack drove back to work, replaying everything over and over in his mind. It was like casting out a fly from his fishing pole—over and over and over and over and not catching a thing.

Now, thinking back, Jack regretted pretending that it was all okay, giving in so easily. He heard it in her voice—her play-acting voice.

I should've tried harder.

The truth of his own weakness as a father still caused his heart to tighten. If only he could've walked back up those stairs and said, "Sylvie, I know you're hurting. I don't know what happened but no matter what, I love you. Talk to me. I'm going to stand outside your door until you do." If he'd done that, maybe things would've turned out differently.

The thought killed him.

There were other missed opportunities. But the one that caused the most discomfort and the one he tried to eliminate from his mind was when he went into the guest bathroom looking for shower soap and dug around in the lower vanity. His hand grabbed an almost-empty bottle of Sylvie's favorite shampoo.

He paused for a moment and sat on the gray cotton rug surrounding the cabinet. When he opened the bottle, the heady scent of oleander and chamomile filled his nostrils and he remembered.

Sylvie had come home for spring break and stayed the week. Dark half-moons were puffed up under her eyes. She'd lost weight, and seemed to want to listen to him and Mia talk rather than start a conversation of her own.

Concerned, he asked, "Sylvie-girl, how's Boulder?"

She offered a faint-hearted smile. "I don't know if college is for me."

Mia overheard and yelled from the kitchen. "What do you mean? Of course, college is for you. Think of your talent." She marched into the living room.

Sylvie and Jack were on the couch, enjoying the late morning sunshine streaming through the two high windows on either side of the fireplace. "It's just the freshman transition thing. Everyone goes through it." Mia looked at Jack. "Right, Jack?"

Jack watched as Sylvie hung her head and rested her hot mug of tea on her knees. He wondered if there was more to her statement, but decided to let her bring up the subject of not going to college if she needed to.

He switched topics without answering Mia. "I thought maybe Sylvie would like to walk out to the new house site. There's still a few snow patches but she'll get to see the excavation spot." Turning to face his daughter, he continued. "There's a view I think you'd really like."

Sylvie perked up. "That sounds great, Dad."

Jack and Sylvie spent several hours strolling through the woods on the new property. The air held a tinge of winter. Large ponderosa pines and Colorado blue spruce trees provided a charming canopy over the forest floor. They startled a deer and some grouse.

"I've been writing a lot," Sylvie shared. "Mostly poems." Unexpectedly, she grabbed his hand. "I'm hoping to publish a few of them soon. Would you like to read them?"

Jack swallowed the lump in his throat and pulled her close. "I'd love to, baby girl." He breathed in her sweet-smelling shampooed hair, cherishing the moment.

It was the last time he had held her like that.

Jack came out of his reverie right before the Eisenhower Tunnel. He nudged Mia. "Hey, we'll be in Denver soon."

Mia yawned. "I can't believe I slept these last few hours. Want me to drive?"

Still lost in thoughts about Sylvie, he replied, "Nope. Thought you'd like a minute though to talk over—you know."

Mia's face darkened, like swift clouds blackening the sky. "Oh."

He breathed deeply, the words hanging between them like shreds of wet tissue paper. Would it get any easier?

twelve

MIA

Seven months after.... Rosewood

There were times when words failed her. She knew it was important to talk before they picked up Tim—to have a plan. Tim would likely have his doctor's hat on, and he would see things through that lens.

Am I ready? Can I see things as they are instead of the way I want them to be?

Jack deserved more than her silence, but it was hard to force her heart to feel something it didn't. Reaching over, he touched her cheek, keeping one hand on the wheel and his eyes on the road.

"Mia?"

Mia's throat felt as parched as the land around their house last fall: wildfire dry. She willed herself to answer. "I know, Jack. I'm just thinking." Thinking was all she could do.

"Once Tim is with us, we'll drive to Rosewood. We're scheduled to meet with Dr. Kanani and his team. All the tests have been done. It's time." Jack's voice cracked a tad on the word *time*.

Time for what? Was it possible to go back in time, like one of those television series? Change things? Change one thing? Am I ready for today?

Mia felt as if she couldn't quite catch her breath—like panicking in water, arms flailing, terrified of drowning.

To distract herself, she looked out the car window at the passing landscape: the Denver suburbs spilling out everywhere as the population on the front range bourgeoned; the familiar warning signs of the seven-mile steep descent onto the plains; the sea of commerce. They drove past Red Rocks and Golden with the Boulder Flat Irons barely in view. Then, further east, she saw the tall white tent tips of the Denver International Airport in the distance.

Mia felt like her words were stuck out there somewhere in the landscape. Still, she managed to voice an apology. "Sorry, I've been such a recluse on the drive." She looked at the glove compartment, knowing Jack deserved more from her. "Thank you for driving."

Jack found an empty space on the top floor of the parking garage, parked, and grabbed their warm down jackets from the back seat. "Here, put this on."

Outside, the wind gusts created mini-snow dervishes from the piles of snow. She contemplated joining those ghostly shapes, staying suspended in their spell. Grief was a beast with no boundaries. It ate her all up: her bones, her stomach, even her skin hurt.

Jack took Mia's hand, his strong, cold fingers wrapped around hers.

Mia nodded to a passing couple in their early thirties, both chatting on their phones, oblivious to the weaving traffic at the departure gates. There were cars, buses, Uber drivers, frustrated traffic police, all with their agendas and schedules. People were leaving on an adventure or just arrived home from one, maybe visiting family, or going up to the mountains on a ski vacation. For a moment, she wished she could be one of those people, free from the sorrow that mushroomed in her heart.

When they reached the airport's arrival doors, the sliding glass opened automatically and a mother with a lovely baby girl in her arms passed Mia and Jack.

Mia watched them and turned her head as they went by. The little girl glanced back, her brown eyes alluding to a tendency toward mischief. Mia imagined the child's delight while causing her parents to squeal when she spilled her milk, or when she threw her doll out the car window.

She let Jack guide her to the passenger arrival area. A glass divide provided a view of the escalator. Arrival mobs were ascending from the underground trains, and people were searching for their loved ones.

Her gaze combed through the swarm of travelers, watching as several packs of people disembarked from the shuttle trains. Would Tim be tanned from the African sun, sport a beard, maybe be leaner or taller since she last saw him?

Exhaustion hit her suddenly, and she felt the strength drain out of her legs. Before she collapsed, she plopped down on a nearby bench. "Maybe immigration took longer than he thought it would."

Jack stood beside her. "Won't be much longer." Folding his arms, he swayed from side to side, seemingly deep in thought. He glanced quickly at Mia and then looked away.

"What's that song again? *Try to enjoy the passage of time,* or something like that."

Mia picked off her nail polish. "I hate waiting."

Thirty minutes later, Tim came up behind them.

"Hey there, been here long? His broad grin bunched up his cheeks. "Sorry, the immigration line was way too long."

Mia jumped up and barreled into his chest. "Tim! You're here!" She closed her eyes and took a deep breath before exhaling.

Jack wrapped his arms around his small family, placing his hand on Mia and Tim's shoulders. They stayed like that for a moment before pulling away.

Jack slapped Tim on the back. "You look good, buddy." In admiration, he pinched his son's side. "Lean and fit as a fiddle."

Tim laughed. "Yeah, well that happens when you work all the time and forget to eat."

Mia looked at Tim, then at the empty space between her and Jack—the space where Sylvie should've been. "Ready?"

They made their way to the parking garage, Jack and Mia each fighting for the next word. Tim seemed different. His eyes looked bigger than she remembered or maybe it was the weight he lost. She hung on to each and every response, hungry for details of his life.

She looked at her son. He'd changed: patted her on the back, listened attentively when she asked him questions, and spoke in a kinder tone. He seemed more empathetic. Maybe something good had arisen from all of this.

Tim talked about the cities and smaller communities where he helped set up medical clinics. "Every small space is filled with vendors selling vegetables, fruits, meats, or fish. People cook outside on wood or charcoal fires. Babies and small children often bathe in the streets. We're trying to develop more modern toilet facilities. During the rainy season, our roads can become impassable."

Visions of Tim driving around the highlands and plateaus of Africa helping others flashed through her head. She noticed a few deeper lines around his eyes.

Wrapping her arms around his thin waist, she asked, "Have you met anyone since Lilly?"

Tim made a face, his mouth twisted to the side. "Are you kidding? I barely have time to sleep, let alone date." As they stepped out into the cold, Mia saw Tim shiver. "I brought you a warmer coat, scarf, and some gloves."

When they climbed into the car, Tim asked, "So…are we going to Rosewood now or…?"

Jack replied, "Thought it might be good to get a bite to eat and then drive to Rosewood. I don't think it'll take long." He continued, "There's a pub I know near the tech center. I think you might not have caught up to the time change yet. Want an early beer?"

Tim slipped into the warmer coat. "Thanks, Dad. I'd like that."

Forty-five minutes later, a hostess directed them to a pleasant booth overlooking a web of tables and a silent karaoke stage.

Mia read the menu front-to-back, twice. Nothing looked appetizing. The thought of a hamburger swimming in grease made her stomach heave. She peered over at Jack. "Think I'll just have a cup of soup."

After they ate lunch, Tim brought up the inevitable. "Tell me about today."

Mia almost succumbed to letting Jack do all the talking, but she knew deep down she needed to start this conversation. "Talking about Sylvie isn't easy; you both know that."

Jack and Tim nodded.

"I believed in a miracle and that she'd improve, you know, get better or at least recover enough that we could take her home. I kept telling myself this was only temporary. But I'm thinking that I might have to face that she won't," she continued.

Tim tapped Mia's hand. "Mom, she's your daughter, my sister. It's hard for me, too."

Mia's eyes threatened to leak a torrent of emotion. She seized Tim's fingers, afraid the wall she'd built to control her sea of tears would collapse, like pulling a block out of a *Jenga* game, and seeing the pieces falling everywhere with a loud crash. Her throat ached and all the words she wanted to say got jammed in her mouth. "I don't know how I'm going to get through today, but at least we're together."

Jack scooted close and put his arm around her. "Yes, we'll get through this together." He motioned to the waiter for the check.

Mindlessly, she watched Jack sign the returned credit card slip while he exchanged pleasantries with their server. She slowly stood, zipped up her coat, and linked her arm through Tim's. "I was wondering if you wouldn't mind speaking with Dr. Kanani before we meet in the conference room? When he talks fast, I have a hard time following him."

Tim gently touched her shoulder. "Of course."

They stepped into the car, drove to the Rosewood Rehabilitation Center, and parked without saying a word. Mia gazed at the aging three-story brick building with dark e-glass windows and the entryway supported by five large pillars. The two maple trees she sat under in the summer looked empty without their leaves. She knew how that felt.

"I'm not sure what to expect, but here's to the best possible outcome…for today, anyway." Mia closed her eyes and attempted to stay calm.

Jack walked behind Mia and Tim. "Uh, hope so too."

Inside the lobby, with its modern chandelier and white pine ceiling, Mia unconsciously inhaled deeply. But, one breath of the uniquely familiar antiseptic smell of the place and her cup of soup threatened to rise up and spill all over the freshly polished tile. Her knees felt unsteady.

She looked around at the light gray walls with the familiar sizable picture of a bridge—a white bridge over blue water that seemed to go on forever. She'd often pondered whether that was a metaphor.

An elderly woman gripped the back of a wheelchair. In the chair, a deformed man, who Mia presumed to be the elderly woman's husband, sat hunched over. A stream of drool fell from his mouth. When the woman passed, she smiled at Mia. But her eyes held an immeasurable depth of sorrow.

Jack laced his fingers through Mia's. "Mia?"

She willed herself to answer. "Yes."

Jack steered Mia through the automatic sliding glass doors leading to the residential unit. Mia thought the gray-brown carpet, with nonskid stops on the stairs, did little to help the depressing feel of the place. They walked past a water fountain and a brightly lit bamboo sign with metal lettering: *Residential Floor*. A new display of Christmas cards and lights bordered the reception cubicle.

The administrative assistant looked up. "Mr. and Mrs. Weaver, so nice to see you. Dr. Kanani is waiting for you in the small conference room."

To Tim, she passed a clipboard with a dozen pages pinned to it. "And Dr. Weaver, good to see you, too. Hope you are not too jet-lagged." Her sitcom laugh sounded rehearsed.

Tim took the clipboard and flipped through the sheets, comfortable and at ease in his doctor persona.

Mia followed Jack and Tim to their meeting place. She could see Dr. Kanani's russet-colored hair through the half-closed blinds covering the large windows. His head was lowered over a stack of files—Sylvie's files.

She recognized the one on the bottom of the pile, bound together with a big elastic band. Mia had memorized every single piece, staying up late in the night and researching anything she didn't understand on the internet, which was a mixed blessing. The internet gave her too much information at two in the morning. All the data made her heart race like she'd been running uphill.

Tim opened the door and exchanged greetings with Dr. Kanani and his small team: an occupational therapist, a nurse practitioner, a psychologist, and the neurologist. He whispered something in Dr. Kanani's ear. Mia took the seat between Jack and the young psychologist, who Mia thought looked like she just got out of college. *What in the hell could she offer?*

She pressed her lips together, forming a straight line.

Dr. Kanani cleared his throat and spoke softly. "Dr. Weaver, Mr. and Mrs. Weaver, there is no easy way to begin this difficult discussion." He put his hand over his mouth and coughed. "As you know we've tried everything for Sylvie these last several months, since—" He shuffled a few papers. "Since May."

It was a stunningly beautiful May morning.

Mia was out at the building site of their new home. A patch of purple columbines was in bloom near the brook that ran through the property. Mia gestured to the flowers, as she spoke to Jack, "Look at these. Aren't they magnificent?"

Jack left the carpenters to come sit with her and take in the view. "I can't believe we are building our dream home. Finally. Tim's done with medical school and he is getting offers coming in left and right. He'll land a great job. And Sylvie in college and thriving."

She leaned into Jack's arms and watched the flowers dance in the breeze. The sun warmed her face. Construction workers pounded nails and took turns on the electric saw. A pop song played from a worker's portable radio.

What a perfect day, Mia thought. She felt the vibration of her cell phone in her jeans pocket.

Jack motioned for Mia to ignore the call, mouthing *not now*. But Mia pulled the phone out anyway and recognized the Boulder area code. For a moment, she wondered if it could be Sylvie. Maybe she was using a friend's phone.

"Hello," she said.

"Mrs. Weaver?" an unfamiliar voice replied. Her voice sounded slightly anxious. Mia recognized that tone.

"Yes, who is this?" She moved into an upright position, her game face on. Suddenly, her face felt hot and her insides started to quiver. "Who, again?" Her heartrate began to pick up speed, faster and faster.

"I'm afraid there's been an accident," the stranger replied.

Her eyes narrowed. "What do you mean, an accident?" She tried to listen to what the person on the other line said.

Jack watched Mia intently; ran his hand through his hair, then massaged his jaw.

Images of what-could-be flashed through her mind. "I don't understand. What are you saying? She's in the hospital? Where? How? Who are you again?" Her voice was intensifying in speed and volume as if she couldn't get enough oxygen, her breaths short and irregular. "Are you sure you have the right number?" Somewhere inside her, she knew she was losing control but she didn't know how to rein it in. "Don't tell me to lower my voice!"

"Mia, give me the phone. Stop yelling." Jack grabbed the phone and started talking. He walked away from her so he could hear. "Tell me that again?"

Mia's shrieking caused the workers to turn off the radio and stop whatever they were doing. The workmen looked at Jack, unsure what to do next.

Suddenly furious, she blurted, "What are you looking at? Get back to work. We're paying you for every fucking minute."

"Mia!" Jack shouted, "Knock it off!"

Shifting back and forth on her heels, she cried trying to absorb what she'd just heard.

The dorm supervisor found Sylvie unconscious and had called an ambulance. When the medics got there, they rushed her to the hospital emergency room. The doctors feared it may have been an overdose.

Mia's mind kept jumping from one thought to another and back again, wondering how it was possible for everything to suddenly morph into something unrecognizable. The gurgle of the nearby stream sounded harsh and cruel, instead of the melodious tone she enjoyed just a few moments ago. The sun seemed too bright. She wanted to rip the colorful flowers out of the earth. A monster beat in a fitful frenzy inside her chest.

Mia's broken memory of the rest of that day was like an aged eight-millimeter film, frayed and thin in places.

She barely recalled Jack's building team silently closing up for the day.

Their rushed, frantic drive over the mountains to Boulder.

Later, Jack told her she bawled like a child, threw up in the car, and kept saying, "I don't understand" over and over and over.

⌇

Dr. Kanani's question brought Mia back to the present.

Tasting the salt from the tears that ran down her face, she didn't like the way the neurologist looked at her.

"Sorry. Could you repeat that?"

Dr. Kanani pursed his lips. "Sylvie has shown no improvement since she was admitted. Her recent brain scan shows little functioning activity. We wondered if you are ready."

"Ready for what?" Mia had the sensation of being squeezed. She watched Dr. Kanani's mouth open, but didn't hear what he said.

The young psychologist clicked her pen on and off, on and off. Mia wanted to rip it out of her hands.

Tim interrupted. "Mom, what's going on?"

Her heartrate rushed and sprinted as if the doctor had injected her with epinephrine. Her palms filled with moisture and her eyes dampened. She looked around the room. *Dammit,* she thought.

Everyone's stares held a hint of pity, making Mia suddenly want to run and hide in the car. She dug her nails into the palms of her hands, willing herself to project a calm she wasn't feeling. "Could we take a break? I'd like to see Sylvie before we continue."

Dr. Kanani shrugged. Tim opened his mouth and then closed it.

To Mia's ears, the nurse's voice sounded a little too sunny. "Of course. I can help if you like."

"No. I remember where she is."

I don't need your goddamn help, thank you very much.

The corridor felt claustrophobic as she walked beside the nurse, who insisted on aiding her anyway. Her feet felt like they had weights around them. She watched the nurse open the door.

And then, there she was. *Sylvie.*

The hard knots in Mia's stomach loosened. Her limbs felt floppy.

Sylvie looked angelic, her light hair like a halo around her head, her skin pale and soft. Her chest moved up and down in gentle melodious waves, the ventilator mouthpiece concealing her lips, her breaths raspy and mechanical.

For a moment, Mia became unresponsive to everything else around her, except for Sylvie, almost as if she was catatonic.

I'm fine, really.

Caressing Sylvie's face, Mia closed her eyes, willing for her daughter to recover, to speak to her, for things to be normal again.

thirteen

SYLVIE

Before - High School

The world felt small. How could it contain everything she was feeling? She gazed through the window above her bed. Outside a bare aspen tree quivered in the wind. She felt a bit like that: stripped of all that mattered, exposed, and scared she might not make it through her senior year—wounded, broken, lonely.

Sylvie tried to fool her parents by pretending to be cheerful and ricocheted their questions. "I'm applying to CU Boulder, Denver U, and of course University of Washington. Do you think I stand a better chance at UW since Tim went there?" Her cheeks bunched up like a squirrel harvesting seeds. Her motto: *nod, smile, agree.*

After Tyler's party, Sylvie stayed home from school for several days. She pushed her face as close to the bathroom heater as she could get without burning herself. "Mom, I feel awful."

Her mom felt her forehead. "Gosh, honey, you're burning up. Do you need me to stay home?"

That was the last thing she wanted. "No. You go to work. I'm not five anymore." She managed a quick smile. "I'm going back to bed."

For two days, she felt sick to her stomach and went to the bathroom often, vomiting up more than just a lingering hangover. Nagging images of Tyler's party replayed in her head, a vinyl record stuck in a worn groove.

When she finally did go back to school, the fear that some of her classmates knew more than she did about what happened at Tyler's party made the hallways feel narrow and skinny, compressing her as if there were endless places for them to gossip. A melancholy seeped into her, like a rain that goes on for days, spilling over the riverbanks and running every which way, a desperate need to keep flowing. She couldn't stop it.

The *what-if* thoughts plagued her. What if her parents found out about Tyler's party? What if they heard rumors about her? What if they found out about Las Vegas? Bandit? What if Tim found out?

She became more jumpy, twitchy, like a little guppy fish frantically gasping for air.

Sylvie also felt ashamed—that everything happening to her was somehow her fault.

After she got home from Las Vegas, she stopped playing online games but silently worried that Bandit might track her down. It seemed strange and way too easy to suddenly cut him out of her life and she fretted constantly that he'd show up and accuse her of deceiving him.

One time, she didn't shut the front door properly and the wind caught it just before it closed, slamming it against the wall and making a loud bang. She startled. A million little prickles erupted all over her skin.

Taking out her sketchpad, she used a charcoal pencil to draw images that complemented the poems in her head. A human arm rested on the earth with the palm up. Underneath the arm, tree roots descended deep into the soil, as if the arm and the rhizomes were one. On the next page, she wrote:

> *I will not rest till I wrestle you to the ground*
> *I will not rest till I stand with you in heaven*
> > *longing to be nothing*
> > *and in being nothing*
> > *I am everything*

She sought advice from Naomi. "I've been feeling pretty anxious lately." She hadn't mentioned the morning after Tyler's party.

"I don't remember much about the party either. Drank way too much." Naomi laughed. "You were such a hoot. Couldn't believe you refused a ride home."

Sylvie fidgeted with the zipper on her hoodie. "Maybe it's just the stress of getting into college or the Bandit fiasco," feeling unsure how to broach the subject. "What do you do when you're frazzled?"

"Cut."

Sylvie didn't get it. "What?"

Naomi's Cheshire-cat grin revealed her crooked incisor tooth. "Okay, Syv. Lesson number seventeen." She touched her fingertips together, forming a steeple. "Self-harm is the quickest way I've found to lighten my shit."

Spellbound, Sylvie listened to Naomi's description of self-mutilation. "First, you gotta get good razors. Get the ones at the hardware store. Super sharp. I cut on my legs."

Naomi rolled up her pants. On the inside of her thigh were tiny scars. "Haven't cut much since I met you. But sometimes when my mom goes off, I get the urge." She demonstrated with her finger. "Start light and then go as deep as you frigging want."

Sylvie went to a small shop in town to buy a package of razors. The store clerk showed her where to find the industrial ones. "These are great for cleaning windows," he said.

Sylvie faked understanding. "Yep. My dad asked for these."

When she brought them home, she hid them in her room and started cutting just after Tim arrived for a quick visit, fresh from all his successes. Her mom and dad acted so proud that Sylvie thought their chests might burst right out of their down vests.

"Let's go for a walk," Tim suggested before a family dinner. "I need some mountain air." He looked at Sylvie. "You coming?"

Snug in their warm coats, the family strolled along a path near the house. Tim let his parents walk ahead and fell in step with Sylvie. "Sylvie-girl, what have you been up to? Heard from any schools yet? Have you been a good girl?"

The way he said *good girl* hit her right in the chest, as if he had thrown a snowball. Her eyes instantly filled with tears; she couldn't speak.

When they got back to the house, Sylvie excused herself and said she needed to go to the bathroom. Locking the door, she held the high-quality blade tightly in her hand. It felt like it could cut through anything. She lightly traced two neat lines across her upper thigh, causing the skin to turn pink.

The hairs on the back of her neck lifted. She sucked in her breath and cut into each line. The blood ran down her leg, the rich scarlet hue flowing in tiny streaks.

An unexpected release washed through her. Taking a deep breath, she somehow instantly felt better, and decided to cut one more line. She made exactly three straight slices and watched the rich red ooze out, mesmerized by the color, until her dad knocked on the door.

"Hey, Sylvie," he said in a low voice. "We're having hot chocolate downstairs by the fireplace."

She heard the plea in his tone and coughed. "I'll be right there." It took longer than she expected to clean up her mess and wrap the cuts in gauze and tape. Only a trickle of blood seeped through.

At school the next day, she confessed to Naomi. "I did it."

Naomi raised an eyebrow. "You did what?"

She sighed. "Cut."

Naomi pulled Sylvie close to her face. "Oh, Syv." She pulled up her shirt, revealing two recent red cuttings on her abdomen, near her belly button. "What did you feel, after you cut?"

Tears welled up in Sylvie's eyes. "Light-headed. A little wobbly." Just saying those simple words helped Sylvie feel like she wasn't alone, almost as if she had a sister, someone who truly got her.

Naomi laced her arm through Sylvie's. "Skip math? Coffee?"

Sylvie had not ever missed math class. "I guess so."

Naomi watched Sylvie's shoulders rise and shook her head. "Let it go. You don't need to go to every frigging class in your senior year."

They snuck off campus, went to a small café on the other side of town, and sat at a table, sipping lattes. Naomi talked about how she couldn't wait to get out of the mountains. "I'm looking forward to living in a city. Enough of this damn small town."

Sylvie exhaled long and slow, thinking about what she wanted. "Well, I don't hate the mountains." In fact, she loved them. "But I think getting away from here will be good." She thought of home—her two-story childhood home supported by big, open timbers, the large living room with the river stone fireplace. She'd rubbed her hands on every single one of those rocks. The wood mantel her dad made from a white pine tree he felled.

Hardwood floors that shone when the cleaning team polished them every year. The kitchen alderwood cabinets stained a chestnut color with their oversized gas stove and two stainless steel refrigerators.

The many hours she sat at the spacious island by herself, with her family.

Home.

She hoped her parents wouldn't build that new house they'd been talking about. A throbbing burned in her chest when she imagined leaving the place where she had grown up.

Naomi touched Sylvie's cheek. "I will always be here for you."

Sylvie didn't want to cry, but she did, as the words chased each other out of her mouth. "Sometimes I want to die. Be free of all that is inside me. Please don't tell anyone, especially my mom."

Naomi flinched, her face turning pale, and her pulse increased by a beat or two. Sylvie's admission scared her. "Always talk to me, right?"

Between sniffles, Sylvie shared her plan. "I'd take a bunch of pills and sleep forever; my worries would be all gone. It wouldn't matter anymore if I didn't become somebody great. My secrets would be gone, too." Sylvie felt a soreness pulsate in her throat and lungs. "Sometimes it feels like too much." She looked Naomi in the eye. "I get tired of feeling the pressure of being…" she paused, "…perfect."

Naomi listened. "Promise me you won't hurt yourself." She grabbled Sylvie's hand.

"Promise. It's only thoughts." Sylvie interlaced her pinkie with Naomi's. "Pinkie swear."

They drove back to campus and Naomi walked Sylvie to her next class. Before they parted, Naomi stated, "I don't care if I'm late for freaking science. It's you that matters, Sylv."

Sylvie hardly heeded the teacher's lecture as she wrote down the assignments, soothed by the mechanical movements of simply writing words. Nodding at the appropriate moments, she was struck by how light she felt. She wasn't sure how long it would last. But for the moment, the relief left her feeling almost giddy.

It didn't last. Within a few days, a hollowness in her chest returned and she lost her appetite. She confided in Naomi.

"I haven't been sleeping well lately. Lots of crazy thinking." Sylvie stared down at her hands. "I'm so tired. I wish I could take some of that white-out we use in class and erase my thoughts; give myself a break."

Naomi rapped her fingers against her thigh as she stared at Sylvie. "We gotta tell someone. What about your mom? She's a freaking psychologist, for God's sake."

Sylvie's eyes widened. "Absolutely not." A cold feeling washed over her at just the thought of telling her mother her secrets. "She deals with this sort of stuff at work. Are you kidding me— I DO NOT want to be one of her patients. Period." Her mother's face after a trying day at work flashed through her mind. "Don't worry. It's just thoughts, remember? I'm not going to do anything, promise."

Naomi shook her head. "I think we should at least give it a try." She snatched her car keys. "How about we just go to your house and pretend it's about somebody else? Like something we heard in the girls' bathroom at school."

Sylvie didn't want to go to her house and playact about her feelings. She dug her fingernails into the palms of her hand. "Why can't we just let it go?"

"Because your mom just might tell us what you could do, you know…to feel better." Naomi clasped Sylvie's hand. "Let me do the talking."

When they got to Sylvie's house, they first went downstairs to the rec room. Sylvie kept hoping Naomi would drop being so hell-bent on helping her. She almost wished she hadn't said anything. Yet, somewhere inside of her, she also knew that something in her head wasn't right.

Naomi took charge. She marched up the stairs, with Sylvie trailing behind her, and walked into the living room. Sylvie's mom sat on the couch, reading.

Naomi cleared her throat. "Hey there, Mrs. Weaver."

Sylvie's mom titled her head. "Oh, hi girls."

Sylvie's chin trembled and tears welled up in her eyes. She instinctively knew her mother would see through their charade. She'd ask all the right questions and find out it was about her. Suddenly, she wanted to fade into the background, as tears fell down her cheeks and kept flowing.

Her mother closed her book. "What's going on?"

Naomi turned to see Sylvie's face. "Um, well…" Naomi hesitated as if she forgot what she was supposed to say. Finally, she blurted, "It's about Sylvie."

Sylvie met her mother's gaze, which showed curiosity instead of the shock that would appear once Naomi told her the truth. It left her feeling as defenseless as a chicken in a fox's den. She had to stop this.

"No, don't," she pleaded.

Her mother glanced at Naomi, then Sylvie. "Don't what?"

Naomi inhaled deeply through her nose, then exhaled through her mouth. She spoke in short spurts. "Sylvie doesn't want to live. Sometimes, I mean. Not all the time. I mean. Like you know." She flapped her hands in a circle. "I mean, like you know that kinda stuff, right? We just thought maybe you could help, sort of." Naomi shifted from one foot to the other, stared at Sylvie, and narrowed her eyes.

Sylvie moved back slightly. *No!* She folded her arms over her stomach and bent forward slightly, her pulse pounding frantically in her chest, knowing her mother would hover again, take charge. She'd have to go to counseling. Her mother might even demand she not spend time with Naomi, her only friend. She wouldn't talk.

"Naomi, I think it's time for us to meet as a family. We can take it from here." Her mother's body went still. "You know the way out." Her eyebrows furrowed. "Thank you."

Once Naomi left, Sylvie lost track of time and didn't listen to her mom or her dad. Their words were muffled in her ears as if they were on fast-forward. *That's it, I'm not sharing my secrets with anyone anymore.* She buried her hurt deep in her heart, a bottomless subterranean ravine of her own making.

The next day, Sylvie went to the counselor appointment her mother had scheduled for her. "I've always had a hard time with change," She shared stories about Nancy and Sally, intentionally leaving out any disclosures about Bandit or what happened at Tyler's party or the recent cutting.

Smile, nod, agree. "That sounds like good advice."

Sylvie made mental bargains with herself. *If I go, then they'll leave me alone. I'll attend all the therapy sessions, participating just enough to pass.*

After her sixth session, the counselor told her mom, "Sylvie's made great progress. I think she is much better."

Sylvie's mother's eyes shone. "I think it was just the pressure of school, a temporary thing, I'm sure."

Sylvie repeated her motto. *Smile. Nod. Agree.*

⌢

That was four months ago.

Soon the aspen tree would burst into a lime-green glory, leaves trembling in anticipation of summer, and she would graduate from high school.

She left her seat by the window for a needed shower. Her hair smelled of Naomi's mom's cigarettes. She covered her body with an oleander-smelling soap and winced when the lather came in contact with a recent cut on her lower abdomen.

She remembered the incident.

In the school bathroom stall, she overheard two classmates talking about her. One of the girls said, "I can't believe Sylvie got the Howard scholarship."

The other girl added, "Yeah, she doesn't even need a full scholarship anyway. Her parents have enough money."

Sylvie wanted to scream…no, she wanted to punch those girls in the face. She hadn't even wanted to apply for the Howard scholarship.

Taking out a razor from her back pocket, she raised her shirt and slashed her abdomen with one swoop, cutting much deeper than she should have. The blood dripped onto the stall floor, creating tiny red splatters against the white tile.

She hit the wall with a satisfying bang as she stormed out of the restroom.

Fourteen

NAOMI

Seven months after.... Rosewood

A gap in the comings and goings of patients, guests, and staff offered an opportunity for Naomi to enter the hospital with minimal detection. She'd memorized every detail about Rosewood, including what went on inside: the bright lights on either side of the sensor-fitted front door; the conference room, occupational health, labs, and business offices on the first floor; the patient rooms on the upper levels; how all the locked doors had code devices next to them set in a metallic frame lighting fixture; the single exit door next to the custodial closet. When she tried to open that door, no alarm went off, nor was there a camera in the hallway.

She peeked outside and noticed the set of stairs leading to a darkened side street.

There were three nursing shifts: six a.m. to four p.m., three p.m. to midnight, and eleven p.m. to seven a.m. Each shift change overlapped with the new set of caregivers. Naomi learned the day and times when she could visit with the least chance of someone seeing her; knew when clinicians made their rounds, when she could slip behind them unnoticed and get through a coded corridor.

The receptionist was new; Naomi didn't recognize her. "Hello there, I'm here to visit Sylvie," she said in her best self-assured voice.

The administrator peered over her chic cat-eye glasses. "And you are?"

"Jeni Snow, Sylvie's cousin." Her smile was so wide it hurt. "You can check records. I've got clearance to see her."

When Sylvie was transferred to Rosewood, Naomi posed as her cousin and hadn't been questioned since. She'd been super-careful with her visits.

The receptionist took her time leafing through the release forms. "Yes, I do see permission for a Jeni Snow to visit. ID, please."

She flashed her fake ID through the wallet window. "It's stuck in there. Do I have to take it out?" Naomi feared her face would split open if she continued with the sweetest-smile-ever charade.

"No, that's fine. Room 317. Evening visiting hours will end soon." The receptionist lowered her head and stared at the computer monitor, already absorbed with her next task.

Easy-peasy, she thought, an expression Sylvie used to say whenever they got away with things they certainly shouldn't have. Naomi walked gingerly through the hallway and drew her soft hat down over her ears. She passed a recessed water fountain and an empty wheelchair next to an AED machine.

When she got to 317, she stopped and looked through the dark glass window. Her heart skipped a beat or two.

Lying in the bed, unmoving, Sylvie's arms looked thinner and pastier; her hair as fair as an imaginary pixie or maybe a character from another world, and as vulnerable as a sleeping toddler. Naomi's eyes flickered with an unexpected welling of emotion.

She turned the handle, went inside, and closed the door without making a sound. Crossing the room, she lowered two window blinds, obscuring the streetlight outside. Then she turned off the light and pushed a chair underneath the door handle.

Naomi climbed onto the bed, lay next to Sylvie, and watched her chest move up and down in a distinct rhythmic pattern. The sound of the ventilator made a constant hissing noise. She placed her ear on Sylvie's chest and listened to the steadily pulsing heartbeat, whooshing blood through her veins, keeping her alive.

Sylvie. Her ideal soulmate.

She thought Sylvie's eyes were as green as springtime in Ireland (even though she'd never been to Ireland, she'd seen enough pictures to know) and loved the quiver in Sylvie's chin whenever she got nervous. The way she approached life. Her cautious tenacity.

Naomi was always floored by the fact that Sylvie hadn't ever realized the depth of her beauty or how magnificent her writings were. When Sylvie recited her poems to her, Naomi almost lost it.

One of the last times they were together, Sylvie whispered in Naomi's ear:

Who will show the sensibility of love
and fix my faulty wiring.
Laugh at my mistakes and remember
to forgive the fractured plastering
which keeps me alive.

It was the loveliest thing she'd ever heard.

To Naomi, Sylvie was like a rare shooting star.

Naomi gently placed her hand over Sylvie's. Her skin felt like a dried-up patch of earth, more like an old lady's skin.

Naomi whispered, "I miss your laugh. Our late-night phone calls. Our private dates." She lifted a strand of her hair and smelled it. It wasn't the same.

Naomi kept talking. "I'm not going back to college or back home. I'm leaving this place, Syv. Gonna travel. Go to some island in the middle of nowhere. Where was the place you wanted to visit? Bora Bora? Tahiti?"

Naomi stopped. Footsteps passed by the door and she held her breath.

She wouldn't have much time.

fifteen

TIM

Seven months after.... Traveling home after Rosewood

When Tim stepped back into the truck, he recalled his mother's meltdown, and the way she crumpled into herself like crushed paper, her face streaked with tears. She shrieked at Dr. Kanani when he followed her into Sylvie's room, grabbing and tugging fistfuls of her own hair, which made her look a bit crazy.

Tim didn't know what to say to her. His dad looked as helpless as he felt.

He didn't object when his mom said, "I need to go home. We'll come another day."

His gut tightened as he contemplated what his parents might have gone through these last months. He clamped his mouth shut to avoid voicing his mounting frustration. The unspoken words about what had just happened, and what they still had to do, hanging around like a bad head cold.

Exhausted, he closed his eyes.

Images of Africa flickered through his mind.

In a grove of indigenous acacias and hardwood trees where his medical team was housed, he spent most mornings now inhaling the loamy air, enjoying the pungent richness of the green, lush earth. Walking to work, the chime of songbirds reminded him that there was more to life than himself, his family, his own kind.

Often there'd be a long line of children and their parents waiting for them.

Julian from Bolivia, with a great sense of humor, usually greeted him first. "Morning, Doctor Tim," and giving him a thumbs-up.

Tim never hesitated to counter, "Morning, Doctor Julian," and spreading his arms out wide to indicate how much work they had that day.

Andrea, a nurse practitioner from Scotland, sometimes surprised the team with tea and scones in the late afternoon. "Ta-ta, time for tea," as if they were playing polo in the English countryside instead of finishing up care for the seemingly never-ending line of need.

Recently he'd taken to swimming in a nearby river after work. He'd lie there on a small beach, whether it was sunny or bruised skies about to burst with torrents of rain, his skin tingling as he pulled in deep, contented breaths.

Wise, honest, Elinah—with full-moon big eyes—often joined him. "So, what did you like most about today?"

"Everything."

A longing spread through his body. He missed them already.

Tim watched the movements of the cars, bursts of speed everywhere, so different from the visions in his head. Ahead, the gentle hills sloped upward to the mountains. Lithe aspen, pine, and heavy spruce trees seemed stitched to the inclines.

He observed his quiet parents, lost in their own thoughts. His dad worried about his mom; his mom was apparently apprehensive about everything. They looked old, worn out.

Tim imagined them younger, full of promise, hope, maybe the way Lilly and he once were.

Lilly. Tim hadn't thought about Lilly in months. Was he finally getting over the break up? It felt like a lifetime ago.

He met Lilly at a college race for a local charity event they both supported, a ten-kilometer run sponsored by the university. In the middle of a packed horde of racers, Lilly stood next to him, stretching her legs by placing one limb in front of her, and then the other.

"Warrior two?" he asked, flashing his best smile.

She laughed. "Why, yes. Do you do yoga?"

Lie or not to lie? "Kind of." He shrugged. He hadn't done a yoga class in years.

Lilly talked about practicing yoga at a studio near the university. Tim listened and was just about to ask her where she lived, when the whistle blew, and they were off, running as fast as they could. Lilly kept pace with Tim. At one point, he had to catch his breath. He was impressed.

When they crossed the finish line, he invited her to break-fast, saying, "Want to get brunch?"

She grabbed a water bottle from the adjacent runners' booth, and drank the entire thing before answering. "You buying?"

Suddenly shy, he answered, "You bet." She made him feel less than sure.

Once at the restaurant, they talked for two hours. He liked her straight white teeth, her shiny hair that fell in a bouncy ponytail behind her back, her tight lean muscles—proof she worked out often. But most of all, he respected her self-confidence.

"What do you like to do besides studying?" she asked.

Wow, he thought. *When was the last time anyone asked me that?*

"Always wanted to learn how to sail. Every time I take a walk on the beach, I look out at those sailboats and say *one day*." It felt wonderful to reveal something he hadn't shared with anyone until that moment.

She nodded and smiled a big, soul-warming smile. "Sounds like you could do anything if you put your mind to it."

Her faith in him made his heart swell. They exchanged phone numbers and texted often throughout the week.

Lilly majored in music and played the violin. Her music department's spring recital was in two weeks. "Would you like to come?" she asked Tim. Blushing, she added, "I have a solo."

On stage in a classy black dress that fell below her knees, Tim thought she looked like a goddess. She picked up the violin and played the most exquisite rendition of *Brahms Violin Sonata No. 3* he had ever heard. It felt as if a spring breeze slipped right through him, lifting him up.

After her bow, her eyes searched for Tim's and time seemed to halt for a moment. A tingling sensation crept down his spine to his toes. He kept clapping after everyone else had finished, but he didn't mind the stares. Lilly was simply the finest person he'd ever met.

They were inseparable for the first two years of their relationship. When they weren't in class or studying like crazy for finals, they did everything together. The best part of his day was when he saw her beautiful face.

He loved that she didn't wear makeup. He believed she didn't need any of that stuff. One of his favorite things to do was to find a new eating place or the best coffee in the area, often ordering just one dish, feeding her bites, and discussing the merits of authentic sushi or Indian curry or trashing the dish, never to return. Being silly together came naturally to them.

He felt raw and real with Lilly, and thought they were destined for a long life together. She listened attentively to his stories.

He shared secrets with her: "Stole my parents' car once and drove 100 mph on a windy mountain road." He trusted her.

When his acceptance to medical school came, Lilly followed him to California, but she struggled, never finding her own tribe, as she called it. She completed her degree in music education and went to work teaching at a local middle school.

She disclosed to Tim: "I miss the squalls gliding across Puget Sound."

Another time, she murmured, "I wished for my mom today. Would've loved to meet her at Zendy's." Her gaze focused on her feet. Zendy's was one of Tim and Lilly's favorite Seattle hangouts.

At the time, he didn't think it was a big deal. He didn't know she would become increasingly unhappy. Hyper-focused on finishing medical school and the details of his own life, he'd forget to meet her for lunch or he'd arrive late for a scheduled date.

Responses of "Hey, sorry," or "What? Was that today?" got old quickly. It wasn't long before things started to feel tense.

Their conversations started and stopped in awkward little jabs. He half-listened to her stories. "Repeat that one more time?"

Lilly's sighs were stretched and prolonged, proof of her growing dissatisfaction. "Never mind, it's not important." He'd counter with, "No, no, tell me." But then he would forget to listen again, the conversation inevitably ending with, "Can we talk about it tomorrow?"

The summer after Lilly's first year of teaching, she traveled to New Zealand with some of her Seattle friends. Tim encouraged her to go as it allowed him the opportunity to concentrate on his promising career, thinking the time apart would be good for both of them. Lilly's recent brooding bothered him—her stiff movements and false smiles, that hard edge to her voice. *Ugh.*

When Lilly returned from New Zealand, she looked fresh and vibrant, like a thirsty rose after a rain. "We climbed Mt. Doom and visited Hobbiton."

He paid attention to her details and even asked questions. "How big were those trees again?"

"They're Kauri trees, silly," she said as she threw a towel at Tim's face. "Dry the dishes." Holding a hand over her mouth to cover her smile, her laugh was wispy and light, uncomplicated.

They had a wonderful two weeks before Tim's attentive self wasn't listening anymore. He faked interest over her newfound attraction to southeast Asia and her latest friendship group, a few musicians who played at various musical venues.

She started coming home late and leaving early. "Let's skip suppers this week."

He spent long hours writing several new investigative articles for the hospital as well as covering for other residents when they needed him and enjoying hanging out with other doctors.

Eventually, Lilly and Tim ended up on opposite sides of a mountain that just kept getting higher and higher, increasingly more difficult to climb.

In early December of that year, Lilly took him out to dinner to celebrate a paper he'd recently published. Tim was delighted at the thought that Lilly might have read his essay. Lilly let him guide most of their dinner conversation, shaking her head at the appropriate times, saying things like "that's nice," or "sounds fascinating." They shared a bottle of Malbec and took their time eating the delicious meal.

He folded his arms over the table. "This is nice. We should do this more often."

"Dessert?" she asked.

"Absolutely," he replied, feeling lucky all over again for meeting someone like Lilly.

Right after the server took their dessert order, Lilly grasped her fingers one by one, a nervous habit he recognized. "Tim, I've done a lot of thinking and have decided to accept a teaching position in New Zealand. Remember I mentioned that? Their school year will begin end of January or early February at the latest."

Shocked, he said, "What? I don't recall that!" Honestly, he wouldn't have missed that detail.

Lilly exhaled. "That's just it. You're too self-absorbed. It's not good for me. I need things in my life right now and staying here and listening to you talk *medicine this* and *medicine that* isn't working out for me. I can't live like this."

She tried to grab his hand, but he pulled away. A red-hot anger exploded in his chest. He wanted to yank the tablecloth off and send every single dish and utensil scattering across the restaurant.

"Why now? I'm in my residency. Could we just take a break for a while and see?" He wasn't ready for the relationship to end—even though, deep down, he knew they had drifted apart.

Lilly's eyes filled with moisture. "I'm sorry, but I think it is best we end things, Tim. Let's just be friends." She blew her nose. "I'll spend the night with Kelly and come by tomorrow to pick up my things." She motioned for the waiter, paid the bill, and left in a matter of a few minutes, leaving Tim at the table wondering what the hell just happened.

He kept repeating the "let's just be friends" part to himself before he also left. Eventually, the anger was replaced with an ache behind his breastbone.

Tim didn't tell anyone about the breakup for a long time. Casually, he explained to his dad and mom when they asked about Lilly, "Oh, Lilly is doing a teacher exchange program in Auckland and will be gone for the rest of the year. It's okay. I'm swamped with work and doing double shifts anyway."

They accepted his answer and he hastily changed the subject. Denial became his best friend.

Almost every single moment of his life became double shifts, completely dedicated to his doctoral practice. He excelled at practicing medicine. Colleagues commented, "You're a beast." When not working, he exercised hard, running a half-marathon, then a full marathon.

One time, he made an offhand comment to an associate about a diagnostic error. "You think you could've tried harder?" He hadn't meant anything by it, but his associate's face got all red.

"Sometimes you are such a jerk, Tim." Then his associate walked away and did not speak to Tim for a week.

In the rare quiet moment, he became aware these remarks were becoming more frequent, and he was pissing people off.

Lilly didn't even send him a postcard from New Zealand.

And then he got the phone call about Sylvie.

That afternoon, in the middle of talking with a patient, he ignored the vibration from his phone in his pocket, twice. Then, he didn't check his voice mail. About an hour later, he received a third call.

This time, he scanned the caller ID and realized the call had come in from his dad. Secretly he hoped it might've been Lilly, even though he knew she didn't live in the same country anymore. Still, he hoped.

He returned his dad's phone call two hours late. His dad picked up on the first ring.

"Tim, oh, I'm glad you called back." Jack swallowed a few times and his voice broke. "There's been an accident."

Tim's palms started to sweat and his gut seized up. He looked for a place to continue their call. He found a cubicle, sat down, and listened to his dad tell him the story of what happened to Sylvie. Before Tim could ask any questions, his dad asked for explanations of the medical terms the doctors had shared with him.

Tim couldn't do it. He wasn't a doctor at that moment— he was Sylvie's big brother, overwhelmed by feeling.

"Dad, I've got to go; I'll call you back later." After he hung up, he sat motionless in the cubicle, letting himself drift away on a ripple of memories.

He remembered the first day he saw Sylvie, this tiny cherub in his mom's arms. Sylvie's light hair surrounded a beatific face, newborn blue eyes, and a crimson mouth. He felt for her warm fingers and put his hand over hers for a moment, comforted by a bond he could barely name then.

"She's beautiful," was all he could say.

He wondered how she would fit into his family, how things might change. Would she play games with him? Would she like to read and invent things and explore?

She didn't do any of these things, of course. Sylvie had her own world to discover.

But Tim yearned for the possibility she might share in his passions. He felt such a deep and abiding love for her, more than he had ever loved anybody besides his mom and dad.

A sharp twinge between his shoulder blades spread down his arms, and he let out a cry.

Another resident doctor named Bernie heard him and walked over. "Hey, Tim, everything all right?"

Tim shook his head. "Just need a moment."

Bernie smiled politely. "Okay," and then gazed at his clipboard. "Got a question for you about the patient in room 504."
He clicked on his pen, ready to write.

Incredulous, Tim looked at Bernie and wanted to roar, "I
don't have the answer! Leave me alone!" Instead, he got up and
walked out of the building. He felt like a wrung-out pair of socks.

Numb and spent and mad, he thought about driving to the
coast and throwing his cell phone so far out into the ocean it'd
never come back. Losing Lilly was hard. But the thought of
losing Sylvie felt like his anchor had vanished.

No... It can't be... It's not true... thoughts swirled around
his brain as he walked aimlessly for miles and miles on the city
streets. Somewhere in the distance, a pigeon cooed. The sun
lowered, the late daylight creating long shadows. Tim's feet
ached by the time he somehow found his way back to his
apartment, around one in the morning. Under the light of his
desk lamp, he opened his laptop, searched and booked a flight
to Colorado, and spent the next several hours before the sun
rose again rearranging his schedule.

He knew his parents believed that he would help them
understand what was happening: what they could do, just as
he also realized they were hoping for a miracle.

Because of that, he tried to be the good son, the proficient
doctor, the one who always got it right, spouting information:
"The poison affected her nervous system. She may be in a
medically-induced coma for a while. There is likely brain injury
and damage to her internal organs."

Nothing helped. They cried. They couldn't sleep and didn't eat much.

Tim watched his parents change from the "always-looked-young-for-their-age" to old—plain and simple.

His dad started to bite his fingernails, a habit he'd outgrown years ago. He didn't shave and his beard grew in odd, splotchy patches, some of the whiskers long and mishappen. Other spots on his cheeks and chin were bald. He forgot to change his jeans. Tim thought if Jack stood outside on one of the Denver street curbs, someone could mistake him for a homeless person.

His mom fell into a soundless spell, as if captured by aliens, and she failed to remember how to communicate. It made his spine tingle and frightened him more than once. He worried about losing his mom, too.

"Do you want me to stay here with you?" he asked them. He privately hoped they would not need him to be by their sides in their vigilant anticipation she might wake up.

His dad encouraged him to take a break. "Thanks, Tim, but no. If you have things to do, please, go ahead. We'll be right here."

He didn't press the issue. "Okay."

He escaped often to the hospital cafeteria with his laptop, feigning he had to work, which wasn't true. The medical wing where he worked had given him leave with full pay. He trolled the web and answered emails. The distraction quieted his otherwise active brain.

One email caught his attention. A colleague forwarded an invitation to apply to Doctors Without Borders. He spent the rest of the day and evening reading about the program and before he left Colorado, he had decided to apply.

Everyone guessed he'd accept a prestigious assignment somewhere in a noteworthy hospital or in a well-off practice. But the ache inside him flourished into this colossal rainforest, and he couldn't see his way through the tangled web of his soul. He needed space from everything he knew. He flew back to California.

The subsequent weeks dragged as Tim filled out paperwork and focused on his future: rented a storage unit for his meager belongings, went to the vaccination clinic, bought an airline ticket, researched about the country where he would be stationed, wrote emails to his new supervisor, excused himself from any social engagements, avoided eye contact, and spoke in one-word answers whenever he could.

Tim left for Africa knowing that Sylvie would never be the same if she recovered, and likely would not improve—not in the way his parents wanted. He understood that the lack of any motor response was a poor prognosis. He'd read the medical reports several times before he told his parents, "I don't think Sylvie will get better. Best to think about how to let her go."

His mom had screamed, "Nooooo! It's too soon! Medical advancements happen every day. People wake up from comas all the time."

Tim wanted to interrupt her. "That's true, but Sylvie's case is different. I've read her medical files. She's not going to recover." But he couldn't bring himself to say the words and switched the topic to something they had to accept—his posting in Kenya. "I'll come home for Christmas." His mom wept until she couldn't hold the phone any longer.

His dad cracked a few jokes to ease the tension. "I might just have to come and see you there." He stopped for a moment, catching his breath. "I'll miss you."

The authoritative barricade Tim maintained so well was at risk of disintegrating and he ended the phone call abruptly. "Gotta go. Remember, you'll see me in a few months." Purposely he omitted it would be a very short visit, and after that, he might not see them for well over a year.

Later, he sipped on a whiskey sour at a pub down the street and watched a football game, grateful for the crazy fans, the loud noise, and the chance to not think or feel for a while.

Not yet ready to process what had happened to Sylvie or the events leading up to his breakup with Lilly, Tim just wanted to be left alone.

Somehow, he managed to take years of feelings and put them in these little boxes that fit comfortably in the corners of his mind, tucked away so he didn't have to open them. But suddenly it was as if they had unwrapped themselves and kept popping up in his thoughts. He felt both oddly relieved and pasty with panic.

When he landed in Nairobi, he vowed for everything to be different: complain less, listen first instead of thinking of what he had to say, show kindness, care more, try to be less aloof— a recent remark he overheard at the nurses' station.

It didn't turn out that way. Almost immediately he became argumentative about the impoverished working conditions.

His supervisor, Dr. Morrie, laughed. "It's Africa, mate. You'll get used it. Relax."

But he couldn't relax. He didn't know how to remain calm in the chaos of inadequate medical supplies, or when one of the medical Jeeps broke down, or when rain seeped through the roof of his sleeping quarters, or after he discovered mice had nibbled at some of his personal supplies.

One time, in the middle of one of his outbursts, Elinah, a stunningly beautiful native Kenyan, stopped counting the syringes and watched Tim. Afterward, she said, "It's just not you, you know. We're all in this together." Her exquisite coffee-colored skin shimmered in the heat. Beads of sweat reflected the light.

She gave Tim a book about the indigenous people. "Might help if you understood where you are."

Later that night, Tim woke and went outside. The air smelled rich and pungent from a recent tilling of the soil nearby. Regrets surfaced like a pickpocket on the streets robbing him of any return to sleep. All the things he wanted to say—no, that he should've said—to Lilly: complimented her when she dressed up; apologized for all the times he didn't show up for a date; bought her flowers; told her he loved her more.

And Sylvie…. Tim couldn't begin to count the ways he had failed her, how she didn't or couldn't reach out to him when she likely needed him the most.

For the rest of the night, regrets left Tim feeling out of sorts and unsteady. He tasted his tears as they ran down his face, as if they had been stored in brine, and knew it wouldn't be the same without Sylvie.

It would never be the same without her.

When Tim emerged from his reverie, they were almost home. Mountains loomed large on either side of the highway. The late day sun sped toward the horizon, the sky a darkish-blue. Having not said a word since Denver, he rolled down his window and gulped a mouthful of fresh air, forcing himself to come back to the present.

"Thanks for driving, Dad," was all he could think of to say.

His dad glanced in the rearview mirror. "Sure, buddy. Glad you got some rest."

Tim rubbed the smooth round stone in his pocket, a recent gift from Elinah.

"Open your hand." She placed a glossy black pebble the size of a small plum in the middle of his palm. "This will help remind you of what's important, yes?"

Tim wished she'd left her soft fingers in his hand for just a bit longer. "Tell me about that kids' game again?"

Elinah's face broke into a childish grin. "Ah, yes. Matata."

She proceeded to describe how the children played: sitting in a circle, feet touching, each taking a turn to name a circular object such as a tree ring or a water ripple. Next, each would identify a figurative expression of round, like family or the cycle of night and day. As players failed to come up with spherical examples, they dropped out until only one remained.

"Tradition has it that the last child in the game will live a fortunate and blessed life." Her words were as clear as a perfectly sung note.

Tim didn't know if the stone would help him or not, but he was going to try to be a better person.

sixteen

SYLVIE

Before – Off to College

S
ylvie sat on the edge of her chair and looked around. Miniature white LED lights hung around the newly stained deck's railing, and the oversized picnic table, swathed in red and white linen cloth, looked elegantly country charming. Long plaid cushions covered the benches. Tied to the corners, colorful balloons bobbed in the breeze. Sunlight snuck through the trees, casting shadows on the freshly mowed grass. Timber beams framed the sizeable sliding glass doors.

She could see the cake through the glass, a luscious lemon sponge with vanilla frosting, her favorite. Her grandma stood at the kitchen island, placing tiny graduation ornaments on top of the cake—the typical square black hat, a diploma, letters spelling *Congratulations* across the rim.

She loved this place.

Sylvie rose and walked across the deck, down the stairs to their garden. She strolled through several neat rows of newly sprouted tomato, squash, and herb plants, stopping to smell the sweet scent of the climbing roses and wisteria vines along the trellises. Underneath her graduation robes, she wore a new dress. The light fabric swooshed against her legs, supple waves moving in an orchestrated rhythm. In a few months, she'd be off to college and leave her childhood home.

"Yoo-hoo!" Her mother yelled from the deck. "Time to go."

Sylvie thought she should be excited to graduate from high school. She should be happy to have her family here. Grandma and Grandpa had flown in from California, Tim too. She should've been elated and super-thankful for the full scholarship to the University of Colorado. Instead, her heart felt like a wound that couldn't heal.

They took two cars to the ceremony. Sylvie rode with her dad. A camcorder lay on the seat between them. Her dad squeezed her hand. "I'm so proud of you."

Sylvie nodded and smiled. "Guess I'm just a little nervous."

"Nothing to be worried about, Sylvie. You are one in a million."

She gazed at her dad. Gray hairs sprouted near his temples. She wished she could bottle his belief in her and take it wherever she went. "Thanks, Dad."

When her turn came to walk across the stage with her diploma, she glanced over at her classmates. She searched for Naomi's face in the sea of happy faces and questioned if her friend had followed through with her plan.

Yesterday, Naomi revealed, "I might not go. It's all bullshit, anyway."

Sylvie wished she could have had the audacity to do what Naomi did and not follow through with the hoopla of commencement. Just the thought of telling her family that she didn't want to walk left her feeling slightly electrified.

Sylvie's family took pictures. They talked with other parents. Sylvie acted her part flawlessly. The principal shook her hand. "Congratulations, Sylvie. Best of luck, not that you'll need it next year."

"Thank you."

Her art teacher walked a step toward her. "You are going places, girl. Never give up on that talent of yours."

"Thank you."

A classmate gave her a fist pump. "We did it!" She fist-pumped him back. "Yeah!"

They drove back to the house just as the sun headed for the horizon, filling the sky with blue, gray, and pink streaks.

In the back seat, Tim spoke first. "Sylvie, you look beautiful. I'm really glad I'm here." He massaged Sylvie's shoulders. "My baby sis graduating high school and off to college."

Her dad spoke next. "Can't believe it. You're all grown up."

A small lump formed in her throat. "Thanks, guys."

Once everyone sat for the post-graduation dinner, her mom rose from her chair. She clanked her wine glass with her fork. "Toast!" She turned slightly to face her daughter. "Here's to the future Georgia O'Keefe or Maya Angelou or…" She paused, shifting her weight toward Sylvie. "You know what I mean." She laughed. "Anyways, we all look forward to watching you succeed and accomplish your dreams."

Sylvie thought about her dreams. They weren't about being famous. They weren't about triumph. She looked at each member of her family. The weight of their expectations smoldered in her chest.

Sylvie's phone vibrated at the same time as her grandma cut the cake. She covertly read Naomi's message from under the tablecloth. *Free tonight? Got a present for ya.*

After cake, she embraced her grandparents. "Thanks for the yummy dessert. I loved it."

She hugged her mom. "Naomi texted. Hope you don't mind if I go out tonight."

Her mom pulled Sylvie close. "Go. You only graduate from high school once."

Sylvie addressed her family. "Hey, guys. Going to catch a few grad parties." She extended her arms in the air, and swung them from side to side. "Thank you for everything."

Tim rose from his seat. "I'll walk you out." He whispered in her ear, "Have fun."

Sylvie dangled her handbag over her shoulder. Together, they walked to the front door, Tim's arm around Sylvie's shoulder, Sylvie leaning into Tim. "Thanks for coming. I missed you."

Tim opened the door for her. He winked. "Don't do anything I wouldn't do."

Sylvie sat on the verandah's front steps and rested against one of the two extensive poles that supported the covered porch. Hearing the *putt-putt* of Naomi's car coming up the driveway, she wondered if Naomi's family did anything special for her. Sylvie stood and waved.

Naomi rolled down the passenger side car window. "Get in, Sylv."

Sylvie climbed into the car. A paper bag with a crumpled hamburger wrapper and an empty soda can lay scattered on the floormat.

"Here." Sylvie handed Naomi a package covered in stylish tissue paper and shiny ribbon. "Happy graduation!"

Naomi lowered her head. "Oh."

Sylvie couldn't wait for Naomi to see what she gave her. "Go on. Open it!"

Slowly, carefully, Naomi undid the ribbon and tissue as if they were gifts, too. Sylvie watched her friend lift the small painting.

"Oh, wow..., Sylv." Naomi whispered, "It's the most awesome gift anyone has ever given me."

Naomi placed the picture on the dashboard. The vivid drawing of two women bathing in a pool of light with a butterfly waterfall held a surprising lure—as if she could just step right into that world.

Sylvie unfolded a piece of paper. "I wrote this poem for you, too."

Naomi read the words.

Everything we have been through
now a cosmic dance
your soul running
free
swirling like atoms
a world
as beautiful
as the beat of your heart.

Sylvie touched Naomi's face. "It goes with the painting."

Naomi didn't say anything for several moments before she seized Sylvie's fingers. "I don't know what to say." She kissed one of her fingers. "It makes my gift seem pretty darn cheesy."

Naomi reached into her pocket and pulled out a tiny piece of paper no bigger than Sylvie's index finger. "I thought we could get high together." She placed the blotter in Sylvie's palm. "Go out to Hummingbird Open Space. I brought a blanket. We can look at the stars as they come out."

Sylvie felt little quivers go up her spine. "What is it?"

"Ecstasy," Naomi explained. "It's not a bad drug, Sylv. It'll just make you feel closer to everything you love. All your worries will be gone."

Sylvie thought how good it would feel to still her thoughts. She could let her concern about going to college, about leaving home, about measuring up to everyone else's expectations, and the hurt buried deep down, disappear. "Okay. What do I do?"

"Put it in your mouth. I'll take mine once we're at the park." Naomi started the ignition. "Fasten your seatbelt."

Sylvie put the itty-bitty scrap of paper on her tongue. Ten minutes later, she felt goosebumps all over and lost control of her body and mind, free-falling into uncharted zones. It seemed to take an eternity to get to where they were going.

Naomi parked in the almost-deserted parking lot. She carefully rewrapped Sylvie's gift and placed it neatly in the back seat, then she helped Sylvie out of the car. "Hey, sit right here until I get the blanket and take mine."

Sylvie sat on the curb, looking like a child waiting for her mother. Feeling a little woozy, she tripped. "Oops." She couldn't think clearly.

The sun set. Muted bands of rose and magenta highlighted the horizon. Naomi spread out her blanket and they lay there, side by side, watching as the stars appeared, each lost in their own hallucinogenic landscape. They hardly spoke.

Sylvie passed the night in a vague distortion. Colors blurred. An elephant and a lion roamed freely and a tree morphed into an eagle. Stars grew increasingly bright, merging with the shadowy silhouettes of the trees. Then a ghost, or a shadow of something dark and creepy, loomed in her peripheral vision. Taking in shallow breaths, she tried to move but couldn't make her body work, so she chose to close her eyes instead. Instantly, a thousand illuminations exploded in her head and she started counting them before succumbing to a deep sleep.

When she opened her eyes, they felt like they were glued together; her throat so dry she could barely swallow. She stared at Naomi and remembered a kiss and the heat of her body.

Naomi caught her gaze. "Finally awake? It'll be dawn soon." She shivered and wiped away the tear on her cheek. "It's cold. Let's go." Naomi drove Sylvie home.

In the silent car, Sylvie thought about her night with Naomi, looking at the stars, with the waning moon emphasizing a drifting cloud. How she treasured the times Naomi reached out and held her hand or stroked her hair. How comfortable and relaxed she felt around her. How Naomi didn't judge or pressure her to be something she wasn't.

She thought she might've asked her about the night at Tyler's, but couldn't say for sure. Sylvie supposed that Naomi was the one person who "got" her, with all her quirks. Together, they were like peanut butter and jelly.

Sylvie shifted in her seat. She looked at Naomi's angular nose and the indentation in her chin. "Thanks for driving me home. Later?" Waiting for agreement from Naomi, she wondered if Naomi felt the same way—comfortable and accepting—or if it was just the effects of the drug they took.

Naomi rested her head on the steering wheel, the sound of the running car in the background. Without raising her head, she muttered, "I need a bed and a shower."

Sylvie leaned closer to Naomi, not enough to touch, but enough to feel something. At that moment, the breeze picked up and a hundred rose petals softly broke away from their stems and floated right in front of the car.

Sylvie nudged Naomi. "I'd love to paint that." Naomi dipped her chin further down and didn't respond.

Sylvie wondered why Naomi might be mad at her. Had she done something wrong? She shook her head, hoping to clear her thoughts, and changed the subject. "Well…goodbye then." She unbuckled her seatbelt and shuffled out of the car. "See ya soon."

Sylvie opened the door to her silent home and soundlessly tiptoed to her room. Crawling in bed with her clothes on, she slept for the rest of the day and evening as if she hadn't slumbered in years. When she woke, her head pounded as if a construction worker was drilling at her temples. Searching in the medicine cabinet, she found a bottle of pain relievers. Swallowing three, she went back to bed.

At breakfast the next morning, the house seemed eerily quiet.

Tim and her grandparents had left. Her dad fixed pancakes. "Blueberries?" he asked.

Sylvie's stomach grumbled. "Yeah, please."

Sylvie's dad placed three odd-shaped pancakes on her plate. "Ready to start work at the office?"

Sylvie gazed at the pancakes. Together they looked like a dinosaur. She laughed; her father had not lost his touch. "Yep."

Her dad continued, "Monica needs help with client files, shredding old documents, and rearranging the staff room."

"I'm working on a set of poems for an upcoming poetry contest and would like to submit a short story as well. Would it be all right to only work half-days?" Her dad agreed and Sylvie began her job, hopeful for the best summer ever.

It didn't happen.

Naomi left to spend the season with her father in Utah and didn't even say goodbye.

Sylvie ruminated that it must've been her fault. Wishing she could remember all the details about the night they spent together, she thought about the ecstasy and how good it had felt to get high. It really had helped with her nerves and even inspired her to write more. But Naomi's sudden departure didn't feel right.

Sylvie spent the summer alone. Monday through Friday mornings, she worked for her father's architectural firm, and left funny cartoons on his desk. In the afternoon, she basked under the sun, mimicking the garden garter snakes. A few times she lunched on the back deck with her mom, but didn't like it when Mia needled her.

"I think you should take a business class and supplement your course load with an honors writing module." Her mother added, "You have so much talent, Sylvie. You need to seize the day."

Sylvie pretended she was listening, but more often she just tuned her out. "Thanks for lunch, but I gotta go write. You know, carpe diem."

"Oh, yes. Of course." Her mom sat up straight. "I'll get the dishes."

Some nights, Sylvie pilfered some of her parents' alcohol. Not much, she thought, just enough to take the edge off, calm her thoughts.

All summer long, Sylvie wrote poems and short stories. As autumn drew closer, she took down all of her wall paintings, wrapping each one in plain newsprint, and stored them in the basement. She removed her poetry from around her door, placing the poems carefully in a portfolio, and labeled them: *High School Writings*. Finally, she repainted her bare bedroom walls white; the color on the paint can read *Pristine Frost*.

Ten days before leaving for college, she bundled up her bedding. "Mom, can I give these to Goodwill?"

Her mom, eager to get rid of the second-hand stuff, approved. "Absolutely. I can buy some new things if you'd like."

Sylvie concurred. Her mom purchased a five-hundred thread-count organic cotton sheet set, an ultra-soft blanket, and a down comforter. Sylvie asked for them to be all white.

When her mom walked into Sylvie's room, it reminded her of an open field in winter, covered with a fresh layer of snow. "Your room looks awfully stark. How about a colorful comforter cover and pillows? Rug? New curtains?"

Sylvie declined. "I like the simplicity. It'll be nice to come home to this." She thought the room would be like a new canvas, a place to record her changes.

She talked to Naomi on the phone. "It's been a weird summer. Are you coming back to your mom's place?"

Naomi hesitated before answering. "No. Driving straight from Utah to Denver. I applied for a job near the community college in Aurora. Thought I'd work during the day and take a night class if I can, or maybe a morning class." Her voice lowered. "My mom doesn't want me back."

Disappointed, Sylvie pressed, "Did you meet any new friends?"

Naomi grunted. "No. Are you kidding me? There's nothing in this place."

Sylvie drummed her foot. "Then why did you go there?"

Naomi switched topics. "Hey, my dad's calling. Let me know when you get to Boulder, 'kay?"

Sylvie wasn't sure how to end the call. "Bye." She thought it such a nothing word.

Firm knots lodged in Sylvie's stomach the day her parents drove her to Boulder. The deep velvet blue sky followed her over the mountain passes.

The time between yesterday and today stretched thin and parched.

Yesterday, she touched every special home spot. Cruxes of magic, she called them. The places where her inspiration flourished: her white and barren bedroom, the window above her bed, the aspen tree outside. In autumn, thousands of leaves fell across a slate-gray sky, leaving her speechless at times. She'd miss her strolls through the garden, sitting under her favorite crimson rose bush.

As a child, she loved opening the spice drawer in the kitchen. The cardamom, ginger, turmeric, cinnamon smells filled her nostrils with promise. In winter, she cherished being wrapped in fleece, writing in the chocolate-colored leather swivel chair next to the wood fireplace. Afterward, she would run a hot bath, watching the burgeoning bubbles, and soak in the tub until the water turned lukewarm. Sometimes, she emptied some of the water, and ran just the hot water again, so she could stay in that toasty luxury for minutes longer.

When summer came, she stretched out on the grass and watched the cloud formations, imagining fairy godmothers hiding in the woods.

Home. Hard to leave.

The same sky greeted her as she stepped out of the family's blue SUV. She stared at the russet block building with three floors. Bassett Hall—her new home away from home. Her dorm room, located on the third floor of the residence hall, had new carpet and the walls smelled of fresh paint. The lobby furniture appeared as if it had not been replaced in a few years.

Once in her dorm room, she sat on the unmade bed and listened. Two girls talked in the hallway. Someone dropped a heavy suitcase and the thump made her bed shake. Elevator doors opened and closed, and multiple cell phones rang.

She caught the laughter of a few students outside on the grass. A police siren resounded off the brick wall of her building and gradually faded into the distance.

Her mom, eager to cast a positive spin on her daughter's leap into adulthood, seemingly made suggestions at every corner. "Would you like help settling in? Should we eat out or in the cafeteria?" Her mom nudged her dad, coaxing him to participate.

Her dad appeared aloof. "Hmm." His eyes seemed cloudy, as if a morning mist got stuck there.

Sylvie didn't know how to not offend her mom and dad, but she really wanted to be on her own. "I think I'll go for a walk first, then unpack later tonight." She hugged them, then tilted her head to the ceiling. "I'll catch up with you in the morning."

She quickly made her bed and left the dorm to walk along the university's stone pathways. A few other students strolled along with her. "Hello," she said politely. No one knew her; this was a new start. She kept on walking.

A small group of men ran past in their CU Buff athletic gear. The smell of hot grease from a nearby barbeque made her wish she hadn't skipped lunch. Her mouth watered at the whiff of burned cheese. A streetlight came on and although the thought of returning seemed sensible, she didn't want to stop.

Maybe Naomi was right. Perhaps leaving her hometown was the best thing for her: a new beginning where she could make new friends, date, even find a writing group, pledge to not drink or do drugs.

She thought if she could be willing to believe everything would be all right, then it could happen. Shaking her head, she wrapped her arms around herself.

When she got back to the dorm, she couldn't fall asleep. Around two-thirty a.m., she got up, turned off her phone, and took four ibuprofen tablets. Just before dozing off, she looked at her roommate's empty space and wondered how things would go once she moved in. She didn't wake up until she heard banging on her dorm door.

"Sylvie?" Her dad sounded upset.

She looked at the clock. Eleven thirty a.m. She was supposed to meet her parents for breakfast at ten at a little café they passed on their walk yesterday. "Hold on."

Opening the door, she stared at her parents' anxious faces and noticed her mom's hair striped with silvery strands. "Sorry. I went for this long amazing walk last night and turned off my phone." She took a deep, steady breath.

I should've at least called and left them a message.

Her mom dropped her shoulders and then hitched them up again. "Oh, that's okay." She gazed at Sylvie. "Lunch?"

Suddenly, her mom's vigil on her emotional well-being felt oppressively hot and stuffy. Even though she had not eaten dinner the night before, she declined the invitation. "No, no. You go ahead."

Her dad coughed. "I'll check with admissions before we leave. Make sure everything is okay." He leaned toward Sylvie and grabbed her chin. "Hey, be good. Have fun. Study hard." Then he pulled her close to his chest. "I'll call you in a couple of days. See how you're doing."

She nodded, like the respectable daughter she was brought up to be. She watched them leave from her dorm window, and waved when they looked back. Her head was full of conflicting thoughts, a congested labyrinth of counting the days until she'd be home again and weighing in on the possibilities of being on her own where no one knew her. Her pulse pounded at her temples and the muscles around her mouth quivered slightly.

About an hour later, Wendy moved in.

She talked nonstop and had more stuff than Sylvie had ever seen in anyone's bedroom: pillows and matching comforter and sheets and stuffed bears and mobiles and shelves and every computer gadget possible, along with her smartphone and tablet and e-book and all those chargers and nice bags for each thing, not to mention her clothes and way too many shoes. She spent the afternoon and early evening filling every usable space with her stuff.

Sylvie watched, partly amused, mostly bewildered, and at times in awe of this creature who would share her living space.

Wendy sported a stylish haircut. Two pale purple streaks highlighted her untreated chestnut color, or at least Sylvie thought it was natural.

Around seven p.m., Wendy asked, "Want to get some food? There's a great sub shop a few blocks from here."

Sylvie's stomach rumbled. "What kind of sandwiches do they have?"

"I like the pressed Cubans." Wendy winked. "I have a fake ID. I'll buy us beer, too."

Sylvie thought about her resolution to not drink. "Maybe just one."

Wendy changed into a pair of short shorts with a tube top and a plaid cotton shirt to go over it. She looked like a model.

Sylvie looked down at her T-shirt and jeans. "Is this okay?"

Wendy smiled a warm, friendly smile. "You look great, like a freshman ready for a fabulous four years."

What was that supposed to mean? "Okay."

Sylvie only meant to drink one beer, but a few people Wendy knew showed up and they sat around and drank several. They talked about the upcoming semester and their respective academic schedules.

Wendy asked, "Sylvie, what are you majoring in again?"

"Not sure yet, but probably creative writing," she responded.

One of the other girls commented, "Cool."

Sylvie thought the evening would've been even better if only Naomi could be there with her, and vowed to call her when she got back to the dorm. But she got back late and talked to Wendy instead.

The next weeks passed in a blur of activity: attending seminars, meeting other students in the residence hall, staying out late, drinking. She even smoked pot a few times.

Every morning after a few too many, Sylvie resolved to stop partying and get to work studying, or making it to the gym. Just these first several weeks of college life and then things would settle down, she thought.

One night she drank until she passed out.

Around mid-October, Sylvie saw a poster at the student union building advertising a poetry slam night at the Run Riot Arts Center and decided to go. It was open mic night. Poets were encouraged to take the stage and read an original verse or sonnet.

She spotted a table near the back. "Can I sit here?" she asked shyly. The two girls already at the table looked to be around her age.

"Sure," one of the girls said. "Jaycee's up next. His poems are mind blowing."

A lean man wearing a white T-shirt and a speckled tie walked toward the small front stage. His dark hair was tied up in a man bun and his thin moustache gave him an aristocratic look. He grabbed the mic. "Hello, you beatniks, freaks, liberals, activists, fanatics, die-hards and most importantly poetry lovers and haters!"

Everyone cheered. Someone yelled, "You da man, Jaycee!"

For the next ten minutes, Jaycee delivered the most amazing rhyme Sylvie had ever heard. The way he almost sang the words had a hypnotic and deeply exotic pull. She listened, spellbound, to his creative saga about a recent tour of Indonesia. She'd always wanted to go there.

> *… when I rose from the water, I was still*
> *my dark hair flamed the encircling wheels*
> *wheels within wheels, breathing in, breathing out*
> *gray days faraway, time without end …*

When he finished, a hush fell over the room, as if everyone and everything had suddenly gone mute. Then, thundering applause shook the room. She jumped up and joined in.

Looking over at the two girls—both also on their feet—Sylvie mouthed *wow* and they both nodded in agreement. After things settled down, Sylvie said, "I didn't know this place even existed until a few days ago." She glanced around the room. "Everyone seems to know everyone."

Ivy introduced herself. "Name's Ivy. Are you a poet?"

Sylvie paused. "I guess so."

Ivy seemed delighted to share all she knew, as if she'd been waiting for someone like Sylvie to come along. "This place is by far one of the best venues in Boulder. We're like family," and continued with tales of the best poets in town. She even shared that Jaycee recently got a book signing deal with one of the Big Five publishing houses.

Sylvie feigned understanding. Every time Ivy mentioned Jaycee, Sylvie stole a peek, admiring his boyish grin and the tattoos on his left arm. He had this infectious laugh that seemed to invite the group at his table to want to join in his fun.

"Do you know him?" she asked Ivy.

"Sure. Would you like to meet him?" It seemed Ivy was on a crusade to get Sylvie to be a member of their poetry clique. Maybe it was working.

Ivy went over to Jaycee's table and whispered something in his ear. Jaycee glanced over, nodded, and followed Ivy back.

"This is Sylvie," Ivy said. "She writes poetry, too. I think we can get her to recite."

"Well, I don't know if I'm in the same league as you all, but I'd like to learn," she muttered. A slow tingle of panic worked its way up Sylvie's spine. Her cheeks burned at the thought of getting up on stage in front of a room of people she didn't know.

Jaycee sat in the empty seat next to Sylvie. "Sylvie, you need to believe in yourself. We're all poets. Just trust and let your inner genius out." He squeezed her hand and his touch made her stomach feel as though it was full of a thousand fluttering butterflies.

seventeen

JACK

Seven months after – The Meltdown

"You guys go on ahead. I'll get this."

Jack didn't know if he could stand another moment with either one of them. Mia's silence needled him as if she was literally stabbing him with little pins. *Why was she being so damn quiet?* She frustrated the hell out of him; being at Rosewood had been tough for him, too. Tim seemed different, less sure of himself, entwined in his own thoughts. *What's happening to my family? How do I reach them?*

A couple of times he rolled down his window on the drive back from Denver. There wasn't enough air in the car for all of them.

Thinking back on the visit, Sylvie looked different. Her pale skin and withered body appeared ghostly, as if she'd already left this world. He knew it in his bones: Sylvie's recovery was highly unlikely. He had to let go of his little girl.

How could he persuade Mia—not an easy task. He loved Sylvie as much as she did and it wasn't just her who had lost a child. Sometimes she acted that way, though, and it took a ton of patience not to yell at her, hit her, *something*.

The charade of being the resilient husband and father, holding things together, being the voice of reason, suddenly felt too much. The holding-in instead of lashing-out seemed more than just burdensome.

He'd always prided himself on his ability to remain calm, even when he got that phone call about Sylvie, but not now. Not any longer.

As soon as Tim and Mia opened the front door of the house, Jack got out of the truck and threw Mia's daypack onto the frozen ground, watching as it slipped and rolled down the embankment, landing with a thud in the snow. Then he raised Tim's backpack over his head and dropped it on the hard asphalt, covered in icy spots. A loud, sharp crack followed.

Unable to contain his feelings any longer, he shouted, "I can't do this anymore!"

A red squirrel ran across the driveway, but not before it had sniffed the fallen luggage and gathered something up in its mouth. He ran after the squirrel, forming snowballs as he went, unleashing them one by one and yearning for a direct hit. The mammal outsmarted him and ran into the woods that surrounded their property.

He followed. In his pursuit, he left the shoveled driveway and found himself post-holing, the snow getting deeper and deeper, slowing him down. The squirrel had escaped up a tall blue spruce and let out a stream of high-pitched chirps, as if to chide Jack for even trying to chase it.

He looked up and tried to locate the animal. A few snow-flakes fell onto his cheek.

He kept going.

A line of sweat formed on Jack's upper brow and pooled in his armpits. One of his legs fell into a tree well, trapping him there for a moment. He hollered and cursed and cried as tears streamed uncontrolled down his face. "Why, why, why?" he wailed.

Images of his silent self in times of controversy and despair and hurt and when his gut had screamed at him to say something flashed through his head. He collapsed forward, freeing his leg, and rolled onto his back. His hot breath produced miniature vapor patches streaming from his mouth.

The late-day lavender light cast the quiet forest in shadowy hues. In a nearby ponderosa pine, chickadees flitted from branch to branch, searching for any end of the day morsels before they burrowed in for the cold Colorado December evening.

His chest heaved up and down as he tried to take in air between sobs, almost as if he was underwater, desperate for just one full breath. Seemingly all things he once held so dear —his marriage, his family, his hopes—were unraveling into something he couldn't recognize, including himself.

He thought he could protect his family, but the fragility of life came out in peculiar ways and he couldn't change that. Salty tears ran down his face, onto his lips, and trickled into his mouth. The taste reminded him of the time he took Mia, Tim, and Sylvie to the Florida coast. There, they leapt up and down in the undulating waves, laughing and holding onto each other. The water splashed in his face and stung his eyes. He swallowed some of the water, too. It seemed like another lifetime.

Nothing seemed like it could be right again.

Since that terrible day in May, his body ached when he tied his shoes for his early morning runs. His head throbbed when his cell phone lit up, thinking it might be a call from Sylvie, even though he knew she was in a hospital bed hooked up to a ventilator. His heart rate jumped from a steady rate to a hurried thumping whenever he heard a young woman's voice. The lunch spots he enjoyed in the past lost their appeal. Whenever he ate there, the food seemed to have no taste.

He used to love listening to music, but sometimes a particular song brought up memories. Sunsets and sunrises and other people's joy somehow deepened his loss. He felt most alone just before bed when all the lights were out and he could stop pretending to be strong for everyone else.

The accumulated emotional toll pressed down like hot stones on his chest.

He sank into the snow and closed his eyes and let himself free fall.

eighteen
JAYCEE
Seven months before – Amour

Jaycee couldn't remember if anyone captivated him more. Sylvie had the most striking face he'd ever seen, immense sea-green eyes, and a slender nose over well-formed lips. She had an elegant, willowy look about her, as though shaped by an ancient god. He wanted to write poetry about her all day long and recite them at every evening venue he could find.

The night he met Sylvie, he stayed up until the wee hours of the morning composing two poems, more sonatas, muttering a line from the second poem before he fell asleep a little before four a.m.

The sun of your smile makes me want to walk on water....

He went to Run Riot every night for a week, hoping to run into Sylvie. He'd given up on the traditional dating scene a few years ago, preferring the informal—or as he liked to call it, *natural joining with someone*—in harmony with his laid-back lifestyle.

On the eighth night, he saw her sitting at the same back table with Ivy and Jenna. He'd known Ivy for two years now and thought her shallow writing not very noteworthy, but she adored him. He liked that.

Besides, she had introduced him to Sylvie.

Sylvie's light-colored hair rolled down her back and bobbed gracefully when she turned her head. The robin-egg blue fleece she wore over a white T-shirt made her appear sweet and fresh —very different from the dreadlocked, cut-up denims girl he was sleeping with at the time.

That night Jaycee rose from his chair and made his way to the stage, grabbing the mic. The audience quiet, leaning in as if they were expecting some big announcement.

"Evening, friends. Tonight, I'd like to read a recent poem." He sought Sylvie's face in the crowd and when he found her, he recited the most tender, heartfelt piece he'd ever written. A pregnant pause followed, the crowd not quite sure how to respond, most hoping he might be talking about them.

"Thanks for listening." Jaycee rose and meandered to Sylvie's table, shaking hands with colleagues along the way, exchanging bear hugs and fist bumps with a few close friends.

Just before he got to Sylvie's table, he stopped for a micro-second and noticed his heart rate had tripled. The nervousness surprised him. It'd been a while since anyone or anything made his legs feel a little wobbly.

"Hey, Ivy, Jenna, Sylvie." He faced Sylvie. Long tentacles of longing unraveled along his spine.

Sylvie cleared her throat. "Jaycee, what a lovely poem."

Ivy pushed closer to Jenna, making room for Jaycee to slide into the space next to her. "Sit. Sit. Yes, that was incredible." Jaycee thought she might've even batted her eyes. After they resettled around the table, Jenna asked questions and Ivy commentated, like a one-act show.

"So, who is this woman you're writing about?" Jenna asked.

Jaycee shook his head. "What makes you think it's about a woman? Could be Mother Nature or a love for a favored pet or my favorite sushi." He laughed.

Ivy and Jenna stared at Jaycee for a moment before they let it pass and conversed about other things: midterms, the upcoming election, the possibility of snow next week, and Jenna's new boyfriend, Max.

"Are you going up to Station X to see Facia?" Jenna asked, turning to Sylvie.

Jaycee touched Sylvie's foot under the table and she startled. "Nah. Think I'll stay here."

Ivy and Jenna continued to share stories, completely unaware of the current passing between Jaycee and Sylvie like mini-electric shocks next to them.

Ivy, bored by Jaycee's lack of interest in her, said, "Well, guys, time for me to head back to campus." When no one asked her to stay, she added, "See you next week."

Jenna yawned and asked Sylvie, "Want to walk back to CU?"

Jaycee interrupted, "Uh, Sylvie asked if I could read one of her poems. I'll walk her back in a bit."

Jenna stared at Jaycee, not quite grasping the implication. She ran her hand through her hair as if she were trying to remember if Sylvie had said that or not. "Okay." Slinging her daypack over her shoulder, she nodded. "Night, Sylvie. Jaycee."

Jaycee watched Jenna leave. He faced Sylvie. "I hope you have a poem for me." Other comebacks danced on his tongue. He waited.

Sylvie stared straight ahead. "Maybe."

"No biggie. I really just wanted to get to know you." He searched her face. "Tell me about your writing."

Tentatively at first, and then with more zest, Sylvie told him about her poetry. "It gives me a way to let my true self have a voice," she said and passed him a folded piece of paper, slightly torn around the edges. She lowered her eyes.

Jaycee unfurled the note and read her words. When he finished, he read it again. He took a long breath in and let it out slowly. "This is good." *More than good*, he thought.

Sylvie brought her hand to her mouth. "Really?"

Jaycee clasped his fingers together and put them under his chin. "Really."

Sylvie's eyes widened as she dug out her phone. "I have a few pics of my canvases that go along with my poems," scrolling quickly until she found them. "Here."

Jaycee took the phone and enlarged the photo for a better detailed view. "You did this?" He stared at the small screen, astounded by the intense images, her method of uniting colors, soft blues seeping through rich scarlet reds. He pointed. "What is that?"

Sylvie leaned in close. He longed for her to touch him. "That is a female mystic."

Fascinated, Jaycee shook his head. "Show me more."

Beaming, she showed him some of her best work. "I love painting just for the joy of painting. I don't do it for anybody else." Later, as they kept on talking, Sylvie shared stories about high school, the ups and downs, even some of what happened with Bandit.

They left Run Riot a little before the place closed for the evening and walked back to campus under the glow of street-lights and the chill of dropping temperatures. When they got to Sylvie's dorm, Jaycee kissed the top of her head, and then her cheek. "Goodnight, dear Sylvie."

Sylvie studied her feet. "Thank you for tonight. For listening." She slowly lifted her gaze, her big eyes worried and vulnerable. "It means a lot."

Without warning, his chest tightened and didn't know how to walk away; didn't know why she had this hold over him. He took a few steps back, recited the last line of the sonata he narrated at Run Riot and mouthed, "That was for you."

Then he turned and ran all the way back to his apartment in downtown Boulder, to the million-dollar loft his family owned.

nineteen

MIA

Seven months after — Undone

All the way home from Denver, Mia fought for control. She fretted she'd just lose it and the rage and pain would explode without control. Once she was in the house, she made a beeline for the master bathroom and locked the door. Then she draped her arms around herself, tipped her head back to look heavenward, and sank to the floor. The tips of her nerves burned beneath her skin.

The wail she let out was more animal-like than human, the sound similar to a lone coyote desperate for its pack. Images of Sylvie floated in and out of her mind, a haunting apparition.

The reality of Sylvie's condition loomed heavy in her frail heart as delicate as an exhale. She didn't have words to explain a mother's connection to her child that had been going on for thousands, maybe millions of years. All that she knew was she'd rather die herself than watch her child die.

She thought she'd made some progress, but seeing Sylvie's white body, her dry, cracked lips and translucent skin, ripped open the wound of trying-so-damn-hard. It felt as if her insides were on the outside. The slightest wisp of air stung her whole body. In the past few months, whenever her feelings overwhelmed her, she escaped to the bathroom, especially after visits to Rosewood.

At first, they went every day. Then their visits slowed to twice a week. This time, they hadn't been back in over a week.

Jack would follow her and wait outside the door. "Mia," he'd urge her. "Come out. Don't do this alone." Pleading with her until she opened the door, he would hug her while she cried or shrieked or beat his chest—or all three. Eventually, they'd find some peace. Jack offered her comforting words: "it'll be all right," or "we'll get through this." And it did help.

Jack saved her from going crazy.

But this time, she didn't hear his footsteps or the familiar coaxing on the other side of the bathroom door. The house was oddly silent.

She uncurled and lay flat on the floor, stretching her cramped muscles, and listened. Nothing.

She reached for a towel, wiped her face, and sat up. "Jack," she called. *Nothing.*

"Tim, are you there?" *Nothing.*

The hallway nightlight showed a darkened house.

Mia found Tim in the guest room, his snores indicative of a deep sleep. Unfolding the comforter at the end of the bed, she placed it over his shoulders, stopping to admire his tanned skin and his long slender fingers.

She remembered him as a child full of energy and questions. "Mommy, how does a camera work?" Later, she found him trying to take a camera apart "to find those pictures," his bright, beautiful eyes and clever mind wanting to understand where the pictures came from.

In that moment, her heart ballooned with love for her son. Consumed by her Sylvie grief, she'd been neglectful of him. It made her sad, how sorrow for one child robbed her love for the other most important people in her life.

Mia looked in the living room, kitchen, and the garage. "Jack?" she shouted.

No answer.

After she checked all the rooms in the house for a second time, she noticed the front door slightly ajar, revealing their truck in the driveway and the passenger door still open. She grabbed her fleece coat, gloves, shoved her feet into an old pair of gumboots and went outside, closing the front door with a resolute click.

Her eyes darted back and forth along the length of the driveway. She saw Tim's backpack on the pavement and a day-pack peeking out from a snowbank. It looked like something had fallen out of Tim's pack. Closing the truck door, she hauled the two bags to the side door. While there, she switched on the outdoor lights to illuminate the surrounding area.

She walked to the end of the driveway and followed a trail of footprints in the snow, leading into the forest. Pausing for a moment, she wondered if she should go back and get a flash-light. In the end, she decided to keep going. The snow became deeper and the going was slow, one foot into a snow well and then the other. Snowflakes, light as dandelion fluff, fell around her and landed on her head. The cold was worsening and she wished she'd worn her fuzzy hat.

Except for the sound of her efforts to move through waist-deep snow, the woodland was quiet, all the creatures tucked in for the night. Fear simmered in her heart.

After about one hundred yards, she saw him in the snow, lying face up, his eyes closed.

"Jack!"

She hurried as best as she could and dropped to his side, wild with worry. He didn't respond to her touch. She placed her ear over his mouth; his breath was barely audible. She shook him and he murmured some gibberish.

Why had he come out here?

Adrenaline poured into her veins like a desert spring rain, seeping everywhere at once. She marched back through the snow, ran to the house, slipping here and there on hidden icy spots.

Once in the house, she called 911. Her hands shook so hard it took three attempts to punch in the numbers correctly. It seemed like forever before she reached the dispatcher.

"My husband is outside in the snow. I think he might be unconscious. You need to come now!" She sounded like she had a bad case of the hiccups. Snatching a wool blanket out of the mudroom closet, she raced back to Jack, a soldier moving through the snow as fast as she could in awkward, bounding hops.

"Jack, can you hear me?" She took off her glove and stroked his face.

Cold.

"How long have you been here?" she whispered. She tried to remember the facts about hypothermia. Was it twenty minutes? Thirty minutes? "You have to wake up! We have plenty of living still to do!"

Suddenly, as if an alarm went off, she repeated the phrase to herself: *plenty of living still, plenty of living still, plenty of living still….*

Yes, of course, she thought. She realized she wanted to do a lot…. To her, it seemed as if she just took off her sunglasses. Everything seemed unusually bright and clear.

Travel to Africa and see where Tim worked.

Show Jack how much she cared about and loved him.

Swim in a warm sea.

Retire.

Grow her hair long again.

Feel twenty inside.

Live for Sylvie.

Right then and there, heavy with sorrow, guilt—and yes, hope—as if a blade had cut right through her, she screamed… and screamed…and screamed.

She'd come undone.

twenty
NAOMI
A month before — Truth

Sylvie. Naomi loved and hated her at the same time, loved her poetic words and hated that she made her feel vulnerable. She detested feeling weak. She wanted Sylvie more than she ever wanted anything in her life, but it scared her something bad.

Naomi thought that Sylvie liked her, too, but she wasn't sure if Sylvie was attracted to her in an intimate way. Even though Naomi was so confident in many ways, she simply didn't know how to bring the subject up.

She might've held back revealing her true feelings because of Sylvie's parents. They didn't like her and she knew it; they viewed her as white trash or a passing phase.

Certainly not good enough for their Sylvie.

At the time, Naomi's resentment swarmed within her like a hornet's nest. She felt crushed when the Weavers didn't invite her to Sylvie's family graduation gathering, even after Sylvie asked.

"She's not family," Sylvie's mom said.

Naomi wanted to shout, "I am, too! I know Sylvie better than any of you can even begin to imagine. I've been there for her when you guys weren't." If they had invited her to their big fancy dinner, she would've gone to graduation, been there for Sylvie.

Instead, she skipped graduation.

Her mom drank too many beers that day and punched her in the head for being "a loser slut." Naomi walked out and grabbed a burger at a fast food joint. The toll of living with her mom, loving Sylvie, hating Sylvie, and resenting the Weavers wore her out by the time she picked Sylvie up for their after-grad celebration.

Naomi bought two tabs of ecstasy for Sylvie's graduation present because of the way it made her feel—carefree, happy, no worries, like riding a waterfall into warm water, and she thought Sylvie would enjoy that, too.

The guy who sold her the drug said, "People fall in love on this stuff." He added, "Take the ecstasy and go somewhere quiet."

She had her speech prepared when she picked up Sylvie, but quickly forgot everything when Sylvie gave her the best present she'd ever received from anyone. Naomi was literally speechless. The painting and poem glided into her heart and struck a nerve so deep she couldn't think straight. Her unrest dissolved as if she was a seltzer tablet in water, all fizzed out. When Sylvie touched her face, her touch softer than an octopus's skin Naomi had once patted at the Denver Zoo, she felt utterly lost.

Laying on a blanket under the stars, she felt the heat of Sylvie's body next to her. Her words trapped in her mouth, and her wounded heart fearful of rejection. Terrified that if she said something, she might lose her best friend. All day, she had pondered what to do—but no answer came. When night fell and her mom started her usual tirade about what a failure Naomi was, she fled to Utah.

All summer long, her thoughts were about Sylvie. Her feelings flowed through her like a slow-moving channel emptying itself into the sea. She yearned to be part of Sylvie's life like a man aspires to marry the girl of his dreams. The desire to cherish and to hold engulfed her in a brushfire so thick she couldn't see.

She thought the escape to her father's place would quiet her impatient heart. It didn't. Her heart jumped every time Sylvie called her. A fervor took hold and wouldn't let go every single time she remembered Sylvie painting, spellbound by her friend's focus and skill as she swept her brush frantically across the canvas. How she memorized the bluish veins on the inside of Sylvie's wrist. She even wished she could've been the brush for just a moment.

At the end of her time in Utah, her mom told her not to come home. "It's been a hell of a lot easier without you, so don't bother coming back."

The words stung. She felt like her mom—probably Sylvie and the Weavers, too—didn't really want her around, either. "Fine. I'll drive straight through. See ya in another life." She wanted to add *fucking cunt,* but she didn't.

Time to move on, she reasoned.

Naomi learned that denial wasn't quiet and submissive, but mean and bitter. The pent-up emotions ate at her, a hollow trough inside herself, needing to be filled—catching her off guard whenever Sylvie emailed or texted her. Unable to express what she felt, she argued with herself when she wrote lengthy emails back. It was a compromise, she rationalized and knew she should at least date someone else, but felt a little stuck. Loving Sylvie messed her up—pure and simple.

In the spring of that year, Sylvie unexpectedly called and then showed up at Naomi's tiny apartment. The streets were covered in about three inches of fresh snow. Sylvie's navy-blue coat had these huge snowflakes all over, as if she was sprinkled in sugar granules. Her hair fell over one eye, just like when Naomi first met her.

"Hi," Sylvie murmured as if she was supposed to be somewhere else.

Naomi smelled her lavender-lemon scent. The feeling of missing her was so strong, it almost caused a physical ache. She rolled her shoulders. "Sylvie. What's up, girl?"

Sylvie started to cry. "Nothing's working out. I didn't know who else to turn to."

She took Sylvie's hand and led her inside. They sat on the torn loveseat Naomi picked up on one of the city's streets, with a *for free* sign secured to the armrest. "Spill."

"Where to start?" Sylvie massaged her throat as if it might help her talk. "I met this guy."

Naomi's stomach hardened. She prayed Sylvie wasn't in love with him. "Go on."

"Well…he's a poet, you see, and he helped me write, discover a bit of who I am." Sylvie's shoulders fell. "I think." She closed her eyes and took a deep breath. "Anyways, at first it was so romantic. I just kind of flowed with whatever he wanted me to do—skip classes, get high together, drink, sleep in." When she opened her eyes, she had a far-away look about her. "Before I knew it, I was failing not just one, but all my classes. How in the hell am I going to tell my folks? And I really don't know about Jaycee anymore. He's way too controlling."

A jolt went through Naomi's body. Maybe things might work out between her and Sylvie after all. She stroked Sylvie's face. "Yeah. It's not been easy for me either."

"I wish I could just go home. Skip this college thing. Be back in my room with the aspen tree, smell my paints." She coiled against Naomi like a kitten. "I feel so lost."

Tears welled up behind Naomi's eyelids. "This growing-up stuff ain't for sissies."

Sylvie reached up and interlaced her warm fingers with Naomi's. "I missed you."

An expanded feeling filled Naomi's chest. "I missed you, too." She let the disclaimer of not loving Sylvie go up in flames and kissed Sylvie's mouth. Sylvie's lips felt silky-smooth and her tongue had a hint of a chai she probably drank on her drive from Boulder.

Naomi's heart started to pump triple-speed and she knew if she didn't say something right then, she'd make some excuse and yield to her hidden spineless self.

"I love you."

Time suspended for a moment as Sylvie sat up and took Naomi's face in her hands. She didn't say anything for what felt like ten minutes, but really was only a second or two. Then Sylvie wrapped her legs around Naomi's middle and laid her head on her shoulder.

"I love you, too."

Naomi felt herself burst open, a summer thunderstorm, lightning strike after lightning strike illuminating the shadows, her brittle heart exploding into a zillion pieces.

W orn out from the travel, the long working hours in Africa, and somewhere in his subconscious, holding on to the slimmest hope that Sylvie might just wake up and everything could go back to normal after their visit to Rosewood, vanished. Just like the possibility of him righting an overturned kayak in the middle of a lake, the chance was close to nil. Tim dragged himself to the guest bedroom, collapsed on the bed, and fell into a deep sleep.

Later, when Kathy—his parents' neighbor—shook him out of oblivion, he couldn't believe all the noise hadn't awoken him: the ambulance sirens, his mom's screeching paroxysm, and cell phones ringing inside and outside the house.

"Tim, wake up! There's been an accident."

At first, he didn't know where he was, or who Kathy was for that matter. Obviously, his internal coding map had ostensibly blacked out due to jetlag.

Rubbing his eyes, he groaned. "What?"

"Your dad was taken to the hospital by ambulance. Your mom went with him." Kathy proceeded to explain to him that his mom found his dad in the snow near the house, "nearly frozen to death, poor guy. He must've been there for a while, crying his little old heart out for his Sylvie. Your mom was screaming her head off."

Two ambulances arrived, along with three other neighbors.

Kathy found his mom's cell phone on the driveway and another neighbor found his dad's cell phone near a ponderosa pine tree. His dad's phone case was cracked, as if he had thrown it at the tree. Kathy added, "It's so unlike him to do that, always the perfect gentleman—kind, and generous. I've never even heard him raise his voice." She shook her head. "Nah. Not like him at all to throw his phone away like that."

Kathy continued, "I put both phones on the dining room table. Seems like there may have been a few calls. I also brought in your backpack and their daypacks. They were outside near the mudroom."

The fog lifted enough for him to mumble, "Thanks, Kathy."

"Well, if you need anything, don't hesitate to call. I'm right next door." She squeezed Tim's arm. "It's awfully cold in here. I'll turn on the heat before I go."

He meant to get up and call the hospital right after he heard Kathy close the front door, but he succumbed to sleep instead. In retrospect, it felt as if he'd taken a sleeping drug, divine to just let go in a way that he'd not done in a long, long while.

When he did finally wake again, he looked at the bedside clock, 2:30 a.m.

He groaned. "Shit."

He turned on a few lights, found his rucksack and lifted it onto his shoulder. A few things inside rattled. Later, much to his dismay, he opened the pack to find most of his gifts cracked or ruined. But he didn't have time to think about that then and headed to the bathroom for a needed shower, sending the plane and Rosewood grime dissolving down the drain.

There were three new messages on his phone: one from the hospital, one from Rosewood, and one from Elinah. He listened to the first one.

"Hey, Tim, it's Joe Finley. I'm a doctor at the hospital. Your dad gave us quite a scare. Hypothermia? What was he doing out there? We have him under warm compresses and are monitoring his breathing. Unfortunately, he is also running a fever, so we're watching that closely. I'm going off shift soon, but there'll be another doc to talk to when you get here. Oh, and your mom is a nervous wreck. I think it's just the toll of the events of the last six months. We sedated her and she's sleeping in the room next to your dad."

Tim combed his fingers through his wet hair, his head full of questions. It seemed everything he thought he knew had come undone, unstitched like a strand of thread caught on a hook, unraveling an entire sweater.

The emergency with his parents took priority and he logged off his phone, thinking to check the other two messages at the hospital. He rummaged around in the front closet for one of his dad's warm coats, since his were in some storage unit a few states away. Searching for the car keys, he found them still in the ignition of the truck.

He tried to piece together the information that Kathy and Joe had both shared with him. Why did his dad go out into the woods and lie down in the snow? Did something happen? Why was his mom shrieking like a crazy person?

Just as Tim turned off the front entryway light, his mom's cell phone lit up and vibrated across the mahogany chest.

Should I take that? Nah, he thought, probably some sales marketer anyway.

The messages could wait.

twenty-two

JACK

Seven months after... In the hospital

As he sank into the snow, Jack thought about a lot of things—but mostly, he thought about Sylvie.

Pain, huge and wide like a swollen river overflowing its banks, burst from his chest like one of those alien movies. He cried like a newborn, wiping his face with his gloves. They got all wet, so he took them off. The tears kept flowing down into his ears and his hat got damp, too. So, he threw off his hat.

A distant hoot of an owl echoed through the forest. His chest ached. He felt stiff and cold and alone.

And then the most amazing thing happened.

He saw her.

No, he *smelled* her first—the distinct scent of the oleander shampoo she used to wash her hair filled his nostrils. She knelt next to him and touched his face. The outline of her face slightly blurred in the falling snow.

Sylvie! The warmth of his heart spreading through his body like a golden light across the horizon.

"I miss you," he choked out between the sobs.

"I've missed you, too, Daddy." She hadn't called him Daddy in years.

"I'm so sorry I wasn't there for you."

She placed her finger on his lips. "You were. You were always there for me."

His chest heaved up and down. "I don't know how to go on without you, baby girl. It's not the same without you. I'm not the same; your mom's not the same. How can we be a family with just the three of us?"

The light flickered around Sylvie's face as if she were encased in a halo. "I love you. I'll always love you." She touched his heart. "I'll be right here, forever and ever. Don't forget me."

"Wait, don't go!" His throat felt sore. "Please, honey, stay with me…."

Sylvie's face faded with the light.

Jack beat his fists against the snow. "No!"

I'll go, you stay.…

Later, in the hospital, the paramedics told Jack, "You were saying all sorts of crazy stuff. You kept telling us to go back and get Sylvie. Hell's bells, Jack, you were in a bad way."

Jack couldn't tell them exactly what happened out there, but something did.

When he finally woke up from the confusion, he knew.

twenty-three

SYLVIE

Six months before.... The Poet

S ylvie skipped gracefully on the light snow covering the sidewalks, passing an elderly homeless man, huddled in a grimy blanket, holding a cardboard sign: *Disabled Vet. Anything will help*. Fumbling around her pocket for a five-dollar bill, she handed it to him.

"Thank you," he mumbled.

Her mom always said, "Don't give them money. They'll just spend it on booze or drugs. Better to donate to the homeless shelters." Sylvie felt sorry for him, though; she thought he needed a break. So what if he spent it on beer or a joint? Wouldn't a moment of relief be worth it?

Sylvie imagined she knew a bit about that.

She continued her walk down Pearl Street until she came to Harvest Café, a modern coffee shop squished between a bookstore and an art gallery. On the sidewalk, Sylvie paused for a moment and watched Jaycee through the café window. Her heart picked up a beat at the sight of him hunched over his laptop, his slim fingers lightly touching the keys. He seemed to have this carefree attitude about most things. She liked that.

A barista brought him a latte. When he straightened to thank him, he noticed her. He grinned and waved. Slightly self-conscious for getting caught, Sylvie tentatively waved back before entering the café.

Sylvie sat down next to him. "Hey there," she said, hoping her words sounded casual and friendly. "I brought my last two poems like you asked." Her cheeks warmed as she took two folded sheets of paper out of her handbag and pushed them across the table. "Here. Read them while I order."

He read them both twice, sneaking glances at Sylvie while she ordered.

There's nothing left inside me but my naked fear
I wait for you in anguish, afraid I'll disappear
come closer, my love
wild waves of longing toss within me,
consuming my tender core
and drown me in a storming sea
so distant from your shore
Alone on a winter night, I search for you with all my might
come closer, my love
devour these ghosts of my past
and let me join with you at last.

Sylvie carried her mug back to their table, stopping every now and again to take a sip of the hot liquid.

Jaycee spoke softly. "Wonderful writing, Sylvie."

"You think so?" Sylvie asked, her heart pumping, one strong beat after another. She gripped her cup tightly, hopefully hiding her nervousness.

"I do," Jaycee said. "You should consider reading them at the Run Riot. Reach for the stars."

She wanted to believe him. However, she thought that if he knew the truth about her, he'd never say that. What if he saw her scars—the ugly, raised bumps on her abdomen and upper thighs. Her throat felt tight, as if she'd swallowed a few stones. "Thank you."

"I'd like you to meet my agent. She's way cool." He took a mouthful of his drink. "You know, we meet people in this journey of life that help make every step an adventure and a mystery." To her, his words sounded like a poem. "You are one of those people."

Sylvie watched the breath Jaycee took, the way his chest rose, then fell. She didn't know what kind of people he was talking about, exactly, but she didn't care. Whatever he said was okay with her.

"All right." She closed her eyes for a quick second to clear her head.

"Do you have time this week?" he asked.

She rapidly nodded her head. "Yes, of course."

Jaycee added, "Let's meet every day for a while. I'll be your mentor."

It had to be good, right? Even if she didn't understand what the *mentor* thing meant. "Where do you want to meet?"

〜

Sylvie wrote late at night and mused during the day about Jaycee possibly becoming her first true boyfriend. It was a conscious choice not to think about the desolate canyon of her failing grades. Just the thought of all those missing assignments made her want to puke. She spent two weeks concentrating on her poetry, along with scheduled meetings with Jaycee to edit and perfect the rhymes, and skipped finals.

She answered the call on the first ring. "Hey, Jaycee."

"Syvie." Lately he'd been eliminating the "l" in her name, indicating they'd become close. "My agent is coming to town tomorrow and wants to meet you. Okay to meet up at Joe's?"

Wow. An agent. "That'd be wonderful."

Sylvie hung up and immediately thought about what to wear and how to make a good impression. Surveying her dorm room, a pile of laundry was heaped in one corner, and the unmade bed hadn't seen crisp, clean linen in a month. *Need to do some laundry.*

A stack of new textbooks with blank assignments sat on her desk. Her still-unadorned walls seemed to glow in sheer contrast to Wendy's side of the room.

She opened her laptop and wrote instead.

The following day, Jaycee introduced her to his agent. "This is Valerie from the Big Bear Publishing Company in Denver."

Valerie, a heavy woman in her late thirties, owed Jaycee's father a few favors. She agreed to meet Jaycee's girlfriend at a coffeeshop. "I have some business in Lewistown and can swing by Boulder, let's say midmorning," she said to Jaycee, her tone taking on a tart tone.

Once in the coffeeshop, she handed her card to Sylvie. "Nice to meet you."

Sylvie, impressed with the silver V on the card for Valerie, thought she was stylishly cultured. "I brought some of my poems." She didn't have a reason not to trust her.

"No need. Jaycee passed on a few." Valerie's eyes were the color of the ocean on a cloudy day, a mysterious blue gray. "But I'll need more. Send them to my email address on the card and I'll get back with you after I've had some time to review, probably not until after the holidays."

Awestruck, Sylvie replied. "I can't tell you how much this means to me." She shook Valerie's hand and watched her leave.

Her agent appointment lasted a whole eight minutes.

Jaycee and Sylvie left their meeting place, a small café near Whole Foods, and walked back to campus through Pearl Street Mall. Their breaths made little vapor clouds when they talked, the air cold and clear. A half-moon had just begun to rise above the trees.

The semester was over. Her dad would pick her up tomorrow.

"So, umm, I'm going to spend Christmas and New Year's at my parents' home on the western slope. Any plans for the holidays?"

Jaycee hesitated for a moment. "Have to be out of town for a bit. I have some family issues to attend to in the next few weeks." He took his phone out of his pocket and scrolled through several texts.

"Oh, it's no problem. I just thought we could continue working and stuff." She didn't want to admit she'd miss their daily get-togethers.

Jaycee put his phone back in his pocket. "When do the dorms open back up?"

Oh, yes, the dorms. "Not sure. But I was thinking of coming back to Boulder before the semester starts. I thought maybe I could spend a few nights at Ivy's apartment." What she really wanted was for him to ask her to spend the night, but she also knew she needed to be honest with him about her past. She contemplated covering her marks with makeup.

Jaycee reached for her hand, pulled off her mitten, and kissed her fingers. "I'll miss you."

She thrilled at the touch. Maybe he'd understand her dark side. "Miss you, too."

They walked hand in hand like elementary kids, stopping every now and again to listen to a musician or watch a street performer act. When they got to her dorm, Jaycee pulled her into a warm embrace. He smelled like moss and overturned soil.

"Where are you going?" she asked.

"The Caribbean."

"Oh, wow, that's cool."

He bent down and stroked her lips ever so slightly. "I'll text you whenever I get a connection."

They agreed to reunite somewhere around the second week of January. She watched him walk away from her dorm lobby. Then she took off her mitten. His scent lingered on her fingers. She hoped somehow it would stay there until he returned.

The following day, her dad arrived right on time. "You look good, Sylvie. Happy."

Her words came out in a mishmash of truths and lies. "I've been focusing on my writing, which seems to be the exact thing I need in my life right now, and meeting new people, and thinking about my future. I don't worry near as much as I used to."

Sylvie half-believed the stories she told him about staying up at night to study, and going to freshman year parties with Wendy. So what if she failed? Spring semester would give her ample time to turn things around.

A thousand tiny deceptions pulled her deeper into a labyrinth of confusion, a muddle of knots and kinks—a jumbled bedlam of her own making. She didn't tell her dad about Jaycee, not wanting to disclose anything about him quite yet. He'd ask all sorts of questions that she wasn't ready to answer.

When they got home, her dad said, "Your mom's dying to see you. Go on in. I'll get your bag."

Sylvie found her mom in the kitchen, baking while wearing a new apron, black with little stars. She hugged her mom from behind. "Hey, I like the new apron."

"Sylvie," she cried and grabbed Sylvie's hands, turning around to face her daughter. "I've missed you."

Sylvie, always smaller than her mom, suddenly felt like her equal.

"How's school? Making any new friends?"

Sylvie hesitated. "A few." Keeping hush-hush about Jaycee felt lusciously addictive. She speculated how to avoid anything about her academia life, or rather lack of. "Can we not talk about my course load right now? I need a break." How long could she keep her failing grades a secret? She'd never flunked anything before.

"I understand. Later. Have you been in touch with Naomi?"

"Not that often. Maybe after break. She decided to stay in Denver." Sylvie shrugged. "She's probably busy with her own life now." Sylvie had forgotten to reach out to her since her relationship had developed with Jaycee. Suddenly, she felt bad about that.

Her mom looked Sylvie in the eye, opened her mouth to say something, but let it pass. She lowered her head and busied herself with the apple pie she always made at Christmas.

Sylvie wondered what she might've wanted to say, but changed the subject. "Think I'll take a shower before dinner."

The next day Sylvie went with her dad to the new property her parents bought to find their Christmas tree. They parked on the newly excavated road, recently snowplowed.

Her dad turned off the ignition. "Ready?"

She zipped up her down coat, scrunched her hair into a fleece hat, and grabbed her lambswool gloves. "Yep."

They walked past a grove of bare aspen. Two boulders lay on top of a snow-covered debris pile. "Thought we'd move those rocks to the front driveway." He gestured to where the foundation would go. "Finally get to build the home I always wanted."

Little twinges nicked at her heart, but she tried to be happy for him. "It's a beautiful place." She turned around in a circle. Tall trees here and there provided just enough open space for views of neighboring mountain peaks. She imagined the iced-over stream running unobstructed in the spring and summer, warbling sounds over the stones. In the distance, she noticed the exposed meadow and spotted a ten-foot-tall spruce at the foot of a large rock.

"Oh, Dad, that looks perfect!"

Her dad carried his small chainsaw as they trudged through the soft snow. When he cut into the tree, the pungent smell of resin filtered through the air. "Shouldn't be too hard to get this thing back home," he said.

Home. Sylvie breathed in lungful after lungful of mountain air, and listened to the breeze combing through the trees, grateful for the tranquility. She thought about hanging her handmade ornaments. "I'll help carry."

Tim arrived on Christmas Eve. When he strolled through the front door, Sylvie sat curled up in her favorite chair. Hisses and pops emanated from the wood-burning fireplace. Lit candles surrounded the mantel. The decorated tree still oozed resin. It smelled and felt like Christmas.

His eyes shone. "Hey there, pretty sis. You look way too comfortable."

Sylvie held her arms out wide. "Bro! Get over here!" Clasping her big brother in a tight hug, she noticed he'd grown a goatee, and seemed gaunt and bony in places. "You look like you've been working way too hard."

Tim, unusually quiet, shrugged in response. "Yeah."

Christmas had an unexpectedly light feel. Sylvie basked in the glow of being with her family and away from the worries awaiting her back at school.

After exchanging gifts, Sylvie had hoped to talk to her brother about a few things. What was his first year of college like? What things did he miss about home? Did it get easier?

But Tim didn't engage in much conversation and he left early the next morning. Sylvie asked her mom, "Why did Tim leave so early?"

Her mother rubbed her left shoulder. "I think things are not going well with Lilly. He said he had to get back."

Sylvie spent the next several days reviewing her poetry portfolio to see if there were any poems she might consider for publication. She unwrapped her preferred canvases and took photos while contemplating if she should bring her paints back to Boulder.

Whenever thoughts about next semester or returning to her dorm bothered her, she pilfered alcohol from her parents' bar, discreetly camouflaging the liquid in her blue snowflake water bottle. She had not yet heard from Jaycee.

On New Year's Eve, Sylvie's phone pinged with a text. *Back 1/5. Dinner at Pasta Lou's? 6? Miss you.* Jaycee ended the message with an emoji of a heart. She thought of his brown playful eyes and his skin tanned from the Caribbean sun. Her heart lifted.

She hollered to her parents, who were slightly out of hearing range. "Looks like I'll be heading back to Boulder soon. Got a study meeting with a college writing group."

Her dad loaned her the old pickup truck. "Keep it. Get a parking permit. You can drive yourself home at spring break."

On January fourth, Sylvie drove back to Boulder and stayed with Ivy. Ivy didn't pry as to why Sylvie needed a place to stay, nor did she seem to care.

"Stay as long as you need to. No worries." Ivy divulged that she had met someone. "He's cute and drives a Mini Cooper."

Wrapped up in a blanket on Ivy's couch, Sylvie rode the waves of emotion rolling through her veins. All sorts of doubts filled her head. Did Jaycee really have feelings for her, or was she reading too much into things? Maybe he saw her as a passing fad. Maybe she was too young for him. After all, he'd finished college. What if he met someone exotic in the Caribbean, a tanned beauty in a bikini?

But those thoughts dissolved instantly when they met. He reserved a secluded corner table near a window, and jumped up when he saw her enter. "Sylvie!" Grabbing her coat, he buried his head in her hair. "I missed you so much."

That notorious lump in her throat formed within seconds. Her head whirled and twirled, tossed like a pile of autumn leaves. The sting of not getting a text from him until New Year's Eve evaporated. Her heart skipped a beat or two, as doubts fluttered out of reach.

They ate dinner under muted light. Every now and again, Sylvie looked out the window and watched the snow falling in big, heavy flakes. Jaycee did most of the talking. Sylvie listened to his stories. She asked questions about his family without being too intrusive, just content to be with him.

After dinner, they walked along the snowy sidewalks. Their boots made imprints in the snow.

Jaycee slipped and fell, taking Sylvie with him. They laughed and she clumsily tried to get up, but Jaycee pulled her to him and found her mouth. His lips tasted like wine and alfredo pasta. A shiver trembled alongside her neck as his tongue touched the underside of her front teeth and lingered for a bit on the inside of one cheek.

"Come back to my place," he whispered.

Suddenly, all she could think of was her scars. Pale ambient light from a nearby streetlight silhouetted Jaycee's face. It was time to tell him. She let him lead her back to his place.

He hurried. She hesitated.

Inside Jaycee's apartment, Sylvie marveled at the expensive furniture and artwork. "Nice stuff." The distraction settled her stomach. "Uh, could we talk?"

Jaycee wrapped his arms around her middle. "Talk?" He nuzzled her ear.

When he gripped her shirt with his teeth, Sylvie tensed. She remembered her blackout at Tyler's. Shame had kept her from asking anyone about what might've happened that night.

Truth was, she didn't know much about sex. Her only knowledge was what she viewed online, seen in movies, read in books, or talked about with Naomi. The most she'd ever done was masturbate with the vibrator Naomi showed her how to use. She couldn't remember ever seeing a real penis.

So, she said, "It's my first time."

Jaycee stopped. "You're kidding me?"

"No, I'm not joking." She hung her head.

Jaycee caressed her chin. "We'll go slow."

"There's something else." She unbuttoned her jeans and pulled them low enough to reveal two scars. "I used to cut."

Jaycee stroked one of her mutilations. "Why?"

Tears rose in her eyes. "I was lonely." She told him about how it started and didn't leave anything out.

Jaycee stared at her scars, then placed both of his hands on either side of Sylvie's face. "It doesn't matter what happened then." He kissed her softly on the lips. "It only makes me want you more." He undressed her slowly, one article of clothing at a time, and caressed the newly naked blemishes with tender touches.

Sylvie thought his balmy lips felt like melted butter. Her body quivered with anticipation.

"You're beautiful," he murmured as he breathed deeply, touching her naked skin. "I've never felt this way before." And then, as if he could sense her feelings, he whispered, "Trust me."

Sylvie relaxed. Reservation and uncertainty left like unwelcome guests as she opened and responded to his exploration of her body; wrapping her legs and arms around him, rocking back and forth in their primal need for each other—a love making ballet, composers of their own concerto.

When Sylvie climaxed, she cried out and sobbed, sending ecstatic waves throughout her whole body. They lay there afterward, not speaking, curled into each other like two small puppies, as if they didn't want to break the spell of their oneness.

Eventually Jaycee fell asleep, but Sylvie stayed nestled in his arms for hours, feeling different, as if she'd been newly born into the world. Gingerly untangling herself from their embrace, she found one of Jaycee's sweaters and went into his living room. The snow hadn't stopped.

Blowing on the window, she fogged it up and drew a big heart with an S and a J, and wrote:

In the innermost recess of my heart
is a door I had forgotten to open
then something crossed the threshold
and filled me with silent wonder
I tremble to name this mystery
my beloved.

twenty-four

MIA

Seven months after... In the hospital

n the room adjacent to Jack's, Mia lay in the hospital bed
for hours, thinking about how much things had changed,
how seemingly everything she knew and all that she was had
unraveled like a ball of yarn, completely tangled now from its
tidy shape. Disconnected from her once-tangible dreams and
her passion for her work, the confident psychologist had been
replaced by an anxiety-ridden recluse. Even her camaraderie
with Jack—their light-hearted happiness—had evaporated. Now
her thoughts were filled with how much she missed Sylvie and
how terrible she felt for distancing herself from Tim.

She'd gone astray, not only from the people she loved but
herself.

Could she forgive herself for not saving Sylvie? She hadn't
known what was really going on with her daughter. Her troubles.
Her hidden world. She had missed important signs. It stunned
her when she learned Sylvie had failed all her freshman classes.

What was she doing? Why did she take drugs? Who did
she associate with in Boulder?

Could she be okay if she never had answers to her questions —that she might never know? Could she open her clutched hands full of guilt and let it go?

What happened to her bright star of a son? On his last visit, he seemed less sure of things. Had Sylvie's death rattled him more than she knew? What if he stayed in Africa?

And Jack…. How could she have taken him for granted these last many months? No, more like years, actually. She'd been self-absorbed and let too many moments pass and she would never be able to retrieve them. The past was over. Her heart stung and ached like an angry welt, swollen and uncomfortable. Her tears tasted more bitter than salty.

The black-haired nurse cooed, "There, there, everything will be all right. Your husband is in the next room. He's going to be okay, too. Doc will be in to check on you soon. You both gave us quite a scare. What were you guys thinking lying there in the snow?" She adjusted the IV drip. "Get some sleep."

Mia felt as buoyant as a balloon freed from its string. Memories twirled….

She carried a tub of water and detergent to the backyard and placed a little pink plastic bubble holder in Sylvie's tiny hand. "Put it in the pail and lift it back out."

She watched as Sylvie dipped her holder into the liquid. "Now what?"

"Watch." Mia gently blew into the circle. A huge bubble formed. It swelled until it separated from its source and quietly drifted into the air.

Sylvie's eyes grew big and round. "Me. Me, me, me try."

Mia held her hand as she tried. "Blow softly."

Sylvie puffed. Several modest bubbles sparkled in the sunlight, creating a kaleidoscope of subdued color. She blew and blew until the space filled around her with floating circles. "Look, Mommy! Me have wings. Just like bird." She opened her arms and whirled around and around.

Amazed, Mia laughed. "I love you, Sylvie-girl."

Sylvie ran into her mother's arms. "Love you, too, Mommy."

twenty-five

TIM

Seven months after... The Hospital

Tim tapped his thumb on the steering wheel and peered out the truck's front windshield. Light snowflakes fell, softly landing on the hood; the air was still and quiet like an indrawn breath. The truck headlights cast a shadow on the patches of ice in the tire tracks where the snowplow had not yet cleared the road, making the trip from his parents' home to the hospital seem longer than usual.

There were only a few vehicles on the road. A cop car passed and the policewoman inside waved. He waved back as if he knew her, thinking it likely his dad did.

At the hospital, he parked far enough from the entrance to have a moment to collect his thoughts. He knew he had to help his parents through whatever the hell was going on. He also knew it was tied up with Sylvie's suicide attempt and the reality of her situation. Once they got back home and had a chance to rest and talk about what happened, he had to convince them to let her go.

Yesterday at Rosewood was hard for everyone. Yesterday? He could hardly believe it was less than a day ago that they had been there.

Sylvie didn't look like Sylvie anymore.

How could he find the right words…not only about Sylvie, but why he wanted to return to Africa. He was hoping to tell them about a place he'd visited just before he left—a protected grove visited often by elephants and wildebeest.

Tim sighed and spoke to the empty truck cab. "Wish you could visit me there, Sylvie-girl," envisioning her under a blue gum tree.

He opened the truck door, and it creaked in the cold. His boots made a crunchy sound on the recently plowed pavement as he walked toward the brightly lit hospital lobby. Through the glass, he saw two nurses chatting with the security guard.

"Evening, or maybe I should say good morning." He smiled, a shallow pleasantry he learned over the years. "I'm Dr. Weaver. Here to see my parents."

One of the nurses chuckled. She had a space between her top front teeth. "Oh, yes. Dr. Stewart said you'd be coming."

The security guard adjusted his holster, lifting his belt over a substantial belly. "But first you gotta go through the detector, just like everyone else."

Tim placed his phone and valuables on the tray. He stepped through the scanner like he did it every day. But for some reason, everything about the encounter irked him. He hated everything: the white walls; the television that blared a commercial for constipation; an elderly man with his arms folded over his chest, mumbling something that sounded like *this goddamn place*; the antiseptic smell; the security guard.

The nurse with the gap between her teeth led Tim to the staff elevator. "I've let Dr. Stewart know you're on your way up. Your mom and dad are on the second floor. Hope everything goes well. Would you like me to show you the way?"

Just the thought of having to spend another minute engaging in small talk made him feel ill. "Nope. Got it. Thanks." He was just about to flash her his personal best smile again when he remembered that Elinah had scolded him on his insincerity. *Pretentious*, she called it.

Tim put his hand in front of his mouth, hoping to turn the smile into something else.

The automatic elevator door beeped, indicating he'd arrived on floor two. He strode onto the newly polished floor, boots squeaking as he made his way to the reception area.

"Hello. I'm Dr. Weaver and I'm here to see my parents and talk to Dr. Stewart."

A young intern jumped up from his seat. "Yes, yes, Dr. Weaver, this way." His shiny naïveté was like polished silver, glinting in the darkness. Arriving at the room, he pushed the slightly ajar door open, and there lay his dad. Tim's muscles felt as if they were stuck in a waterlogged bog and all sorts of emotions hit him like mini-lightning bolts. His dad looked frail and small and vulnerable—not the solid, invincible, prominent father of his youth.

Images of him and his dad rushed through Tim's mind, picking up speed as if his thoughts were on fast-forward.

His dad patiently teaching him how to drive, not once critical of his mistakes, even when he almost ran off the road.

Instead, his dad had laughed and said something like, "I think I did that, too." He remembered their hike up Snowmass. His dad had carried his pack on the way down because he was too worn-out.

Tim recalled watching his dad chop wood, his muscular biceps strained against his T-shirt; both of them jumping off a cliff into Mystic Lake, yelling on the way down; his dad building the new deck onto their old house; and comforting Tim when Maggie broke up with him in high school.

Tim's eyes welled with tears. He sat on the bed and reached for his dad's hand under the heated covers. "Hey, Dad," he croaked. "What happened?"

Jack's eyes fluttered open. "Tim?" he asked. His words sounded raspy.

"Yup, it's me, Dad."

"Oh, buddy, I'm sorry for this."

Before Tim could answer, he heard Dr. Stewart's voice behind him. "Hey, he's awake. Been sleeping for hours. Gave us a scare, didn't you, Jack? We've kept a close watch on him, just to be sure everything is all right, but you should be able to take him home later today."

Tim turned to face Dr. Stewart. He breathed a sigh of relief. Dr. Stewart, well into his sixties, emanated the self-assurance of a veteran physician.

Dr. Stewart pulled his hand out of the pocket of his white doctor's coat. "Nice to meet you, Dr. Weaver."

Tim shook his hand. It felt like sandpaper. "Call me Tim. Good to meet you, too."

Dr. Stewart marched to Jack's side and picked up his patient chart, flipping through the pages. "So, your dad is recovering from hypothermia. His internal temperature got quite low and his fingers got some mild frostbite. He's rewarmed nicely, though."

A nurse came in and checked the monitors. Jack closed his eyes.

Dr. Stewart continued, "He's going to be all right. His pulse is a little low, but otherwise he should recover." With a jerk of his head, Dr. Stewart motioned for Tim to follow him out of the room. They walked to the nurses' station.

Tim said, "Thanks for the info. What about my mom? Is she okay?"

Dr. Stewart put his hands back in his pockets. "Well, Tim, she's been through a lot. But your mom is tough. I think she simply collapsed from relentless anxiety and worry, most of which she kept hidden, not only from you and your dad but herself as well. Not to be trite, but she was putting on a brave façade and couldn't keep it up any longer. The meds should help stabilize her mood." He hesitated. "Did anything happen yesterday?"

He felt a tightening in his throat. "Yeah. We went to Rosewood. Didn't go well."

Dr. Stewart nodded, as if he knew only too well what that meant. "It's been a trying time. He pointed to his mom's room. "Ready for round two?"

His mom, coiled in a fetal position, had the blanket tucked under her chin. She looked like a little girl.

Tim sat on her bed and watched her for a while, wondering what was going on in that head of hers. When was the last time he heard her laugh? She seemed so distant, as if she'd gone to live on some remote island somewhere.

He tried to remember the last time they had fun together. Was it a year ago?

Last Christmas, he came home for less than forty-eight hours. He thought he could forget about Lilly; keep his suffering to himself—steady his shaky heart.

Over Christmas dinner, his mom had asked the question he dreaded hearing. "So, Tim, how's Lilly?"

"Fine," he retorted, without revealing that they'd broken up, and quickly changed the subject. "Looks like we need water. I'll get it." Foolishly pretending that everything would be all right, he left earlier than planned, desperate to get back to an eighty-hour workweek. Talking to his family was harder than he imagined, and he did not connect with Sylvie—staying distant and standoffish.

Tim yawned and moved to the lounge chair near his mom's bed, letting his head fall back against the headrest and shut his eyes.

It seemed like only a moment had passed before he heard his mom murmur, "Tim?"

The sun shone through the window and Tim looked at his watch. "Hey, Mom." He stretched out his legs and rubbed his eyes. "Must've fallen asleep. Glad you're awake."

She patted the bed. "Come here. Talk with me."

He flopped down beside her. She pulled him close and kissed his forehead. "Sorry for this mess." Her eyes had a translucent quality, like see-through glass. "I haven't been myself lately." She placed both of her hands on either side of Tim's face. "I love you." Her voice broke. "I'm sorry, Tim, for not being there for you this last year. I should've tried harder."

She lowered her gaze as if she didn't know what else to say. "How's your dad?"

Tim wanted to connect with his mom. He hoped that she would've really talked about Sylvie, about him, about what happened. Unsure if he should press her to talk more or let it pass, he replied, "Think he's okay. Should we go see him?"

Arms linked together, they walked out of her hospital room with unresolved issues cloaked around them.

twenty-six

NAOMI

One month before... If only...

N aomi finally admitted her feelings, which opened a
dam of thoughts and dreams.

"We could run away together. Start a new life
on a tropical island. Leave Colorado. You could write. I could
wait tables in a fancy resort." Speaking fast, she leaned in close.
Their arms touched.

Sylvie listened, but her gaze seemed blurred by tears. "I
don't know. Things are complicated. I gotta figure out things
with Jaycee first. I don't know what to do about my parents. It
feels all too much somehow. I can't explain it."

Naomi tried to convince Sylvie not to worry about school
and success. "It's a bunch of crap. Look at my dad. He went to
college, joined the army, did what he thought was right and
look what happened to him. Now, he's a basket case—a loser."
Naomi added, "I don't even know why I'm taking that college
business class to be honest with you."

They played a video game they once enjoyed back home,
but Naomi could tell Sylvie wasn't herself, the way she stared
down at her empty hands, slumped over, covering her face

every once in a while. Naomi thought Sylvie should at least bask in the afterglow of their union and not think about things that made her sad. Wasn't that just a little too self-indulgent?

Why doesn't she just snap out of it? Darkness was a choice, right?

She tried again. "We don't need to hide our feelings for each other. It's not like we live in 1920 or something."

Sylvie didn't answer. She just sat there, looking at nothing in particular.

"You're stronger than you think, Syv." Naomi took her shoulders and kissed her. "I mean it."

Sylvie gazed over her shoulder and into Naomi's eyes. "I'm glad I came here."

They spent the rest of the day talking about what they'd do if they won the lottery.

"I'd buy a plane ticket to some balmy, sumptuous island in the South Pacific. Lounge on the beach. Dig my toes in the sand. Drink one of those fancy cocktails under an umbrella." Sylvie laughed.

"That's it!" Naomi squealed. "I'm buying a Lotto ticket tomorrow."

Naomi fell asleep with Sylvie's arms around her, contented, with Sylvie's soft inner thigh close to hers. When she woke, she found an empty place on the left side of the bed.

Her heart sank.

A note on the wobbly nightstand read: "*Naomi, I don't know how to thank you. You've given me hope. Come to Boulder soon and we'll talk.*" A big heart surrounded her name.

She held the note in her hands like a delicate flower blossom. There was still so much she wanted to share with Sylvie: why she went away last summer and her belief that they really could make this work.

Naomi got up, turned on the radio, and found a station that suited her mood. The bass and electric guitar sound resonated off the tiny apartment walls.

Stuck between a gum wrapper and a pencil, she found a cigarette in her backpack, lit it, and blew tiny smoke rings into the morning light…the nicotine soothing her nerves.

Naomi half-heartedly went to her Monday morning class. She tried not to obsess about Sylvie. But she ended up checking her phone every five minutes, chewed on the longer pieces of her hair, and daydreamed about white sand beaches.

Why hadn't Sylvie called? She was done waiting by lunch and sent several emojis to Sylvie—two hearts, a thumbs-up, a beach.

Sylvie returned one emoji of a kangaroo with the words: "Maybe Oz?"

A yearning spread through her chest like a prairie wildfire. "You bet. When?"

Sylvie didn't respond.

Naomi texted back: "I'm buying that Lotto ticket!"

Sylvie called her around midweek, and canceled their tentative date on Saturday. "Still trying to figure things out with Jaycee. Next weekend?"

Naomi, worn out from the constant inner demand to be upbeat, replied, "No problem. If things change, just text. Love you." Her heart felt like it was shrinking.

She waited. But time lagged as if she was waiting for a plane to take off and the flight just kept getting rescheduled, over and over again. On the weekend, she walked to a park near her apartment and sat on a bench, watching two little girls swing back and forth. The sapphirelike sky behind them silhouetted their tiny frames.

The spring snowstorm dumped about six inches of snow just a few days ago, but it had since melted and the hint of summer lingered in the sixty-degree day. Naomi thought about how quickly things change. One moment it was cold, the next warm, and then it would be hot and she'd be wishing for a cooler day.

Drawing a parallel to Sylvie, she shook her head. Naomi had weathered Sylvie's mood swings before and could do it again, convincing herself that her love for Sylvie could trump any hurdle.

Naomi breathed in a lungful of springtime air, clearing her mind of any doubt.

twenty-seven

JAYCEE

Five months before... Owls and Scars

Jeff Torres owned the highest-ranking fracking company in the United States. He'd been on the cover of *Forbes* magazine three times, and had invested his money well. Flush with cash, he bought property all over the world, including a resort in the Caribbean where he and his family usually stayed during the Christmas holidays.

He called and left a message for his son. "Hey there, your ticket will be at the airline booth." His voice dropped. "You know, I'm not getting any younger. Time for you to think about helping out. Your mom and I really want to stay in control of the company. It's essential we secure our future."

Jaycee wasn't persuaded one bit by his father's tirades, although they wore him out. In his mind, the best part about being in the Caribbean in December was just that—being in the Caribbean in December. Everything else sucked.

He tuned out his dad's words about "wasting his hard-earned money" on his pursuit of "writing." Jeff said the word *writing* as if it was a deadly virus.

Jaycee's mom didn't defend his choice to stay in Boulder either, like she usually did. Instead, she stood by Jeff's side, telling Jaycee it was "high time he returned to help with the family business." Almost as an afterthought, she asked, "What are you doing with your time, anyway?"

Jaycee knew that his parents secretly hoped he would tire of writing and pursue a master's degree in business. However, Jaycee never had a knack for the corporate world. Sure, he liked the life of privilege, but he wasn't driven to work nearly as hard as his father. Jaycee figured he could live well on a fraction of the money his dad had.

Jaycee had stayed in Boulder after college mostly to relax after getting his degree, sleep in, take it easy. He had some success with his poetry, but he always wondered if his dad had influenced the publishing company.

Then Jaycee met Sylvie: his goddess, his guardian angel, his other half. He felt like he'd been waiting for her his whole life. To Jaycee, she was this unspoiled being who made him feel whole or complete somehow, like finding a childhood treasure he thought he'd lost forever.

He'd been scared to take the next steps. Loving her might turn him into cotton candy. It seemed easier to keep her on a mantelpiece of his own making, someone to admire from afar than to touch her, let her in.

However, he thought about her all the time while he was in the Caribbean and decided what the hell, might as well just jump in, and he bought her a gift.

One night after a heated conversation with his dad, he strolled over to a local venue. Residents chatted and watched their children still playing outside. A few food stands sold evening fare.

He found the necklace, in one of the off-beat vendor stalls, made from miniscule silver beads and tiny abalone shells with a silver clasp that looked like the letter S. The uniquely genuine piece of art sparkled under the vendor's overhead light, the color of the abalone shell reminding him of Sylvie's eyes.

"How much?"

"Oh, for you only a hundred 'merican dollas," the sly merchant said.

Jaycee handed him a crisp hundred-dollar bill without haggling. "Wrap it up nicely."

When the vacation was over, Jaycee left the Caribbean on bad terms with his dad. "I don't want to take over your company," he'd said more than once, wondering how many times he'd have to repeat that statement.

With a gesture, Jeff dismissed his son's remark. "Let's talk again in the spring, after our shareholder meeting."

As he got in the limousine, Jaycee twisted his hair and piled it on top of his head. "See ya." Once the driver pulled away from the resort, Jaycee texted Sylvie. In Cancùn, he boarded his plane and eagerly awaited landing in Colorado.

Jaycee arrived at the restaurant early and fiddled with his napkin—folding it, then unfolding it. Eagerly he watched the door, attentive to anyone coming or going. Just as he uncrossed his legs, Sylvie walked in, her hair falling in effervescent waves like whitecaps from the sea. Her eyes held the reflection of the restaurant candles, making her seem almost otherworldly. The bones in his body felt like marmalade. It took all his self-control to not jump up and run over to her.

"Sylvie," was all he could manage to say.

Sylvie touched his hand. "Glad you're back."

He jumped up and pulled a chair away from the table. "Sit. Sit. Have you been writing?"

Sylvie sat across from him. "Yes. I wrote plenty while you were gone. Painted, too." She recited a few of her recent verses. "I got inspired by a weird thing. You might think it's gross, but it wasn't for me. It was weirdly beautiful."

Her eyes got large. "I walked on my parents' land and I saw a fox kill a rabbit. The red blood on the snow…." She paused and looked away. "Enough about me. Tell me about your trip."

Jaycee noticed her breasts move up and down as she took a deep breath. "My dad owns a resort there and we met up for Christmas. Didn't write much." He reflected for a moment about how much to share. "Went diving off the tip of Cozumel." Much easier to talk about what he saw in the ocean. "Amazing coral and different colored fish. Spotted a sea tortoise and a stingray."

Jaycee ordered lasagna and Parma Rosa tortellini for Sylvie. They continued their conversation and only took a breather when their server brought their food. In between bites, they chatted as the candles dwindled. Outside, snowflakes began to fall. When the waiter asked if they wanted dessert, they both said yes at the same time, laughed, and settled on sharing a piece of raspberry cheesecake.

He thought the evening unfolded in just the right way. The food tasted fantastic; they ate at an unhurried pace. Being with Sylvie made him feel at ease with the world. He helped her with her coat. "I love walking in the snow."

Sylvie grinned. "I do, too."

They left the restaurant, Jaycee's warm hand in hers. "Let's walk down Cherry Street first."

Sylvie let Jaycee lead her down a few side streets. Sticking out her tongue, she allowed a few snow flecks to melt in her mouth. Out of the corner of her eye, she noticed a pair of wings and pointed, delighted. "Oh, look! It's an owl."

Jaycee lifted his head and watched as the bird silently flew to an uppermost branch of a large blue spruce tree. "I missed you."

She took a long moment before responding. "I think seeing an owl means something special."

Jaycee's heart picked up speed. "Like what?"

Sylvie squeezed his hand. "A new beginning." She smiled. "Maybe something mysterious."

They ran like school children, trying to get close to the owl, but Jaycee slipped and they fell into a soft snowbank. Sylvie landed on top of him and he pulled her in close, kissing her. Tingling sensations exploded down his spine. He wanted her. "Come to my place."

Sylvie tilted her head against his chest. "Okay."

"It's not far." He helped her to her feet and they peered up at the tree. "Looks like your totem has gone home." His pulse tripled. "Let's see if we can run as fast as that owl of yours can fly."

Once they got to the apartment, he opened the door and led her inside. A motion sensor lit up, casting a cozy ambience. He came up behind her and put his hands around her waist. Slowly, his fingers moved under her sweater toward her breasts.

Sylvie tensed. "Can we talk?"

Jaycee groaned. "Talk?" His fingers lifted her velvety bra.

She pushed back. "Yeah. There's a few things you should know."

Jaycee listened to Sylvie explain about cutting herself. "I felt lonely. Scared. Didn't really know who to talk to about things at school…you know…things like how kids can be mean to other kids." She pulled down her jeans over her sleek stomach, revealing the marks. "…and it's my first time."

Sensations moved down his body as his fingers brushed over her scars, letting the information sink in. "I'm sorry." He tenderly kissed her sweet skin and reassured her. "Don't worry. We'll go slow. It's okay. I won't hurt you."

Jaycee took his time with Sylvie, never hurrying, always attentive to what she needed. So much so, that when he came, he was overwhelmed with feelings. The authenticity of their union touched a place inside of him he'd not often visited, leaving him more vulnerable than he'd ever been. He fell asleep tucked in her arms.

Jaycee just didn't fall in love, he nosedived off a cliff without
a parachute, placing Sylvie about as high as a person can get
in another person's eyes, even viewing her self-mutilation as
the perfect flaw, exposing helplessness instead of problems. So
what if she cut when she was in high school because of bullies
and hot heads? He wanted her all to himself.

"Hey, if you don't want to go back to the dorm, you can
stay here as long as you like."

Sylvie sighed. "It's not that. I'm failing all my classes."

Jaycee shrugged. "No big deal. You don't need some pro-
fessor to give you an A. Your talent will rise above all the petty
freshman courses anyway."

For the next month, Sylvie spent more and more time at
Jaycee's place while slipping into his lifestyle—staying up late
and sleeping even later. Breakfast became brunch or lunch.

Some nights, though, she wouldn't eat dinner. "If I fail this
term, I'll lose my scholarship." Her eyebrows drawn together
so tightly they looked like they were one.

Jaycee never worried about money. He pinched her nose.
"You are such a worrywart." Leading her to the bathroom,
he opened a cabinet above the circular sink and uncapped a
prescription bottle. "Here. Take a few of my chill pills."

Sylvie swallowed two without looking at the label. "Thanks."
She trusted Jaycee.

Jaycee had some Xanax, too, but he thought the oxycodone
would be enough. People said they were addictive, but he didn't
believe that because he used them very rarely. Besides, pot
mellowed him out just as well.

Sylvie thought the drugs worked great. She relaxed, often feeling stress-free and peaceful. "Could you give me a few to take back with me tomorrow? I need to stop by the dorm and see which classes I might be able to salvage."

Jaycee handed her a few extra tablets. "Yeah. Sure." He'd been thinking. "What do you think about skipping town?"

Sylvie startled. "What do you mean?"

"You know. Go wherever. Maybe someplace exotic?" He thought of taking her to Bali where they could write, make love, spend their days snorkeling.

"Uh. Well, I don't even have a passport. Besides I really should try to focus on rescuing whatever I can of my freshman year. Think I might spend a few nights back at the dorm."

Jaycee thought about giving her the necklace, but chickened out. What if she didn't like it? "Yeah. No worries." He traced his finger along her jaw. "We have all the time in the world."

Loving Sylvie made him feel like he wore his insides on the outside and that scared him shitless.

twenty-eight
JACK

Seven months after... In the hospital

Jack let the warmth of the heavy blanket lull him back to sleep, adrift in visions of Mia holding Sylvie when she was about three, her fair hair intermixed with Mia's chestnut color. Both of their wide smiles held the promise of a life of joy and happiness.

They were at the county fair and the cowboy band hired for the event played a rollicking tune that made everybody want to get up and dance, including Mia and Sylvie. Little Sylvie wrapped her arms around her mother's neck as they danced, swinging in all directions.

When they passed Jack, Sylvie reached out to grab him. "Daddy dance, too?" she asked.

Jack got up from his chair and grabbed both his girls, burying his face into Sylvie's hair and tickling her as they swayed to the rhythm of their lives.

Sylvie giggled. "Stop it, Daddy."

Sylvie. Gone....

The suffocating loss was pulling him under, deleting the color out of everything. Everyone else seemed to be dancing to music he couldn't hear anymore. He dreamed of building a bridge to cross from the land of not accepting the endless daily sorrow that hurt all over to the acknowledgment that this would be with him every day until he died.

He missed Sylvie terribly, but he also realized how lost he felt in these last seven months without Mia. She'd been devoured by a ravenous sadness, leaving only a ghost of her former self. His chest felt heavy and his nerves seemed to be on fire, wondering how to survive without those two beautiful girls in his life.

Tim would probably tell him it was related to the hypothermia, but Jack felt certain Sylvie was with him the whole time in the hospital. Maybe he was delirious, but he'd swear to anyone who asked that he heard her speak as well.

"Daddy," she had said, "I love you. Sorry for everything. I didn't mean to hurt you. I have to go now but I'll be with you forever and ever."

When she was little, Sylvie used to say, "forever and ever" when Jack turned out her bedroom light.

He tried to make the words work in his mouth, but nothing came out. Instead, somewhere inside his mind, he screamed, "Wait!" Everything felt thick and dense as he sunk deeper and deeper into sleep and a sporadic wakeful moment or two.

At one point, he thought he heard Tim's voice and struggled with wanting to let him know about Sylvie. "She's gone," he wanted to say, but nothing worked. The quicksand state of his mind kept pulling him into the hidden nooks of his brain.

Daylight rays flickered off the walls when he opened his eyes. Tim and Mia stood at the end of his bed, and Mia was gently caressing his feet.

"Mia." Little pinprick sensations made it hard to swallow.

Mia moved to Jack's side, grabbed his hand from under the cover, and bent down to kiss him, her wet cheeks rubbing against the stubble on his unshaven face. "There's so much I want to talk to you about."

He let out a breath. "Me, too."

Tim sat on the other side of the bed. "Hey, Dad."

He gazed into Tim's bright, inquisitive eyes. He still had his beautiful son. A sob left Jack's chest. "I love you." Tears caught in his eyelashes for a second before they slid down his cheeks.

Tim took his dad's hand in his and swallowed hard. "Love you, too."

The nurse walked in and stopped for a moment before speaking. "What a great picture."

Picture. Yes. He couldn't recall the last time anyone took a photograph of the three of them. "I can't remember where my phone is."

Mia placed her hand in her hospital gown. "Oh, I don't have my phone either."

"Uh. Your phones are at home. Kathy found them outside." Tim stood. He groped for his phone in his back pocket. "Here, you can use mine."

After the nurse took the photo, Tim checked his phone.

"Um, I had a few messages from last night. One was from Rosewood." He paused and looked tentatively at his parents.

Jack held on to Mia's hand and wouldn't let go. "Go ahead."

"Hi Tim, this is Dr. Kanani. I've left several messages for your mom and dad asking them to call me back immediately but they haven't returned my calls so I'm going to leave this message and ask if you could kindly call me back as soon as you can. Sylvie passed away about thirty minutes ago. Her heart simply stopped beating. Sorry, Tim. Normally I do not leave messages, but I couldn't reach your parents. Call me. Thanks."

twenty-nine

SYLVIE

Six, then four weeks before... Spring

The whirling tornadoes in Sylvie's mind were an equal match to the cold winds roaring down from Wyoming, sending a relentless howling across the front range.

She watched a willow branch crack, then fall to the ground. A garbage can rolled onto its side, and a lost plastic bag puffed full of cold air swirled upward toward the sky. Spring break had come and gone, evident by the few patches of snow scattered about. The muddy ground was as hard as sandstone in some places, mushy in others, with clusters of crocuses emerging from their long sleep.

Sylvie listened to the announcer on the radio station predicting that Boulder might lose electricity if the wind gusts got any stronger.

Could the wind short-circuit my brain, too?

She looked at the computer screen and reread the email with the official Colorado University at Boulder letterhead.

Dear Ms. Weaver,
We regret to inform you that your scholarship has been terminated due to your inability to successfully

complete mandatory coursework and attend classes as required, per the agreed-upon obligations between your benefactor and the university.

Unfortunately, this affects not only your tuition but all other university fees as well, including lab costs, residency, meal tickets, textbooks, and any outstanding charges that may be on your account.

Our records indicate your scholarship was revoked on April 1. The business office will contact you shortly regarding an updated bill....

Sylvie minimized the screen and viewed her reflection from the computer glass: pale thin face, dark circles under her eyes, puffy eyelids. Looking closer, she noticed a small rash on one cheek.

Next to the computer, a stack of new textbooks remained unopened and a closed poetry journal indicated a lack of inspiration to write as well. She peered at her naked dorm room wall. A load of clean laundry sat in the corner, quiet, still.

Moving her gaze to Wendy's side, there were filled boxes placed neatly on top of her bed, suggesting she would soon move into her boyfriend's apartment, where parties ruled. Sylvie could not remember the last time Wendy spent the night at the dorm.

Sylvie slid open her nightstand drawer and took out two white tablets, and swallowed them with a swig from her water bottle. In her head, she played her latest conversation with Jaycee.

"Babe, stop it." He lounged back in his leather recliner, puffing on a marijuana stub. "A college degree isn't what it used to be. You are perfect just the way you are."

She felt a stinging in her fingers and toes. "I don't know. Do you think it's those pills?"

"You see? There you go again. If it's not one thing, it's another." He reached in his pocket. "Here, take one of these and chill."

When she took the meds, she felt relaxed—sometimes even blissful. "Okay." She curled up in Jaycee's lap and snuggled close.

But the drug wore off quickly and in the middle of the night, she felt strange. Her hands shook and she got sick to her stomach. Unable to fall back to sleep, she burrowed into a blanket on Jaycee's living room couch and watched night bleed into day. She felt exhausted by the time Jaycee wandered into the kitchen.

"Coffee?" he asked.

"Pass. Didn't sleep well." An uneasiness spread in her chest, like an obnoxious weed. "Think I'll go back to the dorm for a bit." The back of her neck throbbed. "Try to sort things out."

A broody expression crossed his face. Jaycee raised his opened hands in the air. "I give up. Text me if you want to meet up later."

How was it possible for things to alter so quickly?

When she and Jaycee first became lovers, she spent almost every moment with him for eight solid weeks and shelved thoughts about school, her family, even inspirational ideas related to her art, feeling happy and at ease with the world. She didn't think about the past or her future. Jaycee offered his chill pills whenever she got anxious, and she downed them without any consideration about consequences.

In the last few weeks, however, she'd begun to experience intense moments of despair that left her moody, quick to anger, and distant, especially when Jaycee dismissed her feelings. She wondered if he liked what he wanted her to be more than who she really was, and that kicked up old wounds that opened and wouldn't scab over. As if she just snapped her fingers, she immediately felt alone, confused by her many feelings and the side effects of the pills, longing to talk to someone who would understand.

Her pulse beat wildly.

Under her phone contacts, she found Naomi's number, and hesitated for a moment before dialing, having not really communicated with her, except for a few emails and a phone call or two since she started college. She missed her friend's crazy seductive laugh and the way Naomi took the most complicated things in life and wrapped them up so small they seemed to fit right in her pocket.

Naomi answered on the fourth ring. "Hey, girl. What took you so long?"

A bolt of joy shot through her. "Naomi!"

Someone in the dorm hallway pounded against the walls. "Hold on a minute." Sylvie put on her coat. "I'm walking outside so I can hear you better."

Once outside, a rising wind whipped her hair across her face. "Hey, thanks for picking up. Sorry I haven't called earlier." She pinched her arm, hoping for a positive response from Naomi. "Wondering if we could get together and talk. You know, like we used to?"

Seconds passed.

"When? Where?"

Sylvie countered, as quickly as a bird with a fox nearby. "Now? I could come to your place. I have my dad's old pickup. You remember? The red truck."

Naomi laughed. "That old thing. Are you sure it won't break down on the freeway?" Naomi had always chided her for not asking her parents for a better car. "Spend the night. We're supposed to get some weather." She ended the call with directions to her place. "See ya soon."

Sylvie felt better. Even the wind had subsided. The forecast called for spring snow, maybe four inches, and for once, the forecast was accurate. The snow began to fall, light goose down fluttering from the sky.

She packed a small overnight bag and drove to a nearby coffeeshop, ordering a hot chai at the drive-through kiosk. The roadways were wet, not icy, so the drive from Boulder to Naomi's apartment near downtown Denver took about thirty-five minutes.

Naomi opened the door before Sylvie had even knocked. "Sylvie," she whispered. "It's so good to see you."

Sylvie noticed Naomi had shaved her head on one side. On the other, her dark hair fell just below her jawline. Lime-green highlight streaks glimmered under the porch light.

Sylvie tried to find the words that were in her heart. "Thanks for the invite."

Naomi brushed the snow off Sylvie's wool coat. "Come in." Grabbing Sylvie's hand, she led her inside.

They sat on a refurbished loveseat next to a timeworn radiator heater and talked like they'd never talked before—a verbal marathon. Sylvie spilled her guts. "I had such high hopes for college: top grades, exciting places to write and paint, working out, not drinking, not taking any drugs, feeling better...." At some point, she began crying. "I lost my scholarship," she hiccupped between sobs. "Jaycee never listens."

Naomi held Sylvie while she rested in her arms like a child being comforted by a parent. "Sounds like you've had a tough go, Syv." She kissed her forehead. "When's the last time you painted?"

Sylvie moaned in response. "For-freaking-ever." Reaching up, she caressed Naomi's lips with her index finger. "Thanks for understanding."

Naomi's eyes misted over. "I love you."

Somehow, Sylvie had always known that. Her love was as natural as rain. "I love you, too."

Naomi pulled Sylvie in close to her chest. "I've always loved you, Syv. Ever since that first day in English class. I just didn't know how to tell you." She lifted Sylvie's silky underwear top and stroked her abdomen; then she moved her hand up to her breasts. "What, no bra?"

Sylvie suppressed a giggle. "No time." Closing her eyes, she let her body fall back against the loveseat cushion.

Naomi undressed Sylvie, one article of clothing at a time, and she gently brushed her lips against Sylvie's newly exposed skin. "Let me," she implored.

Sylvie rode the waves of Naomi's tender loving, her touch soothing and light, soft as a whisper. Naomi ran her finger along the inside of Sylvie's knee, then slowly along her thigh, rubbing her hand over her panties before lightly pulling them down over her hips. Sliding her fingers across the area at the very top of Sylvie's legs, Naomi paused, caressing the area rarely visible in the sunlight.

An excited heat flowed through Sylvie's body as they silently fell into a raw and bruised passion broken only by whimpers and finally wails.

After, they lay together under a ragged comforter, with Sylvie's leg on top of Naomi's. "I never knew it could be like that."

Naomi stretched her arm over Sylvie's chest and kissed her shoulder. "Like what?"

Sylvie spoke as if she didn't want to break the spell. "Sweet." She touched her throat. "Soft."

Naomi moved, shifting to her side. "Let's just snuggle. Be quiet together for a while." She sighed. "Fall asleep."

Although spent, Sylvie couldn't seem to do much more than doze for a few minutes before she awoke, feeling slightly feverish. At one point, she got up to pee and looked at the stove clock in the tiny kitchen—four a.m. She draped her coat over her shoulders and sat cross-legged on the rug next to Naomi's bed, and listened to Naomi's soft snores.

A vision of Jaycee alone in his apartment hovered in her consciousness. The betrayal he'd feel if he knew where she was. Guilt thick as honey flowed into her empty fissures. What had she done?

Do I love Jaycee or Naomi—or both—or neither? Can I love a man and a woman at the same time? Who can I talk to about that?

Sylvie glanced around as if someone might be there to answer her questions, blew out her cheeks, and then released them. Her stomach growled when she uncrossed her numb legs and stretched them out in front of her. She went into the kitchen for a drink of water and looked at the kitchen clock again—six a.m.

Tiny restless bubbles bounced along her veins, her mind racing, searching for solutions to not only her sexuality, but why her head hurt or why her body suddenly got hot—or better yet, why the heavy feeling in her chest just wouldn't go away.

Locating a pen and a tossed piece of paper near the garbage can, she wrote Naomi a note and drew a big heart, leaving it on her broken-down nightstand.

After Sylvie drove back to Boulder, she took some time and walked the tranquil Sunday morning streets. The sky, edged with clouds, allowed for periodic early morning sun breaks and brief glimpses of a never-ending blue. Lilac blossoms popped out from under melting snow.

She thought about her laundry list of failures and setbacks: letting her parents down; her pathetic attempt at college life; giving up on poetry; wanting to be with Jaycee, not wanting to be with Jaycee; wanting to be with Naomi, not wanting to be with Naomi; confusion surrounding her sexuality; knowing she should probably stop taking those pills; and take a break from drinking.

She thought about her paint jars full of color and the yielding texture of the brush against her cheek. A hunger spread across her rib cage as she daydreamed about buying a brand new canvas, clean and white; dipping her brush in an array of color and letting her inside needs spread down her arm, out her fingertips. She smiled wistfully, envisioning the beautiful images she'd create. A weight in her chest lifted slightly as she eyed a park bench to sit on, closed her eyes, and let her imagination flow.

Her phone vibrated in her pocket. She blinked awake.

Sylvie dug around in her pocket and looked at the screen. Jaycee.

What? It couldn't be almost noon.

She answered, "Hey there."

"Hey, I almost hung up. Where are you?" His voice held a hint of testiness.

"I went to Denver to see my best friend from high school." She stopped for a moment to collect her thoughts. "She needed me. Going through a rough spell."

Would that be enough?

"Yeah, okay. I don't remember you mentioning her." He seemed bothered. "I missed you. Lunch?"

"Where?" She agreed not because she wanted to see him, but because she didn't know how to avoid him, wishing with all her heart that she could somehow just go back into her dreams.

Later, at the restaurant, Sylvie played with her sandwich.

Jaycee sensed her lack of enthusiasm. "What's up?"

"Nothing," Sylvie lied. "Just tired. My friend and I talked and talked way into the early morning hours. Maybe we could catch up later?" The weight of her secret hung heavy in her chest.

Jaycee peered into her eyes. "You'd tell me if anything was wrong, right?"

"Of course." She pulled her mouth tight like a stitched seam, careful not to leak something she might regret later.

Jaycee didn't seem convinced, but they parted anyway. Sylvie watched him walk down a hill, his head covered by his hoodie, the tattoos on his neck hidden, looking just like any other man in the street.

She reached into the small silken pouch of her jacket and touched the smooth edges of the tablets Jaycee had given her.

"Here," he'd said, "If you need them." At that moment, her chin quivered and she took a deep breath. *No, don't take them!* her inner voice reasoned.

Using his fingers, Jaycee curled her hand around them. "Chill." Sylvie lowered her gaze and thought about maybe just one, to help her sleep. "Okay, thanks."

Jaycee kissed her lightly on the lips before making strong eye contact with her, hardly blinking. "I'll call later."

Sylvie's stomach dropped and she felt a chill run down her spine; longing to hide, escape from everything, even for a little while.

When she got back to the dorm, she took one, then two, then three, but couldn't fall asleep. *What the hell*, she thought, *I'll take them all.*

thirty
TIM

Seven months after.... Back home from the hospital

T he slight warmth of the sun on his skin did little to lift his spirits. He shivered and looked back at the path he'd created in the snow, so different from the lush landscape of the African village where he lived.

Tim took a moment to admire the architecture of his parents' new home. He could see the mushroom-colored siding peeking through the trees. The high, sloped roof lines with abundant windows allowed for lots of light, and the porch—easily twice as large as the one on their last home—provided ample room for a swing and comfy Adirondack chairs.

Hope they'll be happy here.... The past days hadn't been easy.

He walked back to the house and found his mother in the kitchen. "Hey there, feeling better?"

She smiled weakly. "Yeah, I'm fine."

Tim felt the throb of his heartbeat. "So—let's talk."

Mia closed her eyes for a moment, as if reading herself. "About Sylvie?"

"Well, yeah, about Sylvie, for starters. But also about you. About Dad. About you and Dad."

"Oh, I see." She tucked her chin in close.

"I just want to know you and Dad are going to be okay..." he paused. "I have to return to Africa in a few days, and then...." He picked at a hangnail on his index finger with his thumb. "I don't know when I'll be back."

Mia dropped her head. "I don't want to think about that just yet." She exhaled, long and slow. "Sylvie.... What do you want to know?"

"What did you know about her life in Boulder?"

"That's what keeps me up at night." Mia clasped her hands and sat down next to Tim at the kitchen table. "Not much. I just assumed she was doing the freshman year thing—going to class, meeting new people, going out with friends. I knew she was involved with a poetry group, but I presumed, again, it was affiliated with the university. At Christmas, and at spring break, she talked about her hopes to have her poetry published. She even mentioned taking some art classes in her sophomore year. It never occurred to me to question or doubt her. She was always an 'A' student." Her lip quivered. "She always had so much talent."

Tim cleared his throat. "Do you know who she was hanging out with?"

"I asked at the university, her dorm advisor, and Wendy, her roommate. Apparently, Wendy hadn't lived in the dorm for months. The dorm head mentioned something about a sister visiting her, but that's nonsense. Sylvie doesn't have a sister! I even went to this poetry place but...." She drew her eyebrows together. "Everyone there thought I was some kind of investigator, even though I told them several times I was Sylvie's mom. They'd just clam up and shrug their shoulders or ignore me." She straightened her back. "I still can't believe she wasn't going to her classes…" her voice lowered, "…and that she lost her scholarship."

Tim sighed. "I guess we could keep on trying to figure things out or let it go. It's not like it would change anything."

Mia turned her head and stared out the big kitchen window. Sunbeams lit up the polished walnut flooring. "I wanted to— keep trying, I mean—but it took all my energy to just get through each day." She crossed her arms. "I don't know what I'm going to do now."

Tim thought about how much his mother had changed: her strained laugh, the way her shoulders curled over her chest as if her insides might spill out, her downturned mouth. He wished he could somehow alleviate her pain, but didn't know how. It left him uncertain and not knowing quite what to do. "I was thinking…."

Just then, his dad walked in. "What were you thinking?"

Tim motioned for his dad to take a seat. "We've been talking about Sylvie."

Jack winced. "Oh."

"It's all good. Mom was just telling me about what you know, or more like what you guys don't know."

Jack stared down at his empty hands. "Yeah. It's hard."

"Well, as I was saying," Tim quickly veered the conversation back to what he was thinking. "I'd like to take some of Sylvie's ashes back to Africa with me." His voice softened. "If it's all right with you two."

Mia gazed at Tim for a long moment. "Africa?"

"Yeah, there's this place, you see," Tim leaned forward. "A watering burrow about a day's drive from the clinic. I often visualized Sylvie there, writing under a gigantic tree, her toes digging into the creamy red mud." His insides relaxed. "The colors after a rain, so green you can hardly believe it, and the smell of the earth—so powerful you can taste it." His voice lowered to a near whisper. "And the sky is incredibly beautiful …like Sylvie."

He peered at his mom and then at his dad. They both had tears in their eyes. "So, what do you think?"

His dad spoke first. "I think that's the nicest thing I've heard in months." His lips parted a little. "I think I'd like to go there, too."

Mia suddenly broke out into a broad smile and then brought her hand up to cover her mouth, as if her face muscles forgot how to hold such a gesture. "Oh…that's so…." She gulped a few times. "That would be wonderful." She took a deep breath.

"For the past two days, I thought of throwing her ashes into the Boland River. Remember how green it gets in summer? Almost the color of Sylvie's eyes. Oh, and she used to love to dangle her feet in the cold water and squeal so loud it echoed off the boulders." She hesitated, seemingly lost in thought. "I miss her laugh."

"I'd like to climb up Sunrise Peak and let her ashes drift in the wind." Jack ran his finger along the edge of his shirt. "Free, totally free."

For a moment, Tim daydreamed about Africa, the Boland River, and Sunrise Peak. He loved them all. "Don't see why we couldn't do all three."

He looked at his mom and then his dad. It seemed like they had aged in the last few days, more snow-white strands pushing out the gray in their hair, and new lines forming around their eyes. He wasn't sure it was a good idea for his mom or dad to be traveling to Denver right now. "Remember the advice the doctor gave both of you when we left the hospital?"

Obediently they nodded, as if they were Tim's children.

Jack coughed. "You mean about reducing the stress in our lives? Taking it easy?"

"Yeah, that one. I think you both should really stay home. Even though I haven't been driving near as much as I used to, I know how to get to Denver."

Jack and Mia laughed, and Tim joined in. Tim suddenly felt a lightness in his limbs and an overall feeling of weightlessness. *Maybe things will get better for all of us.* He realized he hadn't yet brought up the subject about how the two of them were doing, but somehow it didn't feel like the right moment, so he chose to wait until another time.

The next morning, Mia cooked breakfast, Tim's favorite— golden waffles with maple syrup.

"Where's Dad?"

"He went into town to fill the truck with gas so you'd have enough to get to Denver. I packed you a lunch." She handed over a neatly filled paper bag. "A sandwich, an apple, cut-up carrots and celery, and a few squares of dark chocolate." She touched Tim's hand.

He noticed her skin, paper-thin with specks of brown blemishes. Curling his hand around her fingers, he murmured, "Everything's going to be okay."

Mia's eyes shimmered in the morning light. "I really hope so."

A few minutes later, Jack walked into the kitchen, and picked up a waffle, biting into the golden crust. "Delicious." He ate the whole thing standing up. "Yep, truck's all ready. Forecast is for sunny skies. Should be against skier traffic; you'll be able to make good time. Thanks again, Tim."

Tim looked at his parents. It would be just the two of them from now on now that Sylvie was gone. He wondered if they would retire soon and what they might do.

Should I ask them to visit me in Africa? Would they like it?

"Okay, I'm off then."

Tim thought that the funeral home director's full silvery beard and brown suit blended in well with the funeral home's pallid walls and tan flooring.

"Good afternoon, I called earlier about picking up…." He couldn't quite bring himself to say Sylvie's name. "Name's Tim. Weaver, that is. The Weavers, I mean."

"Oh, yes. The Weavers. I'll be right back." He grabbed both lapels of his jacket and gave them a tug before walking quickly into another room, and returning with a simple, nondescript urn. "Here you are." Placing a crisp, white copy of the receipt on the countertop next to a bouquet of violet-colored irises, he gestured at the paper. "If you could sign here and here."

Thinking about Sylvie, Tim stared at the container. After a moment, he signed the receipt and placed the copy in his pocket. "Um…thank you." He didn't know what else to say to the man. Was there some kind of handbook for funeral home protocol?

When he picked up Sylvie's ashes, and held them close to his chest, he could hardly believe how light the urn felt. Goosebumps slid along the back of his neck. *Life is so precious.*

Outside the funeral home, Tim pointed his chin to the sky, breathed in a lungful of air, and then walked to the truck. There, he strapped the oblong canister into the passenger seat, gently securing the seatbelt as if the container was alive. After a few moments, he started the truck and began the journey back over the mountains.

Traffic zipped along, traveling bumper to bumper; the inversion effect from the rising cold air trapping the smog, creating a blanket of tawny contamination. Everyone seemed to be rushing to get somewhere. He'd forgotten how crowded the freeways could get, especially in the afternoons. Once over Lookout Hill, the traffic diminished and Tim relaxed a bit, taking in the scenery; the tall, shady trees sewn into the hillsides, the land covered in a soft, white carpet.

He reached for the paper bag and dug out his sandwich, keeping one hand on the wheel and his eyes on the road. With his mouth, he peeled back the plastic wrap and bit into the whole grain bread filled with avocado, hummus, and a creamy sauce, eating the whole thing in about four bites. He was grateful he didn't need to stop at some greasy fast-food shop.

A longing expanded in his chest as his thoughts returned to Africa, and he wondered if Elinah would come with him to the watering burrow where he wanted to spread some of Sylvie's ashes.

The late afternoon light turned a deep, steely gray as he drove through the Eisenhower tunnel. Several vehicles already had their headlights on. Once through the underpass, a few distant mountains appeared ahead of him, shrouded in white.

He turned down the radio, briefly glancing at the passenger seat.

"Sylvie, there are some things I need to say to you." He waited a second, enough time for someone to answer. "I'm sorry for all the times I wasn't there for you." Images of his lack of concern over the years played in his head, like movie-trailer clips. "I don't know what happened in Boulder. I guess I'll never know." The last time he had seen her was over a year ago. "I was engrossed with my own shit last Christmas. Lilly left me and I didn't tell anyone."

He peeked over at the urn. "Guess you were not the only one with secrets." Hesitant for a moment, he thought about Lilly, and how he had not given her a proper goodbye or owned up to his responsibility in the failure of their relationship. Instead, he disappeared from her life without caring about what she might've been feeling, too.

I'll send her a letter when I get back to Africa.

"Anyhow, I wish we could've had more time together. Traveled around and done things as adults." He visualized Sylvie on a safari on the Serengeti Plains, drinking champagne afterward to celebrate their days in the dust. "It isn't fair."

The saying "only the good die young" was true. Sylvie's life was cut way too short.

"Wherever you are, Sylvie, know I'm going to live for both of us," he whispered.

The rest of the way home, through his tears, he mouthed *I love you* over and over again.

thirty-one
MIA

A year after... Spring Cleaning

Mia's heart throbbed from the recent task of boxing up Sylvie's childhood toys to pass on to Childharbor, their local charity for foster children. Outside, the rain turned the backyard into a blurred landscape of muted shades beneath washed-out skies.

Mia was tired of crying, of feeling a sorrow that opened and closed, opened and closed, like a sea anemone. She'd begun to accept the fact that the ache that lived deep inside was likely to be part of her forever. How could it not?

Jack was right. She needed to try and move forward, even if it still hurt.

Elbows on his knees, Jack leaned forward. "I think donating some of Sylvie's toys to children in need would be a good way to honor Sylvie. I like the idea of other kids enjoying her things as much as she did."

Mia agreed, imagining a young girl cradling one of the velvety stuffed animals. "I like that idea, too." She taped shut the last box, containing Sylvie's Animal Elementary game that Sylvie had played as a little girl, Squirmy and Kinta strapped into their desks, and Scooter with her floppy ears.

She reopened the box and held Sylvie's precious toys one more time before resealing it. No one had told her how hard it was to let go of even the smallest things that reminded her of her child, and the fear that somehow she might forget her.

Jack helped stack the packages by the front door. "I found some more of Sylvie's writings. I put them in the bottom of the filing cabinet along with her poetry. Thought we could reread them someday."

She squeezed his hand, grateful for his thoughtfulness. "Thank you."

"Oh, and...uh, I don't think we should give away any of her paintings." Jack rubbed his chest. "I've kept them in the closet under the stairs. All of them." He added, "Think I'll put some of them on the walls in my workshop. You?"

Mia pictured her favorite, a sixteen-inch by sixteen-inch depiction of the Rocky Mountains in spring. A small stream ran through a meadow, turning from blue to the color of Sylvie's hair. "There is one I'd like in the kitchen."

Mia had struggled to reconnect with Jack since the hospital and the conversations with Tim before he left to return to Africa. But the steps to bridge who she was before and who she was now simply weren't there. In unfamiliar territory, she felt her attempts at normal conversation instead of reminiscing about the past were feeble at best.

Yesterday, she made dinner for Jack, surprising him with baked lasagna from her favorite cookbook, paired with a bottle of wine, and chocolate cake for dessert.

Shocked, Jack exclaimed, "Mia, this is great."

Pretending it was no big deal, she countered with, "How was your day? Anything new?"

However, invariably, once they sat down to eat, Mia's appetite faded like a photograph left in the sun. "Guess all that cooking filled me up." They both knew it was a lie, of course. And before she knew it, her mind had trailed off again.

"Mia?" Jack asked. "What do you think?"

"Sorry. What did you say?" Mia shook her head, trying to come out of her fog. Resisting the tendency to backslide into becoming numb to the world around her took all her energy.

Conversation trailed off, and they ended dinner quietly. He offered to load the dishwasher. "I got this."

Mia feigned tiredness and went to bed early. Jack stayed up late, puttering in his workshop. Each was avoiding the truth that the crumbling of their marriage was seemingly too hard to acknowledge.

The day Jack donated the taped boxes, Mia rummaged in them until she found the box with Scooter. Hugging the stuffed animal to her chest, she quietly stowed the toy in the back of one of her closet drawers, hopeful that whenever she held Scooter, the tightness in her chest would loosen just a tad, and she could remember her little girl.

She just didn't know how to find happiness in any other way.

thirty-two
JAYCEE

A week before... The Poem

H e woke before dawn, drank his morning coffee on his apartment balcony, and breathed in the rich scents of spring. A faint light filtered through the trees.

He stayed there until the sun rose, and mumbled to the birds singing nearby, "I'm going to tell Sylvie I love her today." A few birds warbled their approval—or at least that's what he thought. "I mean it. I'm really going to tell her."

A small part of him wondered why he had taken so long to make that decision.

After finishing his coffee, he went inside and found the necklace wrapped in violet tissue paper with a pink cloth ribbon. "Time to give her this."

Jaycee knew Sylvie hadn't been herself these last several weeks and reckoned she needed a commitment from him, some reassurance that the time they spent together was meaningful, even more important than a college degree. He even fantasized about introducing her to his family, and letting her in on a few family matters.

The thought of taking care of her left him feeling light and relaxed. They'd have all the money they'd ever need to travel and write and sleep in, be carefree in love. Images of them running on a white sand beach, sipping margaritas under palm trees on lounge chairs, writing a book of poems, staying up late to listen to a mariachi band rushed through his head.

He dialed her number and got voice mail. "Hey, you. Let's meet up for dinner. There's something I need to talk to you about."

Sylvie didn't return his call until late afternoon. When she reached him, she told him she wasn't feeling well. "Could we do it another time?" she asked. "Please?"

Disappointed by her words, his heart sank. He had the whole evening planned. "Sure, okay. Call tomorrow?"

"Thanks, Jaycee," was all she said.

In the bathroom, he lifted his shirt, and looked in the mirror at the tattoo he endured yesterday. A letter S intertwined with a small iris and a columbine were tucked skillfully below his right shoulder. Sylvie often mentioned how much she loved those flowers. The tattoo was visible proof of his love.

Jaycee canceled the reservation at the Bluebird, but decided to go out on the town. Just the thought of sitting alone in his apartment depressed him. He grabbed a jacket and walked to the Macadamia Brewery.

When he got there, he saw two buddies from college, Jake and Travis. They waved.

"Hey, guys. What's up?" Jaycee fist-bumped Jake, and then Travis.

Jake pointed to a vacant chair at their table. "Take a seat. How've you been?"

They drank a few beers and talked about their lives since leaving college. Jake was seriously dating somebody and had enrolled in an MBA program. Travis was working hard, setting up his own landscaping business. He talked about financial investments and building "his future."

Jaycee listened, but was often distracted by thoughts of Sylvie.

Travis asked, "So, what about you? Dating anyone?"

He took out a picture of Sylvie and showed the guys.

Jake poked Jaycee's side. "She's a looker, all right." Jake examined her picture again. "Hey, I think I saw her walk by here maybe twenty minutes before you showed up." He picked up his beer and took a swig. "Then again, maybe not. Lots of hot babes in this town."

Jaycee didn't engage much after that. Jake's comment about possibly seeing Sylvie bothered him. If it was her, why was she out? Why would she lie about being sick?

Distracted, he paid his bill. "It was great catching up with you guys. Good luck with everything." They parted ways. Jake's words continued to ring through his head like a Buddhist bell, reminding him to be present. He wanted to trust Sylvie but he couldn't let it rest. If he was going to go to the next level, he needed honesty, and to be certain that she wouldn't deceive him.

He conjured up a few plausible scenarios. Maybe she had to run an errand or pick up a prescription. If Jake had seen Sylvie, there was probably a good reason for her being out. The more he thought about it, the more things made sense. Treachery was not part of who they were, he was sure. They were two peas in a pod.

He passed a small flower shop that was just getting ready to close and had an idea. "Sorry, won't be long. Do you have a spring bouquet?"

The storekeeper put down the pots she carried from the curb. "I have some purple and orange tulips left."

Jaycee nodded. "How much?" He paid in cash and watched the seller gently fold the flowers with wisps of green foliage into a tight roll held together with string and cellophane.

Leaving the shop, he whistled a popular tune, confident, sure of himself, of his relationship with Sylvie, and most importantly, their future together. He almost went back to the apartment to grab the necklace, but decided to wait until she felt better. The flowers would be enough for now.

The dorm lobby's front door was propped open with someone's shoe. When he saw it, he laughed. The residents of his freshman dorm did the same thing. He climbed the stairs to Sylvie's floor, passing a group of students with books under one arm and holding a beer in the other.

Some things don't change.

Sylvie's door was closed. Suddenly uncertain, he hesitated before knocking.

Jaycee pictured her face all lit up with wonder. "What are you doing here?" she'd say. He'd gallantly hold up the flowers, inhale their springtime abundance, take her in his arms and proclaim, "I love you." Swept up in his thoughts, he decided an unannounced surprise would be perfect.

"Knock, knock." Jaycee's voice reverberated off the hallway's ceiling, the buoyant tone like the clang of a ship's bell coming back into harbor.

He opened the door.

Sylvie's head emerged from beneath the covers. Her disarrayed hair stuck up in a few places and her puffed lips had smudges of her rose-colored lipstick.

He was about to bow, like out of some corny Shakespeare play, when another head popped out of the covers. The blanket slid from the girl's shoulder, revealing a bare chest.

The three of them stayed frozen in their respective positions, as if someone had pushed pause from a remote control.

Jaycee couldn't fit the pieces together.

Sylvie started to explain in spurts, like she couldn't quite get the words out right. "Jaycee, what?" Her eyes held a hint of shame. She looked at the girl with black hair shaved on one side. "Oh, God." Sylvie slid back under the covers.

The girl had tattoos on her arm. "Hey, dude. Give us a minute."

Jaycee stammered. "I don't know what's going on here but I need to speak to Sylvie. So, would you just leave?" He added, "Did you just call me dude?"

"Whoa. You're a piece of work." The girl rolled her eyes. "I think it best if you just wait outside and give us a moment to get dressed."

He repeated the girl's phrase to himself: "Give us a moment to get dressed?"

Were they naked? Why?

And then it dawned on him. He gawked at Sylvie. "You're a lesbian?"

Glaring at him, the other girl spoke in clear, distinct verbiage, as if she was trying to instruct a child. "L as in lover, E as in egghead, A as in asshole, V as in vagina, and E as in eject. Get out!"

He backed out into the hallway and closed the door. A student winked at him. He wanted to pound his fists against the wall.

Suddenly, all he could think of was to get as far away from Sylvie as physically possible. Jaycee ran down the hallway and took the stairs two at a time, running out the lobby door that had looked charming about five minutes ago, now seemed hideous.

He threw the flowers on the ground and stomped on them, counting his breaths, willing his heart to slow down. A sharp ache grew behind his breastbone and heat flushed through his body. Despair like a wave smashed against his chest. The college paths began to blur.

Sylvie's aloofness suddenly made sense. A tsunami of hurt crashed all around him and in that moment, he felt more betrayed than he'd ever felt.

Sylvie's duplicity filled his head. His faith in her left like a thief in the night, replaced with all sorts of suspicions: had she ever loved him; were there other lovers; had she just used him to get her poetry published?

Maybe there was a reason she hadn't told him about her family. Who was she, really? How many other lies had she told him?

When he got back to his apartment, he locked the door and turned off his phone, throwing it across the kitchen counter.

His hands shook as he poured two generous shots of whiskey in a dirty coffee cup, chugged them and then had two more.

He opened his laptop and wrote. Passionate retaliation jetted out of him. He slammed the keys every now and again, and didn't stop to wipe his wet face until he titled the poem: "My Judas."

thirty-three
SYLVIE
A week before... Trapped

"It'll be okay," Naomi cooed.

Nothing about what just happened would be okay, but she let Naomi believe she was helping. She remembered her motto. *Nod. Smile. Agree.*

"He's not right for you. He's too full of himself. It'd never work out." Naomi's green-eyed monster was out. "Besides, you haven't had a great track record with men anyway."

Flickers of doubt danced in the stale dorm air. "I think you should leave. I've got to talk to Jaycee." Tense, silent moments followed.

Defeated, Naomi got out of bed. She slid her slender legs into her jeans.

"Sure you don't want me to stay?" She reached for the bedside lamp and turned it from dim to bright. "Sylvie, listen to me. I know this kind of guy. He'll always place himself first. Look how he was tonight. He didn't even give you a chance to explain. Instead, he stormed out of here like a spoiled brat."

Sylvie threw back the covers and reached for her sweatshirt. "I don't know." She had feelings for Jaycee and he hadn't done anything wrong. "I owe it to him to be honest at least." Focusing on her bent knees, she tried to ignore the pain in the back of her throat. Most of all she wished she had locked her dorm room door.

"You don't owe him a thing." Naomi sighed. "Let me talk to him. I've got this." She kept moving around Sylvie's small dorm space, seemingly unable to stay in one place for long. "You gotta trust me on this one."

Sylvie brought her finger up to Naomi's lips. "Shhhh, don't worry."

Sweat sheened on her forehead. "You're only going to call him, right? Don't go chasing him."

Sylvie didn't want to admit that she had thought of going to his apartment. "Yeah. I'll call. Don't worry." Handing Naomi her pullover, she walked Naomi to her car and told her she'd text once she had a chance to smooth things over with Jaycee.

Naomi rolled down her car window and mouthed *I love you* before she accelerated onto the street and sped away, the headlights casting a white light on everything.

Sylvie left three voice mails for Jaycee before giving up. Thoughts of going over to his apartment twirled around her head, the looming confrontation full of heated words and hostility. It left her feeling drained and weak, nauseous every time she replayed the scene of him walking in on her and Naomi. He had looked crushed.

Could she fix what had happened? Would he forgive her?

Naomi had also seemed upset. She tried to mask her distress, but Sylvie knew her well enough. The two people she loved were in a lot of pain because of her. And worse, she hadn't a clue what to do next.

She rummaged through the bathroom medicine cabinet, found a couple sleeping-aid pills, swallowed them without water, and crawled into bed, grateful that she had the dorm room to herself. Wendy had moved in with her boyfriend. Sylvie had only seen her a few times since.

She slept in and woke to a robin singing in a nearby tree. For a microsecond, she felt cheery until she remembered.

"Ugh." Reluctant to face the day, she slid back under the covers, and fell back to sleep for another hour.

As soon as Sylvie got out of bed, she checked her phone. No voice mail messages, but she did have two emails from the university admissions department. Both were titled: Please read immediately. Probation status updated.

"Oh, boy. Can things get any worse?"

Unless she passed her finals, she would not be accepted back. Her phone calendar showed seventeen days before finals. She went online and scrolled through the grades for her classes. All Fs. Her stomach contracted. "I've fucked everything up."

She called Jaycee and got voice mail again. "How many times can I say I'm sorry. Please. Can we talk—"

The messaging service beeped and cut her off before she could add how much he meant to her. Immediately she redialed, but got a "full voice mail box" communication. "Darn."

Sylvie took a shower and went to a nearby sandwich shop. Sitting at an outside table, she nibbled at her curried chicken salad and sipped a diet Coke, absorbed in thoughts about how she might remedy her situation.

I could just be honest with my parents and disenroll from CU, or camp outside Jaycee's apartment door until he talked to me or go to Denver and stay with Naomi. Let this whole mess blow over.

The sun peeked out from behind a few clouds. Several students at the other store tables focused on their laptop screens. A passerby texted on his phone.

Sylvie watched them for a while, grateful for the distraction. She threw her half-eaten sandwich in the garbage and walked downtown. A group of lean and fit bicyclists passed her on their way up a hill. A mom clutched her son's little hand as they crossed a busy street. The smell of tacos from a nearby food truck filled her nostrils.

Her mood roiled as she tried to concentrate on anything else but her current situation.

She wished she could go back and change some things: attended classes; told Jaycee about Naomi; told her parents the truth; asked her brother for help. Taking deep breaths, she walked for a while, wondering where she could go. She didn't want to return to her dorm but she had no idea where or who to turn to.

Her hands shook as she dug into her pocket, found two pills wrapped in a tissue, and swallowed them. A wave of nausea engulfed her, and her conflicting thoughts left her feeling a bit claustrophobic, as if she didn't have enough oxygen.

A voice deep inside her head said *stop taking those pills, it's dangerous,* but she didn't heed that advice. She couldn't think about herself when the people she loved were hurting because of her.

Tears rose in her eyes as she pressed a curled fist against her mouth.

thirty-four
JACK

Two years after... Finding hope

Jack lifted his head, set the charcoal pencil down and gazed at the almost-finished sketch—the finest piece of artwork he'd ever done. The sunlight, pouring in from the large window, flickered around the dark portrait lines of Sylvie's face, just as a hummingbird whizzed past in a hurried frenzy to get where it wanted to be.

He stretched, shook out his drawing arm, and rolled his shoulders, watching to see if the bird might alight near the budding rose bush. The return of hummingbirds to the land almost invariably meant warmer days ahead with miles of new field grass growing untilled and free. Jack's chest loosened as he took in the view: a necklace of mountain peaks sprawled across the Colorado blue sky. He left his desk, and walked out to the deck, smelling the earthy breath of late spring, so sweet it almost tasted like honey.

Soothed by nature, Jack listened to his steady heartbeat.

For the past several months, he'd stepped deep inside himself and found something extraordinary: an everglade of creativity bursting through the fog of doing everything for everybody else. More clearheaded than he'd been in quite some time, shapes emerged and his imagination flourished. He drew and drew and drew, cluttering the walls of his home office with landscape illustrations of mountains and birds and cabins and sunsets and sunrises and portraits of Sylvie. As he sketched, his heart pain seeped away, little by little, like water into moss, still alive but rooted in the underbrush. He'd begun to think about the future and what new things he might discover.

His passion for music was reborn as well, and he ended up buying an older piano from a friend, placing it in the living room. Evenings of sonatas filled the empty house and stuck to his soul, like chinking a log cabin with groundcover.

The more he played, the more he recovered from the desert of heartache that had been with him since Sylvie passed away, liberating him deeply. He could hardly contain the outpouring.

As his creativity flourished, his passion for work subsided. Designing a home for someone's else's happiness or listening to a client complain about plans he'd meticulously constructed, only to have to go back and redo the architectural design, just didn't have the same appeal. In the mornings, before work, he started to have these sinking feelings in his stomach, and knew it was time. He met with his partner Ben.

"Ben, I've been doing a lot of thinking." Jack held one elbow while the opposite hand made a fist against his mouth. "I need to sell my share of our architect firm."

An unexpected release of tension swept through his body and he bit his lip to keep from smiling, feeling a sudden urgency to seize the moments: travel to Africa to see his son; meet new people; volunteer at Tim's clinic. Tears welled up behind his eyelids.

Ben nodded. "I get it, Jack."

Jack started writing to Tim, heartfelt letters about all the things he wanted him to know. His last one was almost a confession:

I miss you something terrible sometimes when I think about how far away you are. I don't know if I did anything to make you want to live just about as far away from me as you can get, but if I did, I'm sorry. I feel badly I let work get in the way of going to your soccer games when you were a kid and when I let your mom take you to Washington in your freshman year of college. I should've been there for you. Sorry, again.

Before I forget, thank you—for the hundredth time, I know —for helping your mom and me out while you were here.

These past two years have not been easy and I've had to do a hell of a lot of soul-searching to figure things out. I didn't know my stabbing stomach pains and mental fog I was in were part of my grief, or that my longing to see Sylvie again was why I couldn't sleep. I don't know if I'll ever get over losing your sister, but I'm going to try and be a better dad for you.

I don't know how long I'll live. I guess none of us do. But maybe if I'm lucky, I'll live to ninety, which makes me think of all the things I want to see and do. Number one on the list: seeing you in Africa.

So, how about it, buddy? Mind if your old man flies over there? Maybe we could travel together? I'd also like to volunteer at your medical center. I actually got more monies for my share of the firm than I thought I would, and I want to make a financial contribution to your clinic. Let me know your thoughts....

At first, Jack wasn't sure how Tim would respond to such heartfelt confessions and acknowledgments.

To his surprise, Tim wrote back, lengthy paragraphs filled with his own regrets and disappointments, his own secrets. He opened up to his father about his breakup with Lilly.

I was selfish. Only thinking about myself, my medical degree, my happiness. I forgot to think about what she needed, what her aspirations were, he wrote.

Tim thanked his dad for inspiring him to send a letter to Lilly, not that he expected anything in return. He let his dad know when Lilly sent him a postcard of a Kauri tree with a simple inscription: To be a giant takes time.

About Sylvie, he wrote:

I wasn't really paying much attention that last Christmas I saw Sylvie—too absorbed in my breakup with Lilly—to notice that things may not have been going well for her in Boulder. I should've stayed longer and hung out with her, asked her more questions. I know I can't change the past, but it still hurts.

I wasn't always the best big brother, either, getting a little too sarcastic or putting her down for wanting to spend time by herself or just being downright mean sometimes. Wish I would've reached out more, written her when I was in college, sent her a gift now and again. Guess at the time, I was just so impatient. It might take me a while to let go of my wish to go back and change what happened....

Jack knew a few things about the issues Tim was struggling to express. For him, it was like standing in the middle of a field of wildflowers with a blindfold or wearing earplugs at a symphony; making peace with oneself was not an easy task.

He guessed he'd never be completely healed, but hoped for a soft contentment that he and Tim and his beautiful wife, Mia, would let the past settle into the earth like dust after a rain—marvel at the beauty when they saw the first flower of spring or appreciate the coolness of the air.

The tenderness he felt for Sylvie was still so sharp it was almost pain. But he welcomed it now, no longer recoiling from the discomfort. He talked to her whenever he wanted, sharing little things like the gentle rain that fell on his head and splotched his shirt.

"So, Sylvie, should I just stand here and get soaking wet?" He waited for a bit, as if she was going to answer him. "Okay, then, I'll stay until you're ready to go in." He lifted his face toward the sky, allowing the cool drops to run down his neck.

It was enough to know that his love for her would last until his final breath.

thirty-five
NAOMI

The day before

She released a breath, unaware that she'd drawn it in, and opened the bathroom door, stripped off her shirt and tossed it on the floor.

In the mirror, she caught sight of herself. On the left side of her head, her hair had grown from its close shave to about a quarter of an inch. A stubborn cowlick sprouted a few wiry curls. Her eyes looked sad. There was no point in trying to call Sylvie; she'd obviously turned her phone off.

With a sigh, Naomi turned on the shower and stepped in, letting the blistering hot water pour over her, and watched the soap suds go down the drain. She stayed in the shower until her fingers puckered up, as if she'd been swimming too long. It'd been a long week since she left Sylvie's dorm room and a yearning pushed at her heart, to touch Sylvie's face, talk over things, plan their future.

When she got out, she dried her hair and changed into worn-out sweatpants and an even older T-shirt. The top had a few holes as big as Naomi's foreboding that things might not work out as she hoped.

She hunted through her desk drawer until she found a picture of Sylvie taken in front of her house just before she left for Boulder last August: her windblown hair and arms flung open, the expansive sky behind her with promises of tomorrow, and that smile, as dazzling as a movie star on the red carpet.

Sylvie had sent the photo right after she moved into her dorm. On the back, she'd written: *Naomi—all our dreams can come true.*

Naomi had scanned and saved the picture as her screen saver and waited.

She was still waiting.

She trusted Sylvie would come to her senses and end things with Jaycee. He wasn't good for her; Naomi was certain of it. He'd never respect or care for her in the way Sylvie needed. He'd never give her what Naomi obviously could—unconditional love.

Bright late-afternoon sunlight shone in through her little apartment window. A mass of dust motes frolicked in the musty air. Naomi opened the window and watched a breeze pick up the microorganisms. Her thoughts moved around her head like the motes in the gentle wind.

We should just leave all these fricking demands and pressures behind—Jaycee, Colorado, school, parents. Get on a plane and fly to the other side of the world.

Inspired by her idea, Naomi turned on her laptop and spent the rest of the day and night researching. Her focus was so intent on her task, she skipped dinner. Around eight, she found an island in the South Pacific. The water looked so clear she could see the white sandy bottom, with lime-green palm trees dotting the shoreline. It looked like a place where she and Sylvie could lighten up and relax; where they could wake up in the morning and laugh. Naomi felt the hairs rise on the nape of her neck. What she wouldn't give to hear Sylvie laugh again.

She saved the weblink, opened an Excel document, and calculated travel costs, referring back to the weblink several times as she explored the possibility of going there. Hours went by.

On one of her searches, she discovered a fancy resort on the island, and went to the employment page on its website. To her surprise, she saw an ad: **Seasonal help needed for the upcoming winter.**

Wow! Her insides vibrated with the thought that if they worked all summer and maybe part of the fall—and, of course, saved like crazy—they could leave around October and spend the winter discovering a new life.

Adrenaline rushed through her body and her eyes sparkled. Her text to Sylvie read: *Call me! Got something exciting to share!*

Naomi danced around her little apartment, her head full of plans.

thirty-six
SYLVIE

The night of

The hurt occupied every cell of her body, sucking her into the bleakest place she'd ever been: a dark quarry deep in the marrow of her core, with no light, and little ventilation; so damp and cold it was hard to even breathe. She rocked in place and cradled the twenty-six tablets close to her chest.

Yesterday, numb and spent, she listened to the voice mail twice before deleting. *Your email account has been suspended. Admissions will contact you by mail regarding your probation hearing.*

The university had officially barred her from college. It'd be on her record; her university kicked her out. She shook her head in disbelief at the thought of losing her scholarship.

The second voice mail was from Jaycee. *Stop calling. I don't want to talk to you.*

Why wouldn't Jaycee at least let her clarify a few things? It wasn't that she loved Naomi more than she loved him. She loved them both in different ways.

"Damn," she whispered to Naomi, who wasn't there. She'd forgotten to return her call. "Shit." Her head thumped as if a mini-jackhammer was going off right next to her.

She closed her eyes and thought about what had happened.

Jaycee had not returned her phone calls or dozens of texts. So, she went to Run Riot. It was open mic night. Jaycee rarely missed those readings; Sylvie knew he'd likely be there.

What if I kind of accidentally run into him? Maybe in the context of a large group gathering, things wouldn't feel so tense or altered. Say something like, *Hey, Jaycee, I miss you. Can we at least talk?* Tell him that she hadn't meant to hurt him and explain how Naomi and she were best friends, with history. Surely Jaycee would give her a few minutes to defend herself, to help her process how confused and dark and lonely she'd been feeling.

The more she thought about it, the more it made sense. She wrapped a handful of over-the-counter pain relievers in a tissue, and put them in her pocket.

When she got to Run Riot, most of the tables and nooks were filled with poets and would-be poets. She recognized a few faces and nodded appropriately as she passed them, finding an obscure chair in the back far left corner. Sitting down, she pulled her sweatshirt hood over her head, briefly glancing around the room, which was crowded for a weeknight. *End of semester partying?*

On stage, a woman delivered a sarcastic rhyme about hiking the Colorado trail, and paralleled a few verses about being stuck in the mud as a metaphor to her life. The heat was too much; the cold was too much. People laughed.

She ended with an introduction to the next act. "You all know our next guest for his pointed and brilliant prose. Jaycee."

Sylvie flinched at the sound of his name and sat up straight.

Jaycee took the mic. "Good evening, friends. Tonight, I'd like to recite my latest. It's about deceit and deception. How it can break a man."

Then he said her name. "This is for Sylvie."

Afterward, Sylvie was barely aware of time passing: of people clapping and cheering, of a man asking if she was all right, going outside to a barely warm breeze ruffling through the trees, or noticing a thin layer of clouds obscuring the stars.

She found herself standing somewhere, gazing at something with no memory of how she got there.

Jaycee's words continued to slice into her like miniature razor blades. He compared her to an empty pocket, a thief—that she'd make a career of deceit.

Tears rolled down her cheeks, blurring her vision, and she whispered the last three lines of Jaycee's scathing reading:

No matter how far she travels
she'll never undo what's been done,
and she'll always be salt on my tongue.

She covered her face with her hands briefly before pulling them away, feeling somewhat disoriented, and walked toward Walnut Street, noticing a bright red Cowboy Bar sign. A few students were huddled outside the side door, smoking and chatting. She and Wendy had gone there once; the waiter didn't even ask for her ID.

Sylvie found herself going inside, headed for the bar, and sat down on one of the empty tavern chairs. Loud country music blared from the ceiling speaker.

People all around her talked and chuckled. It felt oddly comforting.

A man came up behind her. "Can I buy you a drink?"

She swiveled her stool around to face him and froze. "Tyler?"

"Well, well, if it isn't the shooter queen." His gaze moved from her face, down to her breasts, and then further to the top of the area where her legs crossed. He touched her neck. "Remember me?"

She tried to move, but couldn't make her body work. Her throat felt so dry she couldn't swallow. A searing agony throbbed in her head. "I don't remember that night."

He lifted a single eyebrow and cocked his head. "Yeah, right."

She wanted to run, but she also wanted to know. "I mean it. I don't remember."

Would he tell her?

He interlaced his fingers behind his head. "Hmmm. Let's see. Which part do you want me to tell you?"

"Everything."

Tyler ran his hands through his hair. "Everything?" His eyes widened and he looked around the pub. "Well…how 'bout I show you how it started?"

Sylvie took a small intake of breath, and before she could answer, Tyler bent down and kissed her ear. Then he whispered, "The best cherry tastes like salt."

Microseconds ticked by. She couldn't breathe.

There, over his shoulder, was Jaycee.

She staggered to her feet, pushed Tyler aside. "Jaycee, wait!" By the time she reached the front door, Jaycee had left.

Tyler came up behind her. "Bye, shooter queen. Maybe I'll run into you another time." He winked and pinched her bottom.

She should've hit him—or at least screamed. But she did neither of those things.

Her brain overloaded with trying to absorb what had happened with Jaycee, with Naomi, and now with Tyler. Her past flickered in and out of her mind, like a candle about to go out.

She ran into the night, hoping to catch a glimpse of him. *Nothing.*

Hot and out of breath, the throbbing at her temples moved to the back of her head. Fumbling with the tissue in her sweatshirt pocket, she fished out a few tablets and gulped four of them without thinking.

Sylvie groped for her phone, resting in the back pocket of her jeans. When she tried to pry it loose, it got stuck in one of the belt loops. "Shit. Shit."

The phone slipped out of her hand and fell to the road. *Crack!*

"Shit. Shit. Shit." The screen looked like an impenetrable spider's web; the apps barely visible. She stared at the broken phone. Sylvie wanted to call Naomi, but her phone simply wouldn't work.

Everything was falling apart….

Her mistakes quickly popped into her head, one after another, as if she was watching a cartoon on fast-forward, leaving her wondering if perhaps she was the mistake.

Images of the morning after Tyler's party drifted in and out of her consciousness.

The memories made her feel dirty—polluted as a mining pond. Her thoughts ran around in circles.

Tyler said something about salt?
Jaycee compared her to salt, too.
What did it all mean?

A restlessness and edginess bubbled in her veins, growing stronger from minute to minute, expanding into her own World War III. Everything felt over the top.

Stillness and spaciousness and wisdom were far away and she didn't know how to reach them. It was like being lost on a mountain with a looming thunderstorm.

She wanted to close her eyes, shut her ears. Ongoing feelings of guilt and worthlessness hovered around her heart. She felt so tired. *If only I could just sleep….*

A young woman about Sylvie's age passed her. "Hey, are you okay?" Sylvie mumbled in response, "Just tired." She remembered her motto. *Smile. Agree.*

The woman believed that Sylvie was telling the truth, and went on her way.

Sylvie's legs felt floppy, but she made them work and walked to her dorm. Time felt like she was stuck on a plane, not moving from the tarmac. She felt out of sync with everything around her.

When she got to her dorm room, she closed the door, and locked it. She opened her bedside table and took out a bottle of sleeping pills.

I just want to stop thinking...

She opened the bottle and lined up the yellow pills into neat rows, as if they were soldiers ready for battle. The hard knots in her stomach loosened.

If she couldn't call Naomi, she could at least talk to her as if she was in the room with her. Pretending was the next best thing, right?

"Hey, best friend, my phone broke," she mumbled. "I know, right? Just one more thing." Sylvie's chest hitched for a moment before she lay her head down on her arms.

She remembered Jaycee's poem. *A sharpened dagger stabbed his heart.*

No, not that one. *She is an empty pocket, a thief, under-payment for crimes, a cancer of deceit.*

No, not that one. *No matter how far she travels she'll never undo what's been done.*

Yes, that one....

"Sorry, Naomi. I'm so sorry," and swallowed a little yellow pill.

"Ah, Naomi. Fuck. I don't know how to be what you need me to be." She pictured Naomi's disappointed face, but didn't like the vision: her lips were twisted to one side and there was a darkness over her eyes, as if she'd turned down the blinds.

"Shit. Can't I feel happy for one frigging second?" She swallowed another yellow pill. Her thoughts began to slow down, surging and jerking like a car running out of gas. The outside world had been a hard place for Sylvie, always feeling a bit like a stranger in a strange land.

When was the last time she felt free?

She reached inside and pulled out a memory she'd almost forgotten.

Tim opened a package of M&Ms with his teeth. A few of the candies spilled onto the rug, rolling like tiny marbles.

Sylvie laughed, amazed at her big brother's talent for using his teeth to open the cellophane. "Can I have the red ones?" The crimson color reminded her of running through a strawberry patch with her mom. Tim picked out the ruby candies and placed them in her tiny hand.

She placed one in her mouth, bit into the hard candy, and let the chocolate melt in her mouth. "Mmm."

Tim picked out the yellow ones and lined them up like little warriors.

He told her, "I eat the yellow ones first because they're strong and brave, like fighters." Then he popped two in his mouth.

Sylvie opened her cradled hand, looked at the yellow sleeping pills, and put some in her mouth. Grabbing the blanket at the end of her bed, she curled into it like a child. "Tim, I'm going to call you tomorrow," she murmured. "Miss you, bro."

Maybe she'd go to Africa and see him. Maybe she could start a new life.

He'd shown her the way out once before: maybe he could again. The thought made her bones feel soft and mushy like melted ice cream, smearing at the edges.

She remembered the most beautiful sunset she'd ever seen riding on her dad's shoulders. The sun had just slipped into its vanishing point, creating picturesque brushstrokes. Carroty orange. Marigold yellow. Rose pink. Eggplant purple. Buttery beige around the edges. She wrapped her little arms around her dad's head, and felt as secure and warm and loved as she had ever felt in her life.

Sylvie didn't know she was crying. "I love you, Daddy." She missed him.

"I'm going to hug you tight when I see you." She opened her palm and swallowed a few more of the little yellow pills. "Boulder's not for me."

Just before she fell asleep, she felt herself spinning around and around and around, just the way she felt when her mom used to dance with her in the kitchen. "My beautiful girl," she'd said.

Sylvie knew in that moment that she was always her mom's special girl and she felt her heart beating in tandem with her mom's. "One heartbeat, one love," her mom used to say.

Sylvie's whisper was barely audible. "I'm coming home."

thirty-seven
JAYCEE
The night of

Jaycee saw her just as he thanked the audience. "Thank you, friends."

Forcing himself to look in the opposite direction, he still couldn't ignore how his heart picked up speed or how his palms started to sweat. Jaycee took a long inhalation and breathed out nice and slow to steady himself. He bowed and left the stage.

An acquaintance grabbed his arm. "Man, that was great. Any bitch I know?"

Jaycee scanned the room, but didn't see her anywhere. "Uh, probably not. Have to go." He shook his arm free.

Pushing through to the venue's front door, he ran into the street, wondering which way she might've headed. In the distance he thought he recognized the color of her sweatshirt in the crowd and raced toward it, only to realize it wasn't her.

Jaycee jogged quickly back to his starting point and began to walk in the opposite direction. Slowly the street grew emptier, the small knots of people untying as they headed toward home.

He turned around and went back. From there, he noticed an alleyway where a group of students sat huddled around what seemed to be instruments. Striding past them, he came onto a larger street, and looked up and down the sidewalks.

Then, he saw her—standing outside the Cowboy Bar, seemingly in a daze. He stopped.

She took his breath away. Damn. She looked as abandoned as an orphan and he suddenly felt sorry for reciting the poem. Maybe he should've given her a chance to explain.

He watched her go into the pub and wondered what she was up to. Crossing his arms, he contemplated whether to go after her. It wasn't like her to go into a bar alone. Maybe he should help her. Maybe she was in trouble.

Jaycee decided to go in.

The bar, filled with primarily the college crowd, had a stale, moldy smell. A few young people played pool while they sipped on their beers. He guessed them to be in their early twenties. Music he couldn't identify boomed directly above him. Two women in cowboy hats drank something fizzy in tall glasses with slices of lime on the rim while a few men watched them.

He scanned the room quickly. Then he saw her sitting at the bar with some guy who looked like he was kissing her.

What the hell? What a fool—not once, but twice!

Jaycee bolted out of the bar and ran as fast as he could, not paying any attention to anyone or anything and didn't stop until he was almost out of breath.

"That's it," he muttered to himself. "I'm done." He wasn't about to fall for any of her tricks again. "She's nothing more than a two-timing bitch."

A fire ignited in his gut, sending flickers of disgust throughout his veins, a grass wildfire out of control. Suddenly, he was glad he wrote that poem and that she heard it. For a moment, he even felt pleased it might've hurt her.

"It's what she deserves."

NAOMI

The morning after

Naomi never had a night terror before that night.

The dream felt so real....

Something came through her bedroom screen, an unearthly thing with no shape or color. It hung over her before devouring her feet, legs, and arms. She started to moan when it ate her stomach and screamed before it reached her neck. It felt like she was drowning. She woke in a sweat and couldn't get back to sleep.

Naomi checked her phone. *Nothing.* She had tried calling Sylvie ten times before she fell asleep and woke up again less than thirty minutes later.

Afraid to shut her eyes, frightened the dream would return, Naomi tossed and turned before she gave up around six, took a shower, and decided to drive to Boulder. Talking to Sylvie in person might solve everything. She picked up coffee at a nearby Starbucks drive-through and got on the interstate.

The end-of-the-week rush hour traffic was bottlenecked at the I-36 interchange and came to a complete standstill a few minutes later. Naomi waited, drumming her fingers on the steering wheel, her nightmare images still appearing every now and again. It left her feeling jittery, as if she was on a ledge of a tall building looking down.

She took a sip of her coffee, hoping to wake up from her internal tornado. "Sylv, where are you?" Finally, the traffic lightened slightly and she was able to move forward. Fifteen miles per hour was better than zero, she thought. The thirty-minute drive took twice as long as usual.

Once in Boulder, she couldn't find a parking place near Sylvie's dorm and pounded the steering wheel, hitting the horn by mistake. The driver in the car beside her gave her a suspicious look. She shrugged and mouthed *sorry*.

Naomi drove up and down a few side streets, but all the parking places were taken. It was as if the universe was conspiring against her. Eventually, she found a corner spot at a bagel shop about six blocks from the dorm. Parking quickly, she locked up, and walked to Sylvie's dorm.

If she hadn't been preoccupied with wondering why Sylvie hadn't returned her calls, she might've appreciated the glorious May morning: the bright sunshine, spiked purple delphiniums in bloom, a faint sweet smell of spring in the air.

But she didn't see or feel any of those things. She had a single-pointed focus: take Sylvie in her arms and persuade her to run away with her.

When the opportunity to slip into Sylvie's dorm presented itself, a student even held the door open for her, she took the stairs two at a time and was somewhat winded when she reached Sylvie's floor. The dorm seemed unusually quiet.

Where is everybody?

She knocked on Sylvie's door and turned the knob a few times. *Locked.*

Naomi tried to jimmy the lock with a paperclip she found on the floor, but it didn't work. Then she saw a dorm custodian down the hall, replacing a lightbulb in one of the overhead lights.

She moved swiftly. "Hey, there. Can you help? My sister hasn't returned any of my calls. I tried knocking on her door, but there's no answer. I'm worried about her. Could you check and make sure everything's okay?" If she said Sylvie was her sister, maybe she'd have better luck.

The custodian put her foot down onto the lower rung of the ladder and peered at Naomi. "What?"

She repeated everything, but this time added a sense of urgency, inventing a story about Sylvie being *really sick.*

"Well, we're not supposed to interfere with student's lives. Them being adults and all." The custodian didn't want to get involved.

Naomi wasn't about to give up. "Please."

The custodian sighed. "All right. I'll call my supervisor."

They waited until her supervisor came. Naomi repeated the whole story all over again and decided to imply the sickness was something dire, like cancer or something.

She laughed quietly, delighted at the thought of telling Sylvie how she got into her room.

The supervisor opened the door.

What's that smell?

Naomi moved toward the curled, still body wrapped in a blanket, leaned over and shook her several times. *No response.*

Leaning closer, she noticed an empty prescription bottle on the bed. She picked it up, looked at the label, and flinched. "Shit!" she exclaimed. "Someone call 911!"

Naomi couldn't remember if she was at the supervisor's side when mayhem ensued or if she had left her body, like she was at the movies watching everything on the big screen. Somehow, she couldn't move. Her thoughts seemed stuck together, as if glued with quick-acting cement.

A paramedic sprinted past her, shouting orders. Another medic performed CPR, then used a defibrillator. Within seconds, a medical team wheeled in a gurney and hooked Sylvie up to an IV. The blare of an additional ambulance in the distance, the screams of students in the hall, and the different ringtones of several cellphones filled her head.

Still, she did not make a sound, her body frozen, a giant ice cube.

However, deep inside her skull, she was yelling—a panicked, ear-piercing sound resembling the shriek of a wild hog as she watched a lion snatch her newborn. An outpouring of emotions fought to come out.

Nothing did.

She would never remember the medics or the dorm supervisor or the custodian leaving, or recall Sylvie being lifted and transported to the hospital. She would never remember if she said anything or did anything.

The world around her was seemingly translucent, almost shimmering.

The only detail Naomi would remember would be walking down the dorm hallway and going outside, wondering where she was. She would forget how long she stood there gaping at the sidewalk, saying nothing, until a girl with red hair asked her if she was all right.

How she found her car and drove to the hospital was a mystery to her. Her legs felt like wooden pegs when she entered the ER. She approached the nurse at the registration desk.

"I need to see Sylvie Weaver." Tears as big as gumdrops welled in her eyes, threatening to cascade into baby waterfalls.

The nurse adjusted her name tag. "Are you family?"

Naomi stammered, "Well, not exactly." She tried to come up with a better answer, but she couldn't access her quick-witted, fast-reacting self.

The nurse curtly dismissed her. "Sorry. You have to go."

"Uh." Her head felt full of cotton puffs. "Where?" Her stomach heaved.

She pointed to the ER waiting room. "There."

"Thanks." Dazed, Naomi walked to the ER waiting room, found an empty chair and fell into it. She brought up her legs and wrapped her arms around her knees, rocking back and forth, back and forth, not sure what to do.

She stayed there for hours and hours while the waiting room filled and emptied with people in their own disasters. She listened, enthralled by a group on the other side of her seating area. They'd brought in a child who had slipped in the bathtub and almost drowned.

A few tried to console the mom. "It's not your fault. Accidents happen all the time."

Others offered words of encouragement. "Your little Melinda is a fighter. Just you wait and see. She'll be riding that new blue three-wheeler you got her in no time."

Their words comforted Naomi as if they were saying those things about Sylvie. The vise grip around her heart slackened just a tad.

She was there when Sylvie's mom and dad arrived. They looked awful. Sylvie's mom's shirt was torn on the side, as if she had ripped it out.

Naomi wanted to run over to them and tell them she was here. But she couldn't get her legs to move. By the time she did stand, the Weavers were long gone, past the security door with an electric alarm that buzzed the right people through.

She steadied herself before she attempted to walk to the visitor station and pushed the words out of her mouth. "Can I see Sylvie Weaver?" She added, "Please, I have to—"

The receptionist interrupted her before she could finish. "Are you family?"

She repeated the question to herself. "No. But—"

The receptionist closed the glass partition, wedging her out. "Sorry."

Everything seemed out of reach as if the world had suddenly shifted into slow motion.

She left the hospital in a haze of wretchedness, repeating the receptionist's question over and over again, and wondered how she could see Sylvie. How could she find out what happened— if she was okay, if she would make it?

How could she become family?

She thought about pretending to be Sylvie's sister. She didn't know how to pull that off. Too close, maybe. A cousin?

She always wished her mom would've named her Jeni. Her thoughts separated a little, giving just enough room for her to create a way to see and be with Sylvie.

Jeni Snow.

thirty-nine
TIM
One year after

The all-terrain vehicle's tires created a crisscross pattern in the magenta-colored sand. Wisps of powdered grit followed, looking like dancing phantoms. Golden sunshine glowed along the horizon, shifting into blushing pinks and an unusual, fiery orange as the light pierced the clouds. The scent of sage and dried mud swirled around them. A grove of gum trees flickered in the distance.

They were almost there.

Tim took her hand. "Thanks for coming." Heat blazed off the dashboard.

Elinah interlaced her long, slender fingers with his. "Of course."

A warmth emanated from his chest down to where their fingers intertwined.

He'd changed since he got back from America. He didn't talk about himself much anymore, preferring to listen to patients chat about their lives. His hair had grown out; it curled along the collar of his short-sleeved shirt.

He came to appreciate his after-work chats with Elinah, following their long hours working side by side. Slowly, he shared little bits of his story with her. She talked about growing up in Kenya. He told her about Sylvie—the good times, and the difficult ones; even the instances when he'd hurt her.

Asking appropriate questions, she listened attentively. The comments she made challenged his thinking.

"You were tough on her, yes?" Elinah paused before continuing. "Maybe you could've been kinder, yes? Been more like a sleepy lion instead of a viper?" She leaned over and wiped the tear from his eye. "I think I would've liked your sister."

Memories crowded the vehicle, filled with water and fuel cannisters. In almost all of Tim's best childhood memories, Sylvie was there. He remembered Sylvie playing hide-and-seek with him in the backyard. She had hidden behind a tree, thinking he'd never find her, not realizing her burgundy skirt gave her away. Her eyes were impossibly large when he snuck up behind her.

"You're it," he said.

Shocked, she turned and opened her mouth. "How did you find me? Did a fairy tell you?"

He bit his lower lip, coercing the laugh to stay inside. "Oh, the fairy. Yeah, she told me."

He watched her run into the woods. "Fairy, I told you not to tell anyone."

His heart contracted a bit, remembering the love he felt then. The love he still felt.

He let out a sigh and pointed. "I'll park right there."

Tim drove the vehicle under a large swooping tree, the long branches almost touching the ground, and turned off the ignition. He picked up a paper bag. In it were some of Sylvie's ashes in a small colored glass jar, her poems she'd sent over the years, and a stuffed animal with floppy ears.

Tim and Elinah strolled hand in hand on the soft earth to a stand of trees that formed an almost seamless circle. In the center, the vegetation grew naturally and abundantly in the rich soil.

He breathed in deep. The fragrant whiff of an aromatic flower filled his nostrils. "She would've loved it here." Opening the sack, he took out the jar, holding it for a moment before he asked Elinah if she'd take out the poems. "Would you?"

Elinah smoothed the manuscript, several pages bound together with handsewn thread. "The first one, right?" At his nod, Elinah began to read out loud, her melodic voice filling the empty spaces.

Shoes
I've walked miles now
seen the sun, loved the stars
looked up and down
explored far
came home, again.

Taped up, broken
seams ripped, tongue frayed
skin turned brown
soul lost.

In knee-deep mud
sticky with time
popcorn, soda, sweaty socks
glued in gum.

Dropped from bridges
left behind
hung from telephone lines
drowned in icy rivers.

Left on foreign sand
been lost and found
on merry-go-rounds
separated from partners.

Survived by dogs
and baby mice
tangled laces
dust and mold
empty places
used, abused, kissed
forgotten.

He unscrewed the top of the container and poured slowly, the dust gliding to meet the earth instead of falling in a straight line. A few particles hovered over the ground. There had been a breeze all day, but at that moment, the wind stopped and the orchard was eerily quiet, as if the trees knew.

Tim let the tears roll down his face. "I love you," he said quietly. "Miss you, baby sis."

In those heartfelt words, he sensed her right beside him, her tiny hand in his.

Goosebumps broke out across his flesh. His face slackened and he felt a release throughout his whole body as if he was encased in muck and someone had sprayed him with a hose. It went against his scientific reasoning that she could be there with him, wrapping him in sweet forgiveness. The feeling wasn't something he could study under a microscope, but rather an invisible waltz between the people he loved.

He would find a way to go on and be the best person he could be.

Grief, a sly thing, would come and go. But he'd be okay, no, more than okay.

He stared at Elinah.

"What?" she asked.

He smiled, a wide smile full of promising things. "Nothing."

The sun began to set and the day drifted toward a lavender evening as he and Elinah walked back to their vehicle. He placed the stuffed animal with the floppy ears between them, right on top of the middle console. "Read me some more of her poems. It'll take a few hours before we're back."

Elinah began with the second poem and recited them all again while Tim drove. He listened to Elinah recite his sister's poetry, hypnotized by her words, and mesmerized by Elinah's accent.

"Elinah, please read that last paragraph again."

Elinah shuffled the papers.

> *And not rest until I stand*
> *with my hands upon you*
> *and not rest until I feel you*
> *in the marrow of my bones*

He remarked, "I wish I could've read more of her poetry when she was alive. Maybe then I would've known."

Elinah cocked her head to one side. "What's that American expression? Hindsight is twenty/twenty, yes?"

He chuckled. "Yeah. Twenty/twenty."

JAYCEE

One year after

The tattoo artist transferred the stencil of his drawing with a moisture stick and placed it on his left rib cage. She showed him where the image would be forever.

"Yep. That's good," he said.

She told him to take a deep breath. "You might feel a lot of pain at first, maybe even a burning sensation. Let me know if I need to ease off."

He dug his fingernails into his palms. "No problem."

The pain came and went during the three-hour session. Sometimes he had an excruciating sting that felt like a hundred bees pricking him at once, other times a quivering vibration that almost made him want to cry out. But he didn't.

He'd have to come back a few more times before the tattoo was finished. He didn't care how much it hurt or how long it took.

She brought a mirror closer to his face so he could view the finished outline. "What do you think?"

He looked at the silhouette. "It's beautiful." He added, "You know, I think you're right. I will go for a bit of color next time."

When he got back to his apartment, he put on some of the ointment she gave him, and turned sideways to face the mirror, gazing at the image. "Excellent."

One of the wing tips touched where his fourth rib bone almost met his lower sternum. The other wing stretched toward his back. The snake in the raptor's talons was shaped in a symmetrically formed S. A piece of an abalone shell around the owl's neck would somehow make the tattoo feel complete. "Next time."

He gently slipped on a clean T-shirt and went out on the balcony. *Beethoven's Fifth* softly played from the overhead speaker set into the tongue-and-groove ceiling. A gust of wind whipped his long hair across his face. The sun headed for the horizon, separated by blue, gray, and pink streaks. The air was warm for May.

It'd been exactly a year ago.

He hadn't heard what had happened to Sylvie right away and by the time he did, it was too late. Too late to change anything. Too late to say goodbye. Too late to try and make things right.

He found out quite by accident.

Someone told him it had been in the paper, but he never saw it. Those who knew of his relationship with her simply thought he must've known and avoided bringing the subject up with him.

He had avoided Run Riot or going out at all in Boulder after that ill-fated evening when he recited his *Judas* poem and followed Sylvie into the Cowboy Bar. He turned off his phone because he didn't want calls or texts from her, and then decided to get away for a few days, going up to his family's cabin in Breckenridge where internet and cell phone service were virtually nonexistent or intermittent at best.

When he got back to Boulder and turned his phone back on, there was a text from a group of fellow poets. So sorry for what happened, with an emoji of two hearts. He didn't think much of it at the time.

It was the bitch he saw in Sylvie's dorm bed that told him. She showed up the day after he got back from the mountains, banging on his door with an incessant pounding that sounded like there were two of her instead of just one.

"Open the door, you motherfucker! I know you're in there!" she yelled.

He wasn't going to open the door at first, but she wouldn't relent on the hammering.

Jaycee was pissed. "What the hell do you want?"

"Open the door, Jaycee. Why haven't you been there?" she implored.

He undid the dead bolt and opened the door just enough to see her haggard face. It looked like she hadn't slept in days. "What are you talking about?"

"Don't give me that shit." A blob of spit landed on his T-shirt.

He recoiled. "You need to leave." He tried to close the door, but Naomi jammed her foot into the crack.

She stared at his face, her eyebrows pinched tightly together.

"I don't have anything more to say to you." Jaycee pressed the door into her foot. "Now, goodbye."

She released her foot and the door slammed. She shouted, "They say she might be brain-dead and they're moving her to a care facility south of Denver." Naomi heaved her body against the door. "It's your fault, you know."

He opened the door slowly. "What are you talking about?"

"Dude?" she asked incredulously.

There's that *dude* word again, he thought. "Listen, whatever your name is. I haven't the faintest idea what you are suggesting here."

She hesitated for a moment before speaking, her voice becoming increasingly unsteady, sharing what had happened to Sylvie in a disjointed torrent of events, gulping in sips of air. "Where were you? Why didn't you at least visit?" Taking a few steps back away from him, she pointed at his chest. "I fucking hate you."

He struggled for composure. "What?" His voice was trip-wire tight and sharp, the news rearranging his face. Shoving a hand through his hair, he looked at Naomi, uncertain what he should do or say. "I was in Breckenridge at my family's cabin. There's no internet or cell service there. I didn't know."

Naomi fixed her gaze on Jaycee. "Whatever." She turned away from him and snarled, "Hope you burn in hell…."

He watched her move toward the elevator. "Wait. Where is she?"

She smirked. "Find out for yourself, asshole."

Jaycee felt numb for days after that fateful conversation. He tried not to remember all that had gone wrong in the days leading up to Sylvie's *accident,* as he liked to call it. If he said the words *suicide attempt,* remorse and guilt filled every cell of his body; a weight in his chest so heavy he could hardly breathe.

He made a half-hearted effort to find out what had happened, where she was and her future prognosis. But the challenges to get information when he wasn't family were daunting. Just the thought of trying to talk to Sylvie's parents made him feel queasy. He was certain they didn't know about his relationship with their daughter.

So, he did nothing. And that created an emptiness he still carried with him.

He stopped going to Run Riot.

He didn't go out. Slept a lot.

His mom worried and thought it might be the pressure to join the family business or the stresses of being a young adult in today's world. She effectively argued with Jaycee's dad to give him an advance on his trust fund.

Jaycee took the money and traveled; touring Indonesia, Thailand, Vietnam, and Japan, hoping new places would erase the memories. It didn't.

He yearned for a light heart and for the day he no longer thought of her.

It never happened.

He returned to Boulder a month ago, followed his family's advice, and went to therapy. The therapist asked a lot of questions, too many as far as Jaycee was concerned. But he answered them as truthfully as he could and learned a few things about depression, anxiety, and mood swings.

Jaycee recognized that Sylvie had been in a lot more pain than he ever realized or understood. He felt selfish for his lack of awareness to what was really going on with her. That saddened him.

Late at night, when he couldn't sleep, he worried. Could he fall in love again? Could he forgive himself? Could he forgive her? Would he ever know the truth about what had happened that night? Had she loved him? The uncertainty was a cruel reminder that he couldn't control everything and that sometimes there were no resolutions.

After he spent hours online researching graduate programs, he decided to apply to three schools he liked in three different states. He would not tell his parents unless he got accepted to one of the universities. It was important to him to achieve this on his own, without their financial influence.

However, he hoped they'd consider his request to set up a philanthropic organization for worthy causes, such as scholarships for writers who could not afford college tuition. He reasoned that he may not find the enlightenment he hoped for, but doing something for others was a start.

Jaycee left the balcony and closed the sliding glass door with a soft click.

forty-one
NAOMI

Seven months after... Free at last

The hiss of the ventilator reminded her with every sound that Sylvie wasn't breathing on her own. The monitor beeped. The indicators droned. The ventilator whooshed.

She asked the nurse, "Will she wake up?"

The nurse replied, "Brain injuries are impossible to predict." The woman patted her shoulder. "It helps to talk to her, you know."

Naomi had been surprised at how easy it was to become Jeni Snow.

She researched online how to get a fake ID. Then she sweet-talked her way with the medical staff at Rosewood, and visited Sylvie just enough times to not draw attention or get in trouble. Naomi went to Rosewood at unusual times, and learned how to erase her name from the visitor contact log. Especially vigilant around holidays, she paid attention to when the Weavers came to see Sylvie and stayed away. It worked.

She unenrolled from her college class and got two full-time jobs, cashiering at Whole Foods during the day and waitressing at a diner at night. Video games became a thing of the past, as well as watching television or going out anywhere like the movies. Working distracted her from thinking about Sylvie or obsessing about the *what-ifs*.

When a supervisor from either job asked if she could help out on weekends or cover another shift, she always said yes. Exhaustion was a great cure for all of her internal angst and worry. She banked almost every penny, and ate her main meal at the diner for free or at a reduced rate. The grocery store let her take home produce and old baked goods they would otherwise throw out.

Naomi let her hair grow out and stopped dying it midnight black. Her natural auburn color shone under the salon lights. To her surprise, she actually liked the bob the Cheap Clips hair stylist suggested.

"You've got a great face for the cut," the stylist said.

She removed her face piercings and found some stylish but simple clothing at a goodwill store, thinking they looked *Sylvie-ish*.

Her one-way conversations with Sylvie—whenever she had the opportunity to see her—brought some relief from her otherwise need to cry all the time. Over and over, she told her how sorry she was that she couldn't help her and how sad she was about what had happened.

"I wish I would've gone to your dorm that night." She detailed how the course of events would have been altered with one simple change. "It's not fair."

On other visits, she was more cheerful.

"Hey, guess what?" Naomi slapped her hands against her cheeks, imagining Sylvie laughing. "My mom got sober!" She waited for a second before continuing, wanting to give her friend a playful swat. "You wouldn't believe it. She's actually kinda nice to talk to these days."

Every time she disclosed another hope, she got excited. "Sylvie, I'm thinking about traveling. Get away from fricking America. Go to that island we always talked about. I'm saving and saving and saving so I have enough for a plane ticket and a few months or more to live. I'm going to do it for you and for me."

In the silence, Naomi thought they got closer than they'd ever been. She felt secretly triumphant about keeping Sylvie's location away from Jaycee—not that he couldn't find out.

But she checked anyway. He'd never been to Rosewood.

Asking the medical team a lot of questions, she learned that Sylvie would likely never wake up. Her injuries were too severe, the overdose crippling her brain. When she thought about those facts and of a future without Sylvie, dark melancholy engulfed her for long periods of time.

The days spun into one another, like silkworms spinning their cocoons or like an ice skater moving into a tight spin at the end of a routine. Summer heat was replaced by cool fall evenings. Naomi continued to work long hours. The only joy she felt was when she marveled at her sizable bank account or when she visited Sylvie.

The snow came. It made her decision to leave America before Christmas an easy one.

She told her work supervisors, "I need to give my two-week notice. I'm leaving the country."

"Oh, where are you going?" the boss at Whole Foods asked.

"Actulai."

"Where is that?"

Naomi smirked. "Cook Islands."

She had learned a few things working at a grocery store and waitressing. And they were skills she could put on her resume in hopes of landing odd jobs as she traveled the world.

However, there was something she felt compelled to do before she left.

In the months she spent talking with Sylvie, sharing her confidences, she watched Sylvie's physical condition deteriorate —bed sores, cracked white skin, muscle atrophy. Eventually, she came to believe that Sylvie wouldn't want to live the way she was living, if one could call the state Sylvie was in living.

Naomi thought it wasn't.

She knew her plan was risky, but judged herself the heroine in doing what was best for her beloved.

So, the night before she boarded the plane bound for the south Pacific, she visited Rosewood, not knowing that the Weavers had been there earlier. If she had, she wouldn't have been as sure of herself as she was that night.

She needn't have worried. They wouldn't have recognized her.

Naomi planned every detail, plotting every step in her head and calculating the time it would take from the moment she entered Rosewood to her speedy departure.

The front entrance light came on at five p.m. The head nurse left around six. The custodian locked the back door at eight, but the exit was easily accessed from the inside. Rosewood had recently installed an alarm on the door, but Naomi thought that might work to her advantage. The staff relaxed between eight-thirty and nine. *Bingo.*

She was the consummate actor with the medical staff. "I'll just be a minute. Just wanted to say goodnight," while blowing out a long breath and smiling.

In Sylvie's room, she climbed onto the bed and cuddled next to her friend. "I'm going to miss our time together, Syv, but it's time." Calculating she had, at most, five minutes, she snipped a swatch of Sylvie's hair and placed it in a silver locket. "I'm taking you with me."

Holding Sylvie's hand, she asked one more time, "If you want to continue living like this, give me a sign. Squeeze my hand or blink. Something."

She waited. Nothing.

She counted her breaths to steady her hand and reached for the pillow.

"Goodbye, Sylvie. I'll always love you."

She loosened the ventilator just enough to prevent Sylvie from receiving any air and placed the pillow over Sylvie's head until the monitor started to beep.

Naomi's research had indicated she might die quickly or linger before cardiac arrest. She quickly placed the pillow back under Sylvie's head, jumped off the bed and fled, racing down the hall toward the backdoor exit.

The sign read: *Alarm will be triggered if you use this door.*

Good. She wanted the commotion, so the nurses wouldn't hear the monitor buzzers warning of Sylvie's impending death.

She ran as fast as she could down two side streets to her parked car, stopping for just a second to glance behind her. Nobody. Pressing the remote key once, she hopped in, turned the ignition, and took off. Checking the car clock, she realized it had taken her exactly fourteen minutes.

She tried not to speed, but the adrenalin was coursing through her blood.

Naomi imagined Sylvie floating away, no longer confined to a bed, held together by tubes, unable to think or speak or move. She looked at the sky through the car window.

"Free at last…."

Naomi parked, made a mad dash through the hotel lobby to the stairwell, ran up the stairs to her hotel room, and swiped the plastic key over the chip reader. The green light lit up and she quickly opened, and next, closed the door, using both the dead bolt and the chain to secure herself in. Her hands shook as her gaze darted to her small backpack and shoulder bag laying on the bed—all that was left of her life in Denver. She had gotten rid of anything that wouldn't fit into those two pieces of luggage. Her heart thumped wildly like an untamed animal locked in a cage.

Sitting down on the bed, she took out the locket and opened it, touching the almost snowy-colored hair. Then she closed the locket carefully, not wanting to disturb its contents any more than necessary.

"I miss you so much sometimes it scares me, Sylv. But I think I can move on. Live again. I think I'll always be living for the two of us."

She let herself fall back against two large puffy bolsters and closed her eyes, taking in deep, long inhalations and exhalations to soothe her galloping heart. *It's over....*

Like a slideshow, pictures of Sylvie twirled through her head: the day they met, watching the stars after graduation, sitting on the loveseat talking about their lives.... Naomi's breathing slowed, her mouth slackened and she fell asleep, not waking until her phone alarm went off.

When she opened her eyes, the first thing she did was touch the locket around her neck. *Ready, Sylv? Plane leaves in three hours....*

forty-two
MIA

Three years after

Mia walked alone on the beach. The waves whooshed against the shore, keeping time with her breathing. She reached down and touched the sand. It felt cool and clean. She wrote a few words with her finger.

Later in the day, the sun dipped behind the hill. She passed a bleached-out log and found a quiet spot next to it, taking out the book hidden inside her shawl.

The cover featured an illustration of a mountain valley with a glacial stream running through, tufts of grass growing on the banks. Unruly patches of wild columbine and irises were sprinkled throughout glimmers of sunlight set in erratic beams.

It was one of Sylvie's last paintings.

In handwritten calligraphy font, the title of the book, faintly off-center, read: *Sylvie's Poems*. Mia opened the book to the dedication page and rubbed her hand over the words: *For everyone who loved Sylvie.*

Mia's heart stung when she turned the pages and reread the poems again, for the hundredth or more times. But the nips and pricks were less these days, reminding her she was healing, learning how to live in the world again and not in her head.

She lost count of how many times friends, family, colleagues, her support group told her that everyone grieves differently. Her grief was a wild beast that knew no boundaries. Unpredictable. Stormy as a winter blizzard or a sudden spring hailstorm, creating havoc in a matter of minutes. It overwhelmed her at times and devastated her on other occasions, the emotion often leaving her scarred and drained, as if someone had literally scooped her insides out.

Losing her baby girl had almost driven her mad. Her thoughts were all tangled up in themselves like a thousand fishhooks dumped into a pail. The pain was ruthless and unrelenting, like pins and needles all over her body.

All the years she worked as a psychologist did not prepare her for the sorrow of losing a child. Her professionalism did not aid her in the guilt she contended with surrounding her feelings of inadequacy as a parent or the questions that would never have answers:

Did something happen when she was growing up? What transpired in Boulder?

The doctor said she had oxycodone in her bloodstream. Where did she get that drug?

Her roommate had no clue. If she wasn't going to classes, then where was she?

No one seemed to know.

The comforting words she offered to others did little to mollify her despair. As she sunk deeper into a sadness that would not go away, she forgot to eat, forgot to take care of herself. She became deficient in much-needed vitamins and minerals. The anemia made her feel tired all the time, and she slumped into a misery of her own making.

Jack tried and tried, but couldn't seem to shake her out of her fall. It was as if she had dropped down a steep slope and all he could do was watch her slide into oblivion.

For the first time in their marriage, he decided not to help her. He let her be.

It left her emotionally stranded on a tiny island and brought her to her knees. She cried and beat at her chest. Eventually, she didn't recognize the face in the mirror, the empty, gaunt face with cavernous lines around her mouth.

She went on medical leave from her work.

Summer came.

In the early fall, she received a letter from someone called Valerie Stern. The letterhead had a beautifully embossed V. She wrote:

Dear Mrs. Weaver,
Let me first begin with my sincere condolences. Sorry for your loss. I had the privilege of meeting Sylvie and reading some of her poetry while she attended college in Boulder. My publishing company would like to publish Sylvie's poetry and would appreciate your assistance in compiling her finest writings into a manuscript for our editor's review. My contact information follows. Thank you.

Valerie Stern

For whatever reasons, the letter woke Mia up from her wallowing self-pity.

She called Valerie the next day. Then she traveled to Denver, and talked to the publishing company. The task of assembling all of her daughter's poems for publication brought light and meaning to Mia's life.

Valerie commented, "You look awfully thin. Are you okay?"

Mia jolted. "Of course."

The comment threw her off. She always prided herself on looking good: expensive makeup, classy clothes, manicured nails, modish haircuts. It bothered her that another professional would actually think something wasn't quite right.

For days, she thought about Valerie's words. She even asked Kathy, her neighbor, "Do you think I'm too thin?"

Kathy nodded. "I've been meaning to ask if there was anything I could do to help?"

Mia went to see her physician, who prescribed she meet with a lifestyle nurse. The nurse, a kind woman who knew a thing or two about self-care, gently steered Mia in the right direction. She met with a nutritionist, a physiologist, and started attending a women's support group.

The support group proved to be just the right thing. A collection of ten women, from all walks of life, had each experienced a significant loss. They listened attentively as Mia shared her stories about Sylvie. They cried with her when she told them about Sylvie's suicide.

Eventually, Mia became friends with Nicole.

Nicole had lost her husband and son in a boating accident. Many of her grief patterns were similar to Mia's and because of that, they formed a close bond, not only when they met for their weekly support, but after when they continued their discussions at a coffee shop.

The comfort of having a friend to confide in softened the edges around Mia's tight-knit psyche. She began to recognize an important truth. Sylvie had learned a destructive pattern from her.

It wasn't good to keep all that hurt inside. Of course, it was something she told others to do, but hadn't known how to do it for herself.

Her mom was like that, too—family sins passed down from generation to generation. She didn't want to keep everything inside anymore.

She told Nicole about her mom. "She just wasn't emotionally there for me."

Nicole took her hand. "I understand."

That's all she needed. Someone who would just listen without judgment, without saying anything in return, without giving advice. Someone who knew what if felt like to go through the deluge of grief. Her heart thawed, little by little.

The first time she slept through the night she was astounded at how good she felt in the morning. She shared the news with Nicole. "I think I've found Nirvana."

Nicole laughed and Mia joined in, their amusement carefree and sunny. Anyone who did not know these two women would never guess at the heartache they'd endured.

Mia devoted hours each day to collecting and assembling Sylvie's poems. She found most of them bound together and sealed in manila envelopes, stored at the bottom of the filing cabinets in the garage.

Jack had labeled each envelope in a somewhat chronological order, beginning with her early writings and ending with the last poems he had collected in her dorm room. Mia communicated with Valerie often, and sent the poems once they'd been copied into the right Word document.

Valerie offered reassurance. "Great work, Mia. Keep it up. We should be ready to publish soon."

Of course, Valerie didn't accept all of Sylvie's poems, only the ones she thought would be a good fit for publication. She didn't tell Mia this, or the fact that Jaycee had contributed a great deal of money for the endeavor. Big Bear Publishing signed a confidentiality agreement with the Torres Foundation to ensure no one would ever know.

The week before Sylvie's book was released, Big Bear Publishing bought an advertisement slot in *The Denver Post*. A full-page ad promoted the new release depicting the handsome front cover and inspirational words from writers and poets all over North America, and even a few from Europe. Run Riot and other notable writer locations in Colorado put up simple, stylish posters.

The book got good reviews, which pleased just about everyone.

Valerie had already pressed Mia for a second book, pairing Sylvie's poems with her paintings.

Mia bought dozens of copies and sent them to family and friends. She propped the book up on the living room mantel, with a picture of Sylvie and Tim on one side and Jack's illustration of the place he and Mia had spread Sylvie's ashes on the other. The three pieces looked lovely together. Jack hung Sylvie's large painting of a moose and a dozen fairies hidden in an aspen forest above the hearth.

Mia missed Jack. They both agreed they needed solo time, time to continue their individual healing process and time to assess their marriage.

Jack had been gone for months as he explored Africa, sometimes with Tim, other times solo. They connected via webcam whenever Jack found reliable internet service. At first, their communications were a bit rigid, but recently they'd become more animated.

"When will you head back to the States?" she asked.

"I don't know," he answered without any hesitation. "Tim and I have a safari scheduled for next week and I want to donate some of the business profits to help fund a new wing at the clinic." He didn't wait for her approval. "I'm trying to decide between naming it the Weaver Wing or the Sylvie Wing."

"Oh, that's nice, Jack." She didn't know how to speak to this straightforward man. "By the way, it's official. I'm retired."

Mia thought of him again as she slumped into the sand, her sarong coming slightly apart. She wondered idly if Jack would like her weight gain. She'd been enjoying herself a lot these days, eating great food and not skipping dessert, and she had watched more sunsets in the last few weeks than she could ever remember. Swam in the warm lagoon every day. Lounged with a glass of wine in the middle of the day. Napped.

Two more days here before I travel to India for my yoga teacher training. After that? I don't know.

A slight breeze swept over the light-colored sand. Mia secured her skirt, pulled the soft shawl around her shoulders, and hugged the book close to her chest. She strolled back to the resort, happy with the thought of eating dinner in the elegant dining room.

When the hostess came to seat her, she asked, "Could I have that table over there?" It was in a secluded spot on the verandah where she could hear the waves lap against the shore. Once seated, she placed the book face up, on the empty placemat across from her, and smiled.

Her server arrived with a tall glass of lemon water. "I'll be your server tonight, ma'am. Can I get you anything other than water to start off with?" Her auburn hair, sporting several bleached blonde highlights, came to her shoulders.

"Yes. I'll have a glass of Prosecco. Thank you." She looked at the server. Something about her face looked familiar, but Mia could not recall where she might've seen her, and let it go.

The server noticed the book. "May I?" she asked. Smiling, she leaned forward to get a better look.

Mia's face lit up. "Of course. My daughter is the author."

The server picked up the book and lovingly touched the front cover. "Maybe you could see if the gift shop would carry some copies. It looks like a wonderful book. I'd like to read it."

The way the server handled the book almost made her cry. "That's a great idea." She always carried a few extra copies. "If you give me your name, I can leave a copy at the front desk if you'd like."

Naomi fingered the silver locket around her neck.

"Jeni. Jeni Snow."

⌒

Shift
Dirt roads
ice banks
snows
muddy swamps
pink ribbons
in the passenger seat
sparkly plastic shoes
pigtails
tiny hands
not strong enough to change the power
Pound the pedal. Split me open. Shift.

Grip tight
push
sometimes like stones
or glass in a blender
older
sitting on her father's lap

learning how to steer
alone behind the wheel
grace and strength
made for off-road gamboling
Pound the pedal. Split me open. Shift.

Laughing in the cab
singing along to a song
drowning out sobs
engine snarled
rusty underneath
ice coated windshield
snow piled in the open back
waiting for her to stand back up
lying there in the darkness and snow
Pound the pedal. Split me open. Shift.

Long conversations spoken to no one
track 12 on repeat
over and over
light from streetlights
tears on the seat
wheels spin onwards
one street to another
muttering curses under her breath
Pound the pedal. Split me open. Shift.

Different, changed, rusted, worn-out
idle, waiting, exhausted
last drive
last run
leave her now
one last time
Pound the pedal. Split me open. Shift.

Reading Group Discussion Questions

1. Early in the book, Mia reflects back on Sylvie's exceptional talent and her initial harassment experiences at school. Do you think Mia missed any signs?

2. Sylvie's transition from the insular protection of home to school and friends was often difficult for her. What are your opinions about why she hid her internal world?

3. The book is infused with metaphors of nature, especially for Jack. What nature images were most meaningful to you?

4. How does Sylvie's life change when she meets Naomi? What does Naomi give her that her family cannot?

5. Tim recognized Sylvie's peculiarities even as a child but never openly shares them with anyone. Identify ways in which he could have impacted Sylvie's life if he had.

6. Think about how suicide is often portrayed in movies or talked about in the media. Compare that to Sylvie's story. What sort of assumptions do you think movies or media might make about suicide? What kinds of falsehoods might they propose?

7. Sylvie best expresses herself through her poems and art. What poetry lines best illustrate Sylvie's deepest thoughts? How did you visualize her artwork?

8. Tim decides to leave the possibility of a lucrative career and work for a nonprofit organization to help others. Why do you think he chose Africa?

9. Owls have special significance in this story. The symbol of the owl has been interpreted differently around the world from Greek mythology to ancient Druid lore to Native American ceremony. What were your takeaways from the owl symbolism in the story?

10. Some readers may question why gaming is villainized in this book. Gaming is not bad, but it is portrayed as such. Or some readers may blame games for Sylvie's mental issues. Is this more apparent because Sylvie is female? Or is it simply her inward pain that had nothing to do with the gaming world? How significant is this in our modern era where female gamers are trying hard to overcome the stigma that games are evil.

11. How might the story have ended if Jaycee had not recited My Judas at Run Riot?

12. The thread of family is woven throughout the book, especially in Sylvie's last chapter. What do you think the author was trying to unveil about a person's last thoughts?

13. The novel does not reveal what happened to Jack and Mia's relationship. Do you think they got back together? Why or why not?

14. Naomi genuinely believes no one could ever love Sylvie as much as she did. Why do you think Naomi thinks this? If the book continued, what do you think might have happened to Naomi?

15. Compare Naomi and Jaycee. How are they alike, and how are they different? Why do you think Sylvie falls for them?

16. Suicide continues to be a difficult topic to discuss in our society. Examine the societal taboos around this important issue.

Wandering

a memoir

Sharon Kreider

AUTHOR'S NOTE

n 1976, carrying a small backpack filled with minimal trekking gear and one change of clothes, I hopped on a plane from my native Canada to England and started my overland solo adventure from Europe to Asia, eager for a fresh start, a new beginning.

I toured the best places in Britain: the Lakes District; Scotland; Wales, followed by a bus ride through France, Germany, and Yugoslavia, heading to Greece. After visiting the Greek Islands, I procured a sailboat ride to Turkey and began the journey to Nepal via Iran, Afghanistan, Pakistan, and India. Once in Nepal, I obtained two trekking visas: one to the Mt. Everest base camp via Sir Edmund Hillary's original route, and the other for Muktinath in eastern Nepal. And I hiked into the Himalayas without a plan, a good map, or knowledge about the terrain.

Traveling through the Middle East and Asia prior to the age of internet or cell phones, the rise in tourism, and the wars of recent years, was nothing short of magical. The world felt vast and mysterious, as if there were secrets hidden in the landscape. Most everywhere I went I got lost, and often had to rely on the kindness of strangers to progress from one place to the other.

On several occasions, especially when in uncharted territory like Iran prior to the overthrow of the Pahlavi dynasty, I had to examine my belief system and ask myself fundamental questions: *What am I doing? Where am I going? Who am I?*

The opportunities seemed as endless as counting stars on a clear night.

At the risk of sounding cliché, I yearned to truly live my life—and the story you are about to read did transform me in almost every way. My sense of smell deepened from all the different pungent, aromatic, and flavorful spices and foods I ate, many for the first time. I listened to Bollywood tunes blasting from Middle Eastern lorries and the soulful sound of Ravi Shankar's sitar in Varanasi. Learning new languages provided another challenge and a profound affair altered just about everything I thought I knew about love, forcing me to discover how to be freer than I had ever been in my life.

At the beginning of my adventure, I knew little about the history of the countries I was about to visit, nor did I realize how much those experiences would alter my view of the world —so much so that I ended up living in India from the summer of 1977 until the early autumn of 1979.

I've longed to write this memoir for many years, especially with the continued unrest in many of the countries I visited. The world seems much more fragile now.

I don't have many pictures of that time since it was difficult to travel with the bulky camera equipment and vinyl film of the 1970s.

However, I have one photo of me, taken in 1978, from an ashram in Kashmir, sitting cross-legged on a woven straw mat, my long hair blowing off my face from a light breeze and my eyes full of wonder.

one

NEPAL—APRIL 1977

Perspiration pooled underneath my shirt as I watched Nepalese villagers working in the lime-green rice paddies and golden barley fields; women in flowing ruby-colored dresses tending the young pastures while the men worked tirelessly alongside them with their hoes. Behind them, the sapphire sky was filled with billowing clouds looking like giant cotton balls.

The bus I chose to travel on, crammed with Indian and Nepalese people and a few chickens, made its steady upward grind on a narrow dirt road. Glassless windows let in the warm morning light and a constant stream of dust. Tattered seats revealed the rusted springs underneath, and pieces of the ceiling paint fell into the crowded aisles. Every once in a while, children would sneak a peek at me, the "Ma'am Sahib," giggle, and then turn back to converse with their families in their native Nepali, their voices soft and rhythmic.

After four months, traversing the land between the British Isles and India, I was finally in Nepal and ready to do the Mt. Everest base camp trek.

I arrived at the Katmandu bus station, a soiled patch of barren earth, in the early evening. Passengers got off the bus and collected their belongings, the late daylight filtering through the haze of kicked-up dirt.

I went up to a tin hut, which served as the bus depot ticket station, and tried to sound confident. "Excuse me, do you speak English?"

The vendor in his threadbare jacket, jet black hair combed back in the style of the nineteen fifties, shook his head from side to side—a typical Indian motion meant to imply *of course, of course.* "Yes, yes, Ma'am Sahib, what is it you need?"

I let out a sigh. "Oh, good, you speak English. Do you know where I can spend the night?"

"Oh, yes, yes, Ma'am Sahib. Freak Street for you." He snapped his fingers and a bicycle rickshaw driver pedaled toward me.

"Ma'am Sahib, Ma'am Sahib," he yelled. "I take you hotel, yes. Best ride here. Best driver, yes. Especially best, Ma'am Sahib."

In the 1970s, most westerners visiting Katmandu stayed on Freak Street, an area where young people from all over the world congregated for the beauty and peace of Nepal, trying to find Nirvana in Buddhism or Hinduism, and for others, in drugs.

Freak Street, with makeshift hotels on either side, could barely accommodate a car. People, rickshaws, cows, dogs, chickens, pigeons, monkeys, and tons of finely powdered dust filled the thoroughfare. The small inns were so squished next to each other, it was hard to distinguish when one lodge ended and the other began. Some entrances were as small as a door frame. Most displayed a clutter of hand-painted signs written in Nepali and broken English. "Hotel Annapurna," "Hotel Yak," or "Hotel Karma." "Best place," "Cheap," "No bed bugs." I picked the cleanest doorway with no litter out front.

A thin Nepalese man wearing a long shirt tended the undersized desk. "Welcome, Ma'am Sahib. You share room?"

"No. I'm alone. Just a single room, thank you."

He stared. "Ma'am Sahib alone? No family? No friends?"

I shook my head. "No. I'm by myself."

"Mmm. No good Ma'am Sahib by her lonesome."

He showed me a tiny area on the second floor with a cot and an open, screenless window with heavy wooden shutters. I didn't think the shutters would do anything to muffle the sound of the street noises, conversations from the next room, or merchants shouting outside.

I paid for the hotel room, dropped my backpack off at my room, and went out to find something to eat. There were several small restaurants near the hotel, but I ended up buying *chapattis* and rice from a street peddler, preferring to stand and watch the sky turn from light orange to bluish purple with one or two twinkling stars.

When I headed back to the hotel, I paused to admire the quaint city: terra-cotta sculptures; red shrines, golden *stupas*, monastic courtyards, and exquisite stone statuettes; old buildings with carved images of gods and goddesses and sunken water-spouts; a trader making chai over a pail of crimson charcoal; dogs eating the day's scraps; chanting from a nearby temple; a family carrying their children on their backs.

It felt as if I had stepped back in time.

〜

The next morning I waited in line for several hours at the Nepal Tourist Bureau, a small primitive structure, for my turn to apply for a trekking permit into roadless Nepal. I listened to a group of scientists and climbers, trying to gather information for my trek as questions swirled in my mind.

Would I meet any of these people later? Would the original route to Mt. Everest base camp be a wise choice? Would I see any other trekkers during the first week of travel through the jungle?

"Next." A small Nepalese man motioned for me to come up to his booth. "Your group?"

"No, I do not have a group."

"Sherpa?"

"No, I'm doing this on my own."

His eyes widened. "Porter?"

"No. I have everything I need in my pack. I plan on taking rupees to pay for shelter and food at tea houses or maybe stay with families."

At the time, it never occurred to me it might be wise to, at least, be a little afraid.

After all, I had been traveling alone for six months. During that time, I had survived an uprising in Iran, an attack from a Bulgarian truck driver, heat stroke on the road to Syria, and was almost robbed at an Afghani border crossing.

He put down his pen and opened his mouth as if to say something, then picked up a metal stamp pad and embossed my permit. "You pay sixty-four rupees," he said, and shook his head.

I counted out the blue and pink rupee notes, "Ten, twenty …sixty-four," placing them in a neat pile on the counter and picked up my six-week permit.

The man mumbled something that sounded like, "Lonesome no good."

I compiled a list of things to do before leaving Katmandu: buy peanut butter and a pair of used wool socks from the Expedition store near Freak Street; find a tailor in the central market to repair my jacket; go to the bank and get one hundred and fifty American dollars converted into one-dollar-equivalent rupee notes. At the time, one American dollar was worth about eight rupees and tea houses on the trek charged only a few rupees for a simple room and local food—maybe fifty cents a day. Basic food items consisted of rice, whole wheat *chapattis*, curried lentils, spinach or potatoes, and an abundant supply of tea. Cheese and yoghurt were luxuries.

Katmandu, the capital of Nepal, at an elevation of forty-six hundred feet was surrounded by the tallest mountains in the world. The two-thousand-year-old nerve center sat in a large bowl-shaped valley and supported a flourishing Hindu and Buddhist society. Most of the people spoke Nepali, but English could also be heard in the marketplace.

A small outdoor store owned by two American men nestled among the local vendors. This store sold imported groceries: packages of freeze-dried foods, cans of fruit, condensed milk, and tins of peanut butter, as well as a wide variety of used expedition equipment and hardware. I bought a small can of peanut butter and a used pair of wool socks for the same price as a three-night stay in Katmandu.

"Yah, yah, we flyin' to Lukla, then hiking—ah—Thyanboche," said someone in a small group of European men. I guessed them to be from Switzerland.

"We're taking the bus to Pokhara and then doing the Annapurna Sanctuary," asserted two Americans.

"I'm hoping to catch up with two of me mates near Ama Dablam," uttered an Australian man. A woman looked at me but said nothing.

I decided to join in on the conversation. "I'm doing the Mt. Everest trek starting southwest of Jiri, the original starting point. You know, where Hillary started his trek before the road extended farther north."

"Well, I think it's a lot of unnecessary hiking, if you ask me. Why walk those extra weeks when a sixty-dollar plane ride can land you within two days of Namche Bazaar? Useless if you ask me," said one of the American men as he easily slipped his large backpack over his muscular frame.

"I want to see it. I think it'll be fun to be in an area where foreigners have not been for a while. Maybe, I'll catch a glimpse into what Nepal looked like before tourism arrived." I was thrilled to be going into a part of the country where people grew their own food without modern machinery, did not drive cars or watch television, or even listen to the radio.

He smirked. "Suit yourself."

I watched him saunter out the door. Our styles could not have been more different.

Next morning, en route at last, I swayed in my seat as the rudimentary bus, overflowing with mostly native peoples, heaved its way up the valley and then zigzagged higher into the foothills before disgorging all of us on the side of the road.

Chaos ensued, with families and porters fighting to claim their luggage or merchandise. Men shouted, women consoled crying children, a few boys peed in the nearby bushes, chickens clucked, goats bayed, and dogs barked. Then the bus driver waved, turned the bus around, kicking up a cloud of dirt, and headed back to Katmandu.

Porters and families put their hefty loads into oversized baskets and lifted them onto their backs with an attached strap stretching underneath the basket and continuing over the crown of their heads. Much of their cargo weighed at least eighty or a hundred pounds. Barefooted, some porters didn't even use the basket; they simply manipulated the strap to rest huge boxes of commodities on their backs.

Self-consciously, I slipped on my twenty-pound pack and followed them in my snug hiking boots.

It didn't take long before we reached a precipitous, northwestern-facing hill and the crowd thinned into a lengthy line. The trail, wide enough for one person, went straight uphill— no switchbacks, just steep, rocky terrain.

Feeling a little panicked, I checked the small, handwritten map given to me at the permit station. *Is this it?*

Struggling to find Nepali words to ask if I was on the right trail, I asked a porter who passed me: "Janu? Namche Bazaar?"

"Ho. Thada. Namche." He pointed to the top of the hill and asked a few other questions I could not understand.

I replied with the one Nepali word I knew to mean *thank you*. "Dhanyabad," and paused for a moment. *Wow, this is tough.*

The steep incline left me fighting for breath. I fell behind quickly.

After a vertical, thousand-foot climb to a ridge, followed by a two-mile walk along a slender footpath, I saw my first destination spot in the distance and stopped to rest; quickly realizing all the people from the bus were long gone. I had tried to keep pace with the sherpas and porters, but they zoomed up the slope seemingly like long distance runners.

The sun, an orange ball, slipped behind a jade green hillside.

As I approached a picturesque settlement of thatched homes on a knoll above terraced paddies, about a dozen or more dogs started to yelp and bark wildly before they formed a pack and came running straight toward me.

They rapidly made a circle around my body, showing their teeth, their backs raised for attack; growling and howling like feral creatures ready for battle. One of the dogs started to nip at my boots. Terrified, my whole body went rigid and my stomach felt hard and hot like a brick in the sun.

Suddenly, a silver and black dog jumped as high as my throat and my heart picked up speed. Disoriented, I looked around, gauging if I could back away or escape.

Then, in my peripheral vision, I saw an older man, who I assumed to be the village elder, emerge from a very small hut. He waved and started walking, trailing several children behind him. When he was about twenty feet away, his mouth broke into a huge smile and my breath released slowly like a deflated balloon.

The dogs raced to their village leader and proudly trotted back with him. Their snarls diminished to high-pitched yaps as if they were trying to convince their master, "She is not one of us. Don't let her in."

When the distance between us closed, he extended his hand. His wrinkled eyes sparkled in the fading light and his skin color was brown and leathery from years in the sun.

I extended my hand, eager to cement our camaraderie and quiet the dogs.

The moment I touched the elder's hand, two of the larger dogs ran behind me and bit into my calves with such viciousness, they tore through my pants and into the skin, leaving four enormous, deep puncture wounds. My chest tightened as if I couldn't get enough oxygen and my fingers went numb. I thought I was going to pass out.

Time suspended for a moment, and then, everything seemed to move in slow motion.

The elder, along with several other village men who seemed to me to appear out of nowhere, ordered the dogs away, and apologized in their native tongue—or at least they acted contrite. The dogs retreated to their respective homes, occasionally looking back at me as if to say, "remember who's boss."

The chief began to shout commands. Two village men grabbed my arms and helped me walk into their community.

Dazed, I felt no pain as I limped through their village before we stopped at a diminutive shelter with a straw roof. An older woman, stooped over a walking stick, emerged through a doorway covered with a muddy blanket. The village elder spoke to her.

She had long, white braids pinned to the top of her head and a smile that creased across her robust face; the glisten in her eyes resembling a clear morning after a rain. A woven plum-colored jacket fit snugly around her slight frame and a russet-colored skirt covered her felt boots. She said a few more words to the head villager, took my hand, and led me into her simple home.

I couldn't take my eyes off her.

Squinting in the dim light, I laid down on a wool blanket. The woman lit a few candles and busied herself for the next several minutes boiling water. When the water was hot, she gestured for me to remove my pants and lie face down. Chanting, she placed hot cloths on my wounds and washed the damaged skin. Every time she touched my skin, I flinched.

After that, she rubbed a lime-colored ointment all over my lower legs, placing a little bit extra on the open areas, which felt cool and comforting, and ended by wrapping my calves in clean strips of white cotton.

By candlelight, I watched her make tea and bake flat bread on her primitive stove. We didn't speak.

She put an ashen powder in my tea and said something that I thought meant, "drink it all."

I don't remember much after that because I fell asleep.

The next morning, I woke to the sun streaming through the doorway. *How long had I slept?* I looked around and saw no one, only dust mites dancing in the golden light.

Blood had dried through the cloth bandages. When I unraveled the cotton bands, my calves looked like a patchwork of blue, green, and black. The adrenaline rush that overrode the pain the night before had since passed and now my legs howled in a chorus of complaints. My head throbbed. I felt confused and insecure.

What to do? Go back to Katmandu? What if I had rabies? What if the punctures got infected? Do I need stitches?

As I mulled over these thoughts, the medicine woman came in. She touched my calves and nodded. I got lost in her eyes for a moment when she touched my face, her caress velvety smooth, and swallowed the lump in my throat. As I drank tea, she methodically reapplied the ointment and new strips of fabric.

My heart sunk at the thought of turning back. It was only day two.

I just couldn't let this stand in the way of my dreams, so I decided to not listen to the *what-ifs* and packed up.

When I emerged from the hut, a woman from the village offered me two warm *chapattis* wrapped in a clean rag, and a mango. The young boy, who I assumed was her son, handed me a walking stick.

I looked at these gentle people and placed my hands in the prayer position. "Namaste. Namaste. Dhanyabad."

Grandmother watched me leave the village and waved every time I turned to look back. When the trail came to a bend and

I could no longer see the community, I stopped, folded my arms under my breasts, and looked at what lay ahead. Miles of heavily vegetated hills undulated sharply and incessantly to meet snowcapped peaks in the distance. *That seems like a long way.*

I sat on a rock outcropping and closed my eyes. My legs hurt. My shoulders ached from carrying a twenty-pound pack. The hip belt dug into my low back. I doubted my ability to go another step.

Feeling like a six year old, I burst into tears.

In the weeks to come, I would learn that the long route into the Himalayas consisted of countless ridges and passes —an extensive skyward journey into a magnificent, massive mountain system; ascending one day to a high ridge or pass only to descend into a valley the next day with a fast river flowing at the bottom.

Crossing these rivers was sometimes challenging, as they were usually nothing more than narrow, unsteady bridges made of wood and woven fiber strung from a tree on one side of the river to another tree on the opposite shore.

I often felt a little like a character out of *Lord of the Rings*, except I was alone, not with a band of friends.

two

CANADA—1959

One of my earliest memories was sitting on a man's lap with his hand down my white underpants. He touched my private parts and stuck his finger inside of me. I didn't want him to do that and when I tried to squirm away, he held me tighter.

"Sssshh. Stay still," he whispered in my ear.

We sat in a rocking chair on an open verandah facing a street. I watched a car drive by, wishing I could be in that car.

When the man had had his way with me, he stopped and put me down. "Just don't stand there, pull up your panties."

I glanced down at my underwear around my ankles and quickly lifted them under my dress.

I never could put a face on that man.

When I look back on my early childhood, the only memories I recall are of me crying. Standing on a bridge with tissue stuffed in my pockets, my father said, "Smile."

I just kept sobbing.

In the summer of 1959, just before I turned six, a woman with red hair and red lipstick, dressed in a purple outfit with matching high heels, took my hand and said, "Let's go for a walk."

We strolled down a street, past the house with the white wraparound porch and the house with the blooming rose bushes. Confused, I asked, "Are you really my mother?"

The woman stopped walking and slowly bent her knees until her bottom touched the top of her shoes. Her eyes glistened with moisture. "Of course, I'm your mother. Don't you remember?" She smoothed my wild hair and shook her head.

I didn't remember; it'd been so long. I'd been living in what my father called "a boarding house," which sounded better than orphan or foster home.

My father alleged, "I didn't have time to take care of you. I had to work, and I needed to hang out with my buddies. You know, get a beer or two."

I whimpered and whined a lot in the orphan home. The beds seemed like cradles for giants. I had difficulty climbing into the bunk bed assigned to me and when I finally did settle in, I was afraid to get up in the middle of the night to pee. What if I couldn't get back into bed? I'd have to sleep on the cold floor, which happened sometimes.

The outhouse was in the back of the farmhouse. It smelled like rotten garbage and was so dark I couldn't tell what might be prowling in the nearby thickets.

One time, an older boy locked me in the outhouse. I blubbered, "Let me out! Let me out!" He laughed, "Crybaby, crybaby, misses her daddy."

I wept and screamed until an older kid came out to use the latrine. "What are you doing here?" he asked.

I didn't answer and ran back to the dorm as fast as my little legs could go.

When I asked my father why he didn't come to the home very often to see me, he stated, "I couldn't stand coming to see you because you'd bawl your eyes out all the time. Thought it was better to just leave you there."

Things must have gotten worse for me at the boarding house because he ended up calling my mother. "Jeannine, I can't do this anymore. Please come and get her as soon as you can."

Wearing her lovely purple outfit, my mother took a train south to Toronto and went straight to my dad's place. Once there, she marched in and announced, "She is going to live with me from now on."

My father yelled at my mother. She shouted some obscenity back.

When they stopped arguing, my mother found my small, dilapidated suitcase and began stuffing my meager belongings into it, all the while muttering to herself, "What? The lock on this thing doesn't even work."

My best assumption was that bad things happened in the orphan home, but I could never be sure. I pushed those memories so deep inside my consciousness they got all twisted up with my nightmares.

That same day, we got on a train and traveled to a small mining town in northern Quebec. I couldn't stop ogling this woman—I still didn't believe she was my mother—and I watched her every move; the way she ate her food or crossed her legs or talked to me.

"You're going to like your new home." She blew her nose. "I still can't believe he didn't enroll you in school."

My stepdad, Noel, and my two-year-old brother, Tony, met us at the station. Noel roughly pushed me into their beat-up truck. Tony cried all the way back home, a trailer located off a narrow dirt road with a tool shed out back. A clothesline drooping with hanging laundry swayed in the breeze.

A week later, my mother enrolled me in a Catholic elementary school. They changed my last name. I spoke in one-word answers, or shook my head or nodded whenever my mother talked to me.

First grade reminded me of the orphanage: lots of kids yelling on the playground, all the students crammed together at long tables in the cafeteria, having to raise my hand to ask to go to the restroom.

I became increasingly nervous to go out for recess, afraid I might get stuck out there and not know how to get back into the school. Summoning up my bravery, I asked Sister Frances, "Can I stay in here with you? My tummy hurts."

She let me clean the blackboards and shake out the felt erasers, and offered me encouragement to get caught up with the other kids because I missed kindergarten. She even hugged me when I wept for no rational reason.

I loved her traditional dress: the long robes swishing together when she walked, the clink of the rosary around her neck, the spotless white-and-black wimple. Her eyes sparkled when she saw me each morning and her hand felt like sunshine when I placed my tiny hand in hers.

One day I stayed after school to help clean the classroom. Sister Frances sang, "Dominque, nique, nique…nique, nique, nique, nique." I sang along in my high-pitched voice.

Halfway through the second song, my mother came into the classroom. "What are you doing here? It's almost *four o'clock!*" She stared at Sister Frances and pressed her lips into a thin line.

I knew that look. *Watch out, Sister Frances! You'll have to kneel in the corner!*

Without saying a word to Sister Frances, my mother yanked my hand and dragged me out of the school.

When we were home, she shouted, "Off to your room! Come out when you are ready to apologize."

I couldn't stay after school anymore, but I still loved Sister Frances, who continued to shower kindness all year long and looked out for me throughout my unruly elementary school years. This kind woman placed a card on my desk with an inscription *Never give up*, winked when I passed her in the school hallway, listened to my silly stories, and forgave my neediness.

She knew a childish game of patty-cake or singing a silly song healed—not kneeling in a closet.

three

NEPAL—APRIL 1977

A s I trekked into the precipitous Himalayan foothills, soft countryside scenes greeted me at every turn: yellow and pink lilies, billowy white clouds, gushing streams, bits of color here and there like splattered paint on an artist's canvas.

Nepali families worked in green terraced hills. When I entered their small communities, local villagers burst into grins, reminding me of school children meeting a new teacher for the first time.

I felt vulnerable after the dog attack and frequently thought about my mother. This surprised me, considering we'd never been close. The walking stick provided a critical comfort and for the most part, dogs stayed away. Nonetheless, my bones always went soft on me whenever I met a strange mongrel.

In those first few days and weeks on the trek, I noticed how everything in Nepali society revolved around the core value of caring for each member of the tribe. This was such a contrast from the emotionally distant family I grew up in, where children had to behave and be quiet.

I watched as Nepali families showered their children with hugs and smiles. Relatives shared food and chores and worked together as they lugged as much water from the wells as they could carry, sometimes singing and chanting while precariously balancing jugs on the top of their heads. They then took delight in distributing what they had with one another.

Toddlers and schoolchildren appeared happy: running around playing games, laughing, skipping, and humming sing-song rhymes. It reminded me of my own childhood jingles: *not too big, not too small, just the size of Montreal.* Their mirth oozed a satisfaction I rarely felt as a child.

After several days into my journey, I stopped at a small thriving community of ten thatch-roofed homes about the time the sun in the western sky produced long shadows. My boarding home for the evening had a separate guestroom with polished wood floors and a covered deck overlooking the valley. Mountain rhododendrons in crimson bloom circled the perimeter, the smell intoxicating the air with sweet-scented breezes.

The lively mother of the house, wearing a long skirt covered with a garnet-colored apron, offered a basin of warm water for washing up. Drawing a tattered cloth closed around the bed area for privacy, I undressed and took a sponge bath using a rag and a tiny piece of white soap laying in the bottom of a porcelain bowl.

I eyed the cotton bandages around my calves and tried to convince myself not to worry about infection—or worse, rabies. The once-white material, now gray, was frayed and knotted in places. I took my time unraveling the plain strips and could hardly believe it when I saw that the blue-black bruising had subsided to a golden color. Even the puncture wounds had completely closed.

When I pressed down on the fading bruise, the skin felt lithe and young—no pain, tenderness, or sensitivity. Flexing my calves showed no sign of tightness or unevenness and it looked like I would not have any scarring. *Amazing.*

I dressed in a clean pair of jeans, now faded to a stonewashed blue, and a checkered cotton shirt made silky-smooth from many hand washings. Leaving the drawstring pants and top soaking in the same water I used for a sponge bath, I opted to rinse them out later.

When I pulled the curtain back, the late afternoon light flickered on the hand-hewn floorboards and warmed the soles of my feet. Refreshed and relaxed, I looked at my pack on the bed and remembered what was inside.

To celebrate the miraculous recovery of my wounds, I decided to open my one can of peanut butter and eat a spoonful. If I ate a tablespoon every few days, it could last until I reached base camp and give my body that much needed extra boost of energy.

Digging around in the bottom of my pack, I found the can tucked efficiently away, under my only other pair of socks and a jacket. The peanut butter tin had a resealable top with a piece of aluminum foil to guarantee freshness. This foil cover ripped off easily by pulling an attached tab. *Swoosh!* Underneath the foil lid, the peanut oil floated on top, revealing creamy nuts underneath and a rich aroma smelling like home.

Could I eat just one spoonful?

Suddenly, two precious brown eyes gazed into my own. The house mother's five-year-old daughter then stared at the peanut butter. Her dark hair in two braids, tied with golden ribbons, swung gently from side to side.

How did she get here so fast? I didn't hear a sound.

"Kannus, ke?" she asked.

I caught the word *what* and maybe *eat*.

Surely, she wouldn't want some of my prized peanut butter. Maybe I should put it away.

She opened her mouth, revealing two missing front teeth.

A warmth radiated across my chest and I took out my spoon from the pack's side pocket and gave her a dollop.

When I looked down to scoop up a larger serving for myself, there were three other pairs of sweet eyes watching me.

Where did these children come from? That took, what, four seconds for them to get here? What to do? Share or not to share?

And then, there were four more children. Within about twenty seconds, I went from being alone, with thoughts of satisfying my hunger for protein (or maybe just for comfort), to contemplating allocating several teaspoons worth of beloved peanut butter among eight children.

I observed their eyes, glued to the can of peanut butter. *Will they ever get the chance to taste this Canadian staple?* This might be a culinary apex in their lives.

Of course, I needed to share.

No sooner had one of the children swallowed their ration, giggling, and chewing slowly when several more children arrived. The entire settlement's children must've been in my room and if any more came, I would have nothing left.

"Tapaiko naam ke ho?" a small, barefooted boy asked.

What is your name?

"Ma'am Sahib." The native people had difficulty pronouncing "Sharon," so I stuck to what was simple.

Another girl, around seven years old, whispered, "Dhanyabad," peanut oil dripping down her chin.

"Ramro, ramro!" cried two little three-year-old girls. *Good, good!*

I dished out more servings, laughing when their eyes lit up like fireflies at their first taste of this gastronomic pleasure. Within minutes, the feast had ended.

"Namaste, namaste," they yelled, leaving my room to play outside.

Alone, I looked at the empty can of peanut butter. Not a smidge was left; it was completely licked clean.

I walked out onto the terrace and watched them play a game using a stick and a ball made from odd pieces of material. They danced, shouted, and sometimes waved.

Chuckling, I yelled out, "Namaste!"

The sun ducked behind the foothills casting silhouette shadows of the children's fun on the grass. A hummingbird buzzed by on its way to the cherry flowers surrounding the house.

Not long after that, the children went to their homes, skipping and whistling. My host family called me for dinner, and we sat cross-legged on straw mats as earthen clay pots of rice and lentils were passed around. Silence filled the room and we ate carefully with our right hands, our left hands tucked neatly behind us.

In Nepal, and in other Asian countries at the time, there was no toilet paper. Instead, the left hand was used for cleaning oneself with water and soap. The right hand was used for eating. It was polite to always place the left hand behind you when consuming food with the local people—something I had learned while traveling in the Middle East.

The house mother's daughter reached over and squeezed my right hand just before I could scoop out a rice portion. She took the ladle, measured a hefty serving, and placed it in my bowl.

I glanced at this family, so relaxed and at ease with one another, tenderly sharing a meal, and swallowed. Their palpable warmheartedness filled my heart while my eyes threatened to leak a flood of emotion, my feelings spilling over like a garden hose left running…trickling everywhere.

ACKNOWLEDGMENTS

Thank you to Judith Briles, the Book Shepherd, for tirelessly bringing this book to an audience; Barb Wilson, editor, for carefully editing these pages with insight and humor in the work; Rebecca Finkel for her artistic book cover and design; Natalie Kreider for the captivating drawing on the front cover as well as the Sylvie title font; and Julie Ulstrup for the author photographs.

Thanks are also due to the thousands of children, adolescents, and their families that I had the privilege of working with over the tenure of my working career as a Mental Health Professional.

I am eternally grateful to my husband Rea, my son Peter, and my daughter Natalie who have supported me without condition, and given me courage, steadfastness, and love, without which I could not have written this book. A special recognition has to go out to my wonderful daughter Natalie who read all the earlier drafts, offered such invaluable vision, and inspired me to keep going when I thought maybe I should just retire. I love you to the moon and back. . .

MEET
SHARON KREIDER

 Inspired by her former career as a Mental Health Therapist and Suicide Prevention Trainer providing counseling services for over 10,000 children, adolescents, and their families, Sharon now weaves the psychological and emotional qualities of the human condition into her writing to help shed light on many relevant issues facing society today.

Born and raised in a small northern Canadian town, she left home at an early age to travel the world, and eventually settled in Colorado for many years where she penned Sylvie, her first book. The siren call of the Pacific Northwest lured to her new writing home: several acres of wild, natural land to live a quieter life close to nature surrounding the idyllic home she and her husband built.

Discover her blog, *Finding Solace in all Things Great and Small* at **www.SharonKreider.com.**

Sharon's memoir, *Wandering*, will be available 2022; a poignant story focusing on her younger years when she hopped on a plane and flew from Canada to England to begin a 3-year solo journey overland to Asia. It's the rest of her story …

HOW TO WORK
WITH SHARON

Sharon Kreider is an exceptional storyteller, weaving the psychological and emotional fabric in women's fiction.

Bring her to your Book Club. Participation can be Virtual or In-Person. To check her availability, email her at:

Sharon@SharonKreider.com

www.SharonKreider.com

Connect with her on social media:

 SharonKreiderAuthor

 KreiderSharon

 sharonkreiderauthor

 @sharonkreiderauthor